SUE TOWLER

ISOLATION

A New Zealand Historical,
fictional novel; based on fact

Typesetting by PublishMe-Self-publishing, New Zealand
www.publishme.co.nz

Cover photo – Erewhon Station and Clydesdales - by Sue Towler

AUTHOR'S NOTE

This book was inspired by a true story; however, the storyline and the main characters are purely fictional and are not intended to bear any relation to any person or persons living or dead.

The details surrounding much of this story are fact based and have been derived from historical archives. Most of the places mentioned can be found on a New Zealand map with the exception of Flaxbush Station, Stony Downs and the Arrowsmith run, these names are fictional. The snow storm of 1867 and the flood of 1868 did occur, details of which can be found on line. Excerpts from Papers Past, sourced through the National Library of New Zealand, make for interesting reading.

I was saddened to learn that one third of migrants from Europe died within the first 3 years of coming to New Zealand. I am a descendant of English migrants, my Ancestors arrived here in 1874. My Great-Great-Grandfather was the first white baby to be born that same year in Fielding which, back then, was just a small settlement in the middle of the North Island. Thankfully my family line was strong enough to survive and thrive in those difficult times, allowing us to live on in this beautiful country we are privileged to call home. I love writing about the New Zealand High Country, the stunning scenery never ceases to take my breath away.

Website: www.sue-towler.com

I welcome your feedback on my facebook page -
http://www.facebook.com/susy.co.nz

DEDICATION

I dedicate this book to my dear friend and Editor, Lorraine Miller (WordsComm) for taking the time to edit and proofread my story and help me get it finished. Thank you

OTHER BOOKS BY THIS AUTHOR

ELIZABETH'S DIARIES

BRIGIT

PROLOGUE

James Morley stood at the foot of his late wife's newly dug grave, head bowed, hat removed. His shoulders shook a little, by all appearances giving way to the pent-up grief and guilt that had been haunting him since his wife's death. The Reverend Joshua McAllister and his wife Alice stood quietly by at a respectful distance.

'What do you suppose happened to her?' Mrs McAllister whispered to her husband.

'I doubt we will ever know for sure my dear,' he sighed sadly.

Neither of them noticed the figure huddled behind a tree on the far side of the church yard clutching a journal to his chest, hot tears streaming down his face. He watched, fists and teeth clenched in rage, as James Morley mouthed a few words then turned abruptly on his heel and walked purposefully across the manicured cemetery lawn to the waiting arms of his lover. They walked arm in arm out of the cemetery gates where James lifted the lady onto the waiting horse and cart, and they rode away into the setting sun.

Confident that nobody else was around the man emerged from his hiding place among the trees and made his way to the same grave site. He stood for a moment reading the words painted on the plain white wooden cross at the head of the dirt mound then sunk to his knees and began to sob uncontrollably. It was as if a damn of emotions had broken free inside him and in a way perhaps that is exactly what happened.

'Shhh,' hushed Alice McAlister, as she and her husband made their way back to the Vicarage, 'did you hear that?'

'What is it you think you heard my dear?'

'It sounded like…, listen there it is again.'

They both stopped walking and listened to the sound that merged in with the birds settling themselves onto their night time perches. Alice's heart stopped and a tear formed in her eye.

'Oh my, Joshua, if that isn't the sound of a broken heart then I surely don't know what is.'

This story is inspired by the strength and bravery of the pioneer women who, with their husbands, ventured far away from their homes to places unknown across vast expanses of seemingly endless oceans. Some found themselves drawn to the majesty and promise of the mountain ranges of central South Island, New Zealand hoping to tame and farm the land. Some were successful in their ventures, sadly, many were not.

New Beginnings - October 1859

Meghan leaned against the damp wooden railing of the ship, arm stretched high, waving to her family who she knew would still be waving back at her from the disappearing dock in the misty distance. She knew they would no longer be able to see her as the ships wind-filled sails pulled them further and further out to sea, but she didn't want to stop this final connection she held with them.

With a pang of guilt James watched the tears rolling down his new bride's cheeks. He'd never known such a close-knit family as Meghan's, his upbringing was cold and regimented in comparison. His father was military, his mother a nurse. They had moved a lot, so he never bothered to make friends. He put his arm around Meghan's shoulders and pulled her close, she didn't resist.

'Have I done the wrong thing Meg, taking you away from your family?'

She turned her tear stained face up to his and smiled.

'No, my love. I am terribly sad to be leaving them of course, but I know in my heart that we cannot stay living in a family cocoon forever. At some stage we all have to leave the nest and I believe my time has come. Besides,' she laughed, 'it's a bit late now don't you think?'

Meghan eventually stopped waving and thought back to the weeks and months of planning it had taken to prepare for this journey. James had been offered surveying work in the Canterbury region and registered with The New Zealand Company being formed to colonise New Zealand. Passage had been booked for him and his then bride-to-be, on the ship the *Roman Emperor* due to depart on Saturday 1st October 1859. Much paperwork had to be filled out and strict instructions were issued and expected to be adhered to. Meghan and her mother had dutifully and painstakingly fulfilled the list of requirements to be packed into trunks for the new settlers.

The following articles are the least which will be deemed sufficient for the voyage: --
For each Bed:
1 Mattress, 1 bolster, 2 blankets, 6 sheets, 1 coverlid.
For Males
6 Shirts, 6 pair of socks, 2 pair of shoes, 2 complete suits of outside clothing, 1 hair brush and comb.
For Females
6 Shifts, 2 flannel petticoats, 6 pair of stockings, 2 pair of shoes, 2 gowns, 1 hair brush and comb.
For each Person.
6 Towels, 3lbs. of marine soap, a knife and fork, a deep tin or pewter dish, a spoon, a pint drinking mug, a hook pot.
Provisions, cooking utensils, medicine, and medical attendance, are supplied aboard.
The owner's name should be marked on each box.
Passenger's luggage must not measure more than ten cubic feet.
Each person must have one or two canvas bags, as boxes will be kept below in the hold.

Now everything was done, they were aboard the ship, there was no turning back. Meghan leaned into the comfort of her husband's arms and sighed.

'This is it; this is the start of a new life for us James. I wonder where it will take us.'

October 1859
Aboard the Roman Emperor

Dear Mama, Papa and my dearest brothers and sisters,

I felt my heart would break as I watched you all getting smaller and smaller standing there on Gravesend Wharf. When our lighter reached the side of the ship, James and the deck hands helped me climb aboard and then he and our cabin trunks and luggage followed. The first thing I noticed was the number of other passengers all standing around looking as bewildered and uncomfortable as we were. There seemed to be a lot of confusion as more and more people were being loaded aboard. Some were weeping openly, others sniffing into their handkerchiefs. James and I stood to one side and watched the luggage being stowed below decks. I could hear the sounds of various animals on board. Until that moment I had not considered that we would be travelling with animals. Not that I mind, as you know I love animals, I just never imagined them on board ships.

And so here we are on Saturday the 1st of October 1859. We are leaving dear England for who knows how long and heading in to who knows what adventures.

Wednesday, 5th of October. We are settling in a little to our new life at sea now. Our cabin is small but comfortable. There is a small chest of drawers fastened to the wall and our canvas bags stack nicely in the corner which is where I am sitting while I write to you. I leave the bed for James as the poor dear has succumbed to sea sickness and spends most of his time in bed. I spend a lot of time on deck to give him peace. The evenings are my favourite time of the day. The seas seem to be a little calmer then and the sky puts on such a dazzling display of colours as the sun sets below the horizon. The meals are surprisingly tasty and fresh. I don't know what I was expecting. I guess they will become less fresh as time goes by.

We have been at sea for around 10 days now and have run into a storm. The wind is extremely fierce and has been blowing for several days. I am finding it difficult to write at the moment.

I don't know what the date is, I have lost track of the days so please excuse the lack of dates on my diary entries. We are now off the coast of Portugal. The winds have stopped now but we were being tossed about as great waves rose up beneath us, dropping us down into the troughs between them. I must admit that although I find the size of the waves a little terrifying, I am also fascinated by the way the ship pitches and rolls up and over the top of them. James has recovered fairly well from his sea sickness although when it is rough he succumbs to the vile affliction once again. At times like this I leave him in peace and spend many an hour up on deck holding on to the side of the ship for dear life whilst at the same time being mesmerized by what is happening around me. I am not surprised to find that apart from the sailors, I am almost alone on the deck although they often suggest I might be better off down below. If they get really gruff with me, I know they are only looking out for my wellbeing and I duly oblige, after all they know the ocean better than I ever will.

It's been a little more than two weeks since my last entries. Nothing much has been happening to write about. We have seen land again and are moored in a bay off the coast of an island called Tenerife. Here we are without wind; I think the term used is 'becalmed'. There are other islands here as well and upon enquiry I am informed they are the islands of Palma, Gomera, and Ferro. We have been sitting off the coast of these beautiful islands for three days now. James is well again and joins me on deck and together we lean on the side of the ship gazing across to the islands trying to imagine what life would be like in such beautiful places. The most breath-taking time of the day here is in the early evenings as the sun is setting. The skies are the most beautiful deep blue and the moon casts a silver light across the water to us. It is almost indescribable. I wish I could capture the image and send it to you. Perhaps I should learn to paint.

Since James has joined me on deck again we have met up with some of the other travellers. For some reason they avoided me when I was out on my own but now that they have gotten to know us as a married couple, I am sure we will exchange pleasantries whenever we meet. There are a few families with children, heading for a new life together. I am not sure I would be taking my children on such a journey but the children I have seen seem to be enjoying the adventure. A lot of the travellers are on their own, young men leaving home to try their luck in a new land and a new life. There are several young couples like us, a few older ones and a few older men on their own. Two of them, brothers, have been to Australia and have held us enthralled telling us of the exciting adventures they have had there. One of the men is a poet and sits on deck all day observing his surroundings and writing in his journal.

We have left the islands now and I must tell you of a little bit of excitement we had today. There was much commotion from the cook's galley. Apparently, he had spilled some fat on his fire while he was cooking which created much alarm until the fire was successfully extinguished. A fire aboard a ship in the middle of the ocean does not bear thinking about.

It seems to be getting a little warmer now. The seas are smoother and the sailing conditions much improved. Today we saw the strangest thing, a fish with wings. Truly. These fish fly up out of the water in an arc and down into the water again. I have never seen or heard of such a thing. One of these fish even flew up on to the deck of the ship. It was quickly grabbed by one of the deck hands and passed around for everyone to see. The wings of the fish were about 18 inches from tip to tip but if it wasn't for the wings it would have looked just like any other fish that we would see in a fishmonger.

Again, I wish I could capture the image for you.

November, 6th Sunday. I know this because we had a church service today and the Vicar mentioned the date as it was the Captains birthday. We have services every Sunday which helps us keep track of the weeks at least. The lovely Vicar and his wife are heading to Canterbury too. Today we gave thanks for our survival of the storm we had yesterday. It was rather frightening and there was what I later found out to be chain lightning. It looked like forked lightning, but it seemed to zig zag between the clouds. Fascinating but frightening all the same. My goodness what an adventure we are having.

We have once again become becalmed and the weather has been absolutely dismal. Everything is wet, or at best, damp. We just seem to be wallowing around as if in a giant tub. One poor young girl succumbed to the dampness and has been buried at sea. My heart goes out to her dear grieving parents. It is raining hard outside, much like it used to in the Highlands Papa.

We had a little excitement today which helped to stave off the misery which has been settling over us due to the awful weather. A large shark fish came close enough for us to get a good look at. Some of the sailors attempted to catch it but came off second best. It was most entertaining and gave us all something to laugh about.

The winds picked up markedly today and we seem to be off again at great speed. I heard one of the sailors say these were the trade winds. I don't know what that means but the sailors seemed to get excited about it.

It has been another week at sea and I sometimes wonder if we will ever reach our destination. I have lost track of the days and weeks. It feels a little foolish having to ask someone what day it is. The temperature is dropping the further south we go. I am grateful for the heavy woollen coat you gave me Mama; I wear it most days now when I am up on deck. Thank you.

What wondrous sights we have been seeing these past several days. There are enormous birds circling around the ship. I have never seen the like, even in my school books. One of the passengers seemed particularly interested in the birds and I asked him what they were. He told me the largest ones were albatross; there was a smaller similar looking bird which he said was a mollymawk. Now isn't that a funny name for a bird. There were pigeons and mutton birds and several others which I have forgotten the names of. It is wonderful to see the beautiful giant birds drifting gracefully about the ship. Some of the young men try to capture them but I don't think they will succeed. At least I hope they don't.

Christmas has now been and gone. I purposely did not write during this time as I felt so melancholy and missed you all so very much that I did not feel like writing. Christmas aboard the ship was more fun than I thought it would be. The families had come prepared for Christmas at sea and had bought gifts with them. For those clearly on their own and for the crew, we womenfolk rummaged around in our trunks and found enough bits and pieces to make kerchiefs and neck scarves like the sailors wear and notebooks for the more scholarly gentlemen. Christmas dinner was as special as the cook could make it with the rations he has left. We were all terribly grateful. We sang and ate as if we were in a great banquet hall, it was such a jolly time.

One day the captain lowered a small boat over the side and several people, scrambled in. The Captain had spotted some unusual ripples in the water a short distance away and when they rowed up to them, they discovered a large mass of seaweed full of little fishes. The men attached the seaweed to the boat and then towed it back to the ship. It seemed to take an awfully long time, but they did get there eventually. But the best was yet to come.

9

After lunch the Captain made arrangements for ropes and a chair to be fitted so he could lower us ladies down to the boat so we too could go for a row around the ship. They lowered champagne into the boat followed by the ladies who were lowered on the chair one by one, laughing and squealing in absolute delight. And yes, I must admit I did do a bit of squealing too but oh it was so much fun. James and three other husbands also came with us and we were rowed around the ship while we sipped on champagne. It seemed to be so much warmer on the surface of the water and the rise and fall of the waves was so much greater in the small boat. When we pulled up alongside the mass of seaweed someone suggested we try and catch the little fishes. A small makeshift net was produced and with great hilarity and more squeals of delight we managed to catch quite a number. We caught enough for everyone to have their fill at dinner that night. Fresh fish, what a delight. They were only about five inches long, but they were very tasty. Some of those who ventured out in the small boats during the day were showing signs of sunburned necks and faces that evening at dinner. The weather has been warm at times but certainly not enough to cause sunburn, or so we thought.

The outings in the small boats seemed to wake everyone up again and get them excited about their future. It seemed as though we had all gone into some form of stupor being crowded onto this ship day in and day out with nowhere to go. I am pleased to say that throughout the latter part of this journey, once James finally overcame his sea-sickness, we have thoroughly enjoyed our days together walking and talking with other couples on deck during the day. At night we talk or read or play games in the dining room with other guests. The time seems to pass by. We tend to lose all track of time.

We had a wonderful New Year's Eve party on deck with music and dancing and singing into the wee small hours. Even the small children were allowed to stay up to see in the New Year. 1860. I wonder what life will be like for us this year. It is difficult to believe that we have been on board this ship for three whole months. At times it seems as though it has been forever and that we did not have a life before this.

We have been cruising down the coast of Australia and are now heading towards New Zealand at last. There is an air of anticipation and excitement on board. We are beginning to imagine a life other than that which we have lived for the past four months.

January 26th, we have arrived in New Zealand! We have been sailing up and down the coast for almost a week since passing Stewart's Island at the south end of the country. The land is tantalizingly close, but the weather has prevented us from docking in Lyttleton Harbour. It is most frustrating but it is wonderful to finally be here and to be so close to land. It does look most inviting. The colours of the sunrises and the sunsets are magnificent, and the birds surround us in their hundreds. Once again, the beautiful big albatross, mollymawk, seagulls and so many others circle overhead screeching and calling.

The landscape is most unusual. There seems to be several layers of hills and valleys that change hue with the rising and setting of the sun. I see palls of smoke drifting slowly up into the air. It seems peaceful although from where we are moored we can hear little else but the sound of the waves breaking on the rocks along the shoreline. When one sees the amount of spray that flies up into the air as it breaks over the rocks it is no wonder that the sea must be calm and the wind blowing in the right direction before we can dock safely.

A boat from shore was sent out to welcome us today. They wanted to know how many of us had survived the trip, I think. One of the other passengers who knew the Captain quite well told me that there were 213 passengers on this trip. There were three births and three deaths so that number didn't change.

There was some consternation when our Captain asked if the ships the 'Robert Small' and the 'Burmah' had arrived and was told no, not yet. They set sail before us.

This morning we were treated to fresh beef steaks and potatoes for breakfast, courtesy of the Pilot who welcomed us last evening. You have never seen the likes in all your born days. Not a word was spoken and every face without exception was lit up in ecstasy as we ate. We had not had such a meal since we left England.

February 1^{st,} 1860. We have found lodgings in Christchurch while we look for a house to rent. The day we disembarked was glorious. The

11

sea was calm at last, the sun was shining, and the sky the clearest deep blue. We walked down the gangplank and felt a little unsteady as though we were still moving, it was the most unusual sensation and not what I would call pleasant, but we were finally on dry land and that in itself was a blessing.

We were housed in a very basic lodging over night while we waited for our cabin trunks to be unloaded. These were then placed on the back of small drays and sent on ahead of us while we followed on foot. The climb up the hill was quite the challenge, even more so for the horses and wagons. James pointed out that a tunnel had been started at the base of the hill which, by the time we got to the top of the hill, I realised would be most advantageous. However, once we stopped and looked back down from whence we had come we were granted the most breath-taking view of the sparkling waters of the ocean and the hustle and bustle of the harbour far below. In front of us the countryside spread out in vast plains reaching to mountain ranges in the distance, some with snow on their tops. We stopped here for a time to regain our strength from the steep climb and take some refreshments.

By the time we reached Christchurch it was late afternoon. The weather was hot and sticky, we were both wet with perspiration when we reached our lodgings and very pleased to find that a tub would be made available for us to bathe in at our convenience. It was heavenly to slide into a tub full of delicious warm water. The hostel owner had even brought in some divine smelling sprigs of Lavender to sprinkle on the water.

We were relieved to hear that the ship, Robert Small, did arrive safely four days after us but tragically the Burmah was wrecked along the coastline with all 50 lives and many head of stock lost. I am so very thankful for the blessings God has given us to have travelled and arrived safely after such a long and adventurous voyage. One hundred and seventeen days at sea, that is a very long time.

Mama I have discovered the beautiful Bible you tucked into our travelling trunk and have begun reading it again. It gives me great solace. Thank you.

I have missed the post this time as the mails leave on the 23rd of each month but I will leave this letter at the Post Office so that it might go with next month's post. I know you will be anxious to hear from us. James has secured a position as a Surveyor already and I am presently a lady of leisure, which has given me ample time to walk along the streets and browse through the stores. Not as well stocked as our stores at home but very interesting all the same. I have had to purchase some lighter clothing for both of us as it is so much warmer here than it is at home.

I sat on a stool outside the boarding house in the sun yesterday without my bonnet and last night I noticed I was glowing pink. I'm sure James thought I had been at the whiskey bottle.

Mama, Papa, James asks if you would kindly pass this letter on to his parents to read. He sends his love and best wishes to everyone and promises to write himself once we are more settled.

All our love,
Meghan and James

14

Christchurch 1860 – 1864

By the end of March 1860 James and Meghan were renting a small cottage in Christchurch. James position as a Surveyor had him spending days and sometimes weeks away at a time leaving Meghan bored and restless. She was used to being busy. She had spent most of her teenage years working alongside her father during his time as a shepherd in the Highlands. They were the happiest years of her life and she was bitterly disappointed when her mother became seriously ill and they had to move back in to town. During her mother's convalescence Meghan took over her role in the household and cooked, cleaned and looked after her siblings. It was a relief when her mother eventually got her strength back and was able to resume some of the household chores again. Meghan didn't mind the work or helping out, she simply preferred to be outdoors.

James Morley had walked into a store one day and literally bumped into Meghan as she was making her way out with an armload of groceries.

15

'I knew right at that moment that I would marry you one day,' James told Meghan on their wedding day.

Meghan was still looking after her siblings at the time but only because she hadn't decided what else she wanted to do. She was enamoured with James and enjoyed their outings together. James talked endlessly about wanting to go abroad. He hated England, he hated the weather, he wasn't close to his parents, and there didn't seem to be much holding his interest once he had gained his Surveyors Certificate.

'I want to see the world Meg, there has to be more to life than this dismal place. I need to spread my wings.'

Meghan had smiled indulgently at first but eventually became caught up in his enthusiasm. They drifted along for a year or so before James, on impulse, responded to an advertisement in the paper calling for applicants for positions in New Zealand. He decided not to tell Meg in case nothing came of it.

But something did come of it. They were wanting qualified Surveyors and James suited their requirements. He took Meghan out to dinner one evening and broke the news while they waited for their desert. She was stunned.

'New Zealand?' she squealed. 'You are going to New Zealand?'

'Not without you I'm not, will you come with me? We could get married and ...'

Meghan's trembling hand flew to her gaping mouth.

'James Morley, what is all this?' Meg was stunned. 'Out of the blue you say you want to get married and you want me to go with you to New Zealand! All in one breath! Oh my Lord, oh my goodness.' And with that she excused herself and ran out of the dining room.

James was mortified. Had he underestimated her? He certainly wasn't expecting such a reaction. But then what sort of reaction had he been expecting? He paid the bill and raced outside to find Meghan. He spotted her on a park bench across the road. As he drew near to her he could see she was taking in deep breaths and trying to control the tears threatening to spill down her cheeks. James sat beside her and took her hand.

'My love, I am so sorry to have landed all this on you at once. To be honest I have been thinking about it for some months now and I hadn't considered how this would affect you coming out of the blue like that.'

'Is it James you are in love with, or is it all this silly talk of a life in New Zealand?' Harold Winstanley asked his daughter that night after James had asked for her hand in marriage. The question caught Meghan by surprise. She thought about it for a moment then laughed.

'Both Papa, I am in love with both.' She threw her arms around his neck. 'Be happy for me, please.'

But Harold Winstanley was far from happy when James announced they would be leaving England as soon as they were married. Harold loved his eldest daughter and would miss her terribly, but apart from that he feared for her safety and wellbeing in an untamed land far across the ocean, and far away from his protection.

Meghan went out almost every day and walked around this new and as yet unfamiliar town, enjoying the hustle and bustle of activity. Her favourite place was at a table in the corner of a small sunny room in a house on the main carriageway. The lady of the house, realising that there were no refreshment establishments in the new town suitable for ladies, had taken it upon herself to turn her sunny front room into a ladies tea room. Her husband was out of town on frequent visits to the local farming community, so she staved off her loneliness by sitting and chatting with her clients. Meg enjoyed watching the street's activities from the lace trimmed window. She envied the men and women loading their wagons with supplies from the hardware store further up the street and heading off to places she could only dream of.

The blacksmith across the road from the Hardware Store was kept busy shoeing horses. Meghan would stand for hours watching the Smithy at work. She loved the ringing sound of metal being pounded on metal as the hammer hit the anvil. She loved the hiss of the steam as the burning iron was thrust into cold water, and the way the Smithy shaped not only horseshoes but tools as well. Every now and then Baldy, as the Smithy was known, would look up at Meghan and give her a wink. She intrigued him. What on earth was a pretty young thing like her doing hanging around a blacksmith shop? He found the courage to ask her one day. Putting his hammer down on the anvil he'd wiped his hands on his leather apron and cautiously approached her as she leaned against the door in the sun.

17

'What's a pretty young lass like you doin' hangin' around a dirty smelly place like this then eh?'

Meghan smiled up at the man.

'He must be well over six feet tall', she thought. In answer to his question she said, 'I love the sounds and smells and I love the horses. I used to work in the Highlands with me Da back in Scotland.'

'You don't sound very Scottish.'

'My father is Scottish, my mother is English. My father worked in Scotland for a few years before we moved back to England.'

'Oh, I see.'

'Can I try it?'

'Try what?'

'Can I try to make a horseshoe?' Meghan didn't think he would agree but she was cheeky enough to ask anyway.

'Now why on earth would you want to make a horseshoe?'

'Because I used to help Da change the shoes on the horses and I always wondered how they were made.'

Baldy looked around to see if anyone was watching. He wasn't sure of the protocols of allowing a young woman to work alongside him in his dirty old workshop.

'It's alright,' she whispered, flashing him a devilish smile, 'I won't tell if you don't.'

Baldy threw his head back and laughed till his belly ached.

'Cheeky wee thing aint ya. Well, we best get something to cover up that pretty dress of yours, you will have to wear one of my leather aprons. It will be way too large for you but it's the best I can do.'

Meghan was delighted. She threw on the clean coverings Baldy found for her and tied the leather apron twice around her trim waist. The rest of the afternoon was spent with both of them in fits of laughter as she learned to handle the heavy hammer and hit it against the anvil, which she succeeded doing some of the time. They both enjoyed the day so much that Baldy readily agreed to teach Meghan the work of the blacksmith any time she liked.

James never found out about this time Meghan spent with Baldy until well after they had left town, but he would often wonder why his wife sometimes smelled of soot and smoke. He put it down to the coal range being in need of a clean out.

In the evenings when James was away, Meghan would read or do embroidery. She loved spending time curled up by the fire on a cold wet day reading books about New Zealand farming practices. She had no doubt that she and James would eventually become farmers and she wanted to be ready. She was also quietly gathering a collection of items for a glory box. She wasn't able to bring much with her when she left England, so she decided to start putting things together now, for their new life.

It was February 1862 - Meghan was preparing vegetables at the kitchen sink for her dinner when she saw James come galloping down the street. She wasn't expecting him back so soon. She wondered why he was in such a hurry and started to think that perhaps something was wrong, until she saw his face. A huge grin stretched from ear to ear as he leapt down from his horse and ran up the path to the front door. Meghan flung the door open.

'What is it James?'

'You won't believe who I met up with today,' he laughed as he picked her up and swung her around the room.

'Who?'

'Samuel Butler.'

'Who?'

'You know, the man we met on the ship coming over.'

'Oh, the writer.'

'Yes, that's him. Well he introduced me to his neighbour, Mr Phelps, who is managing his farm at Mesopotamia and he's offered me a job if I want it.'

'So, what did you tell him?'

'I said I didn't have much farming experience, but I was keen to learn and that you had worked in the Highlands with your father.'

'So, what did he say?'

'He said he was looking for a farm labourer and if I wasn't afraid of hard work and a very basic lifestyle then the job was ours.'

'This is very exciting James, but why you, when you haven't had any experience?'

James smiled ruefully, 'Well he wants to buy more grazing blocks and will be needing a surveyor and thought my skills in that area would be most useful.'

19

'How soon can we leave?'

'Does that mean you want to go then?'

'Yes, of course I do my darling, so when do we go?'

'Well, I talked to my boss at the office and he said he would be sorry to see me go, but if I could work out the month, he would be most grateful and said he'd pay me a bonus for the work I've done.'

James and Meghan adapted quickly to life on Mesopotamia, Meghan more so than James if the truth be told. She fell in love with the high-country mountains so reminiscent of the Highlands although the weather here was a lot warmer and drier. James would go off each day with the head Shepherd leaving Meghan at home to do the household chores. Their cottage was smaller and more basic than the one they'd had in town, but she set about making it homely with lace curtains and embroidered linen. When there was nothing to be done in the vegetable garden and the laundry and baking had all been done, Meghan would venture over to the stables and ask if she could take one of the horses out for a ride.

The Station owner had a spoilt daughter who had lost interest in the beautiful bay mare he had purchased for her and was happy to allow Meghan to exercise her. Meghan would take a sandwich and a bottle of tea in a knapsack and make her way up in to the hills carefully following the well rutted trails. She would sit on the side of the mountains and soak up the scenery below while the horse grazed on whatever sustenance it could find. Sometimes she would lie back and gaze up at the fluffy white clouds dancing across the deep blue skies and dream of a life on their own farm.

Once a month on a Sunday Meghan and James would join Mr Butler, Mr and Mrs Phelps and their two daughters, the domestic staff and farm workers as they rode on drays to a small chapel on a neighbouring block. The Minister would do the rounds of his Parish on a regular basis but sometimes the weather or unexpected circumstances would mean they would be without a Minister. On these occasions the owner of the Chapel, who had been a curate in his younger days, would take the service. Everyone was happy for him to lead them in prayer and song in the Minister's stead.

When they returned to Mesopotamia, the domestic staff would spring into action and set up the dining room for a late luncheon. Meghan and James thoroughly enjoyed these afternoons. They learned so much from the experiences of the people living and working alongside them. The afternoons generally lasted long into the evening when left-overs were served up and much alcohol was consumed.

They had been working on Mesopotamia Station for over a year when James came back from checking a flock of sheep across the river.

'How would you like to take my place while I go and do some surveying further up the valley?'

'Take your place? You mean stock work?'

'Yes, I mean stock work. You are more than capable Meg. You are very adept at riding and I know you have taken note of everything we do when you have come out with me during the round-ups. You don't have to do any shearing or crutching, but Mr Phelps is happy to teach you if you want to.'

'Oh James, you do have a way of throwing things at me unexpectedly,' she laughed.

'Is that a yes?'

'Let me have a talk with Mr Phelps first. I know it is unusual for a woman to be doing farm work but if he is prepared to teach me then I am certainly prepared to learn. I didn't tell you before, but while we were living in Christchurch I learnt to shoe horses.'

Now it was James' turn to be dumbfounded. 'Shoe horses? How, when, who...?'

'Baldy from the Blacksmith shop showed me. I used to spend a lot of time standing in the doorway watching him and eventually he let me have a try.'

James pulled his hat back and scratched his head. 'Well I never. You are a dark horse aren't you.' He picked her up and hugged her to him as she laughed and begged him to put her down.

Mr Phelps had been keeping an eye on young Mrs Morley. He was impressed with her riding ability and she seemed to enjoy being out and about with the stockmen whenever she had the chance. He sat across the table from her now as Mrs Phelps set cups of tea and biscuits before them.

'So, Mrs Morley, you are keen on becoming a stockwoman then?'

'Yes, very much so. I loved helping my father in the Highlands back home and I must admit I have really missed it.'

'Well, I know it's not the done thing, but I also know that the womenfolk who are working hereabouts on the land are working just as hard, if not harder than some of the men. I have great admiration for a woman who knows what she's about and is not afraid to try new things and work hard. Mrs Phelps here was a land girl before I met her, but marriage and children have forced her to work indoors these days.'

Mrs Phelps flashed him a knowing smile but said nothing.

On a handshake over a cup of tea, Meghan became a farmhand and James went back to surveying. Once again, he would be gone for a week or two at a time as he explored and surveyed unchartered valleys deep in the mountains. He would come home full of stories of stony river beds reaching from the base of one mountain range across to another, sometimes a mile wide; of waterfalls cascading down the mountainsides falling into the quiet rivers below and turning them into raging torrents; of the tussock covered grassy flats alongside the rivers which would be suitable for grazing; of grass covered hills and snow covered mountains; of run-holders he had met and the stories they told of their life in the high country. He had fallen in love with the land even if he hadn't fallen in love with farming.

It took James almost a year to complete surveying the areas assigned to him. As his tenure was coming to a close one of the run-holders told him about a 2000-hectare block way up the valley that was being put up for lease. James called in to the Land Office when he was in Christchurch two weeks later. He didn't tell Meghan what he was up to, he didn't want to get her hopes up.

He raced into the house all excited after his visit to Christchurch and was disappointed to find Meghan wasn't there. He got the fire stoked up and put the kettle on to make a cup of tea while he waited for her to return.

He was sound asleep in front of the fire when she finally walked in the door at dusk.

'Where have you been? I've been waiting for you for ages!'

'We've been penning the sheep; we start shearing tomorrow. Why has something happened?'

'Yes it has. You had better sit down my love.'

Meghan was beginning to get worried. James looked very serious as he knelt before her and took both her hands.

'Mrs Morley,' he began, 'you and I are now the proud lease holders of 2000 hectares of land.'

Meghan looked at him for a moment, stunned.

'Once again James Morley, you have thrown me into turmoil. Are you going to do this often?' But a smile was curving her lips as it dawned on her what he had just said. 'Truly James? You have found us some land?'

'Truly my love, I have.'

'Where? Have you got a map? Show me where?'

James pulled a bundle of papers out of his satchel and spread them out on the table. Taking up the map he had acquired from the Land Office and laying it beside his surveyor's map he patiently outlined the area that they were to lease and where it was situated on the larger map.

'That's not far from here James. But how do we get in to such a remote place? Do we have to cross someone else's land?'

'Yes we do. The land borders Flaxbush Station and the owners are happy for us to cross through their property. In fact, the man in the Land Office said they are a lovely family and very welcoming.'

'I wonder what Mr Phelps will think about us leaving?'

'I spoke to him and Mr Butler before I went to Christchurch and they have given us their blessing and any help we might need. They are all for people setting up and farming the land here, after all that is what we came here to do, is it not?'

'It is,' she sighed, 'it truly is.'

They purchased two saddle horses from Mr Phelps at Mesopotamia. Meg had watched her mount being born and had spent a lot of time with him as he matured. When he was offered to her to break in and ride she was delighted and burst into tears when Mr Phelps eventually offered to sell him to her. James was able to purchase the horse he had been riding on the farm. He was a bit older but solid and reliable and he had a kind eye, James felt comfortable with him. Meg named her horse Jasper; James horse was already named Gus.

November 1864
Flaxbush Station

James and Meghan were to travel by horse and wagon as far as Flaxbush Station taking as much as they could load onto the wagon. There would also be two pack horses tethered at the rear. They were told it could be another eight to ten months before they would be able to leave the property and replenish their supplies. The rivers would dictate their access to and from their run holding and they were heading in to Autumn. It wouldn't be long before it snowed and the rivers ran too high for them to cross. But this didn't bother James and Meghan, they were far too excited to begin life on their own farm. They felt confident they had enough supplies to last them.

They set a steady pace on the first two days of their journey while the going was good and the horses fresh. By the third day they were getting a little weary, but their spirits were still high. They came up over a hill around mid-morning and to their delight there stood before them a large lake, perfectly still, reflecting the surrounding trees. They stopped and stared in amazement.

'What a wonderful sight this is,' sighed Meghan. 'I had no idea it could be this beautiful so far inland. You never told me about this lake.'

James reached out and taking her hand in his held it to his lips. 'I wanted to surprise you my darling. This and so much more awaits us, just you wait and see.'

'Can we stay here for the night? Please James, I know you are excited to get to...'

James held his finger to her lips. 'Hush, yes of course we can. I was going to suggest the very same thing. We could have pushed on and stayed here last night but I wanted you to see the lake just as I did, in the calm of early morning when it is still, with the surroundings reflecting in it.'

They sat for a while just taking in the natural beauty around them before making their way around the side of the hill down to the flat tussock covered grassy area beside the lake. They pulled up close to the water, tethered and unpacked all six horses and let them graze, drink and rest. James rigged up a canvas shelter attaching it to the side of the wagon closest to the water so they could sit in the shade and enjoy a view of the lake. He then set up a stone fireplace, and using the wooden stakes normally reserved for the bracing of the V-shaped tent, pushed them into the hard ground on either side of the fire bracing them with rocks to support them. He placed a metal rod across the fire wedging it into the V-shape formed by tying three stakes together at the top. He had fashioned these stakes himself before they left Mesopotamia. He liked to work with his hands and under the tutelage of Mr Milne, the carpenter on the farm, he had learned valuable skills, the kind that would be useful when it came to building their house and furniture.

James and Meghan sat down at the water's edge on rocks warmed by the morning sun. They almost held their breath as they tuned in to the sounds around them. The water as it washed gently over smooth rounded stones, the munching of the horses as they grazed, the buzz of insects, and a variety of bird calls from the bush behind them. On the far side of the lake the mountains loomed deep blue in the late summer morning. Soon they would be completely covered in a thick white blanket of snow and look altogether different and even more remarkable. The undulating land from the base of the mountains running down to and flattening out at the lake was brittle dry and brown at this time of the year.

'I can't see how this land could feed much stock James.'

Meg was sipping on strong tea from her tin cup as she studied the land around her.

'It doesn't at this time of the year, that's why they send them up in to the hill country. Surely you learned that at Mesopotamia Meg.'

'I did but there was a lot more flat pasture there than there was hill country and they did grow crops as supplement feed so I guess they would farm differently there than the farmers would here, especially as the farms encroach more and more into the higher mountainous areas.'

'Yes they do. I guess we will learn more and more as we go and some of it by trial and error I suspect,' replied James ruefully.

Behind them the hills were covered in dense forest and alive with bird song.

'This must be what heaven is like,' whispered Meghan, not wanting to disturb the sounds of nature.

'Yes, I guess it must,' James whispered in reply. He reached down and untied his boots then stripped off his woollen socks. Easing his feet into the crisp cold water he let out a long sigh of relief and satisfaction.

'You should try this Meghan, it's wonderfully soothing.'

Meghan did as he suggested releasing her feet from her tight leather boots and sweaty socks. Then she too relaxed as the cool water soothed her tired aching feet.

'I could stay here forever,' she sighed, closing her eyes and lifting her face to the sun.

'And who pray will fix my dinner this evening?' laughed James.

'Oh, I am sure you are quite capable of doing that yourself James. After all, you do it when you are out surveying. Maybe you can cook for me tonight for a change.'

'I've got a better idea,' laughed James as he jumped up and pulled Meg to her feet. He picked her up and waded out into the lake to hip height threatening to drop her in to the cool clear water. She squealed and clung to his neck, but she knew he wouldn't do such a thing. Sure enough, he waded back to the water's edge again but set her down deep enough for the water to soak the bottom of her dress up to her knees.

'Oh James, now look what you've done, my skirts are soaked.'

'Well you will just have to take them off now won't you,' he teased.

When she had stripped to her pantaloons and bodice, he drew her down to the ground beside him and slowly and gently made love to her, the warming sun bathing them in a golden light.

They ate bread and cheese and drank the cool water from the lake then slept for an hour allowing the sun to warm and heal their bodies. By late afternoon James had caught and skinned a rabbit. Meg cut up some potatoes and carrots and all of this was simmering away in a pot over the hot embers of the fire. As the sun began to dip towards the horizon James grabbed Meg's hand and said, 'Come with me, I want to show you something.'

Curious she allowed him to lead her into the forest behind their camp. They fought their way in through the undergrowth for a short distance until they came across a fallen log.

'Sit down here,' James whispered and holding a finger to his lips said, 'listen.'

The variety of beautiful sounds coming from the birds settling down for the night was overwhelming. Meg had always loved birds and thrilled at the variety of songs she could hear. She gasped as a large green bird flew down close to them then flew up to settle on a branch above their heads.

'The Maori call that one a Kee-aa,' smiled James. Did you see the bright orange under its wings?'

Meg nodded, 'I did, it was stunning, 'she said breathlessly. 'I've never seen such a beautiful bird.'

'There are many beautiful birds up here Meg,' he smiled. 'Look, I brought this for you on our last trip to Christchurch.'

He pulled a small book from his pocket and gave it to her. It was a collection of bird sketches and descriptions he had found in a bookstore. He knew how much she loved birds and he thought the book might help her identify the ones she would come across when there was no-one around to tell her what they were. Meg traced her fingers gently over the images on the pages, tears welling up in her eyes.

'Oh my love, this is the most perfect gift, thank you so much.' She leant over and kissed him tenderly on the mouth. 'You are such a thoughtful man.'

'I have marked the ones we are most likely to encounter here and further up the valley. There is the Saddleback, Pihoihoi, Kokako, Rock Wren, Wood Pigeon and the Tititi-pounamu.'

'What unusual names.'

'Some of them are the names given to them by the Maori people.'

'Pounamu, isn't that the green stone that the Maori people treasure?'

'Yes, I believe it is.'

'Do you think we will see any Maori people living in the mountains?'

'I don't think so. They don't much like the cold, or so I am led to believe.'

They sat in silence for a while longer before following their noses back to their delicious smelling rabbit stew.

They reached Flaxbush Station late afternoon the following day and were warmly welcomed by the owners. The Hopkins family consisted of the mother, Gladys, the father, Henry, and their three rather lively, ruddy cheeked healthy looking children. Meg just couldn't picture them sitting quietly at a dinner table speaking only when spoken to as had been the case in her formative years.

'My my, what a wonderful welcoming committee you all are,' smiled Meg. 'This reminds me of my family back home.'

She fought back a tear at the thought and quickly swallowed the lump in her throat which didn't go unnoticed by Gladys Hopkins.

'Come along my dear let's get you inside where you can freshen up and rest before dinner, you must be exhausted, it is a long way up here isn't it.'

'Yes, but it's worth every mile when you have such beautiful surroundings.' she replied.

Gladys and Henry Hopkins had been at Flaxbush Station for many years and were well established with a comfortable homestead featuring three bedrooms, a large kitchen dining area and a separate lounge room. There was a long-drop out the back and further away there was a wooden structure for storing food. Along one side of the house sheltered by a row of trees was an orchard with apple, quince, cape gooseberry and peach trees. A short distance up the track was a large woolshed and pens all sectioned off with wooden fencing.

'Did you and Mr Hopkins build all this?' Meg asked looking out the back door across to where Henry and James were talking outside the woolshed.

'Not all of it. The house was only a two-room hut when we arrived. We built on once the two younger ones arrived and Henry and his brother Daniel built the woolshed. His brother has a building business in Christchurch which has been such a blessing. What about you two? What are your plans?'

'Well, James tells me our first home will be a one room hut for now which I am sure will be ample for us. Once we have children, I am sure that will change things as it did for you. That's if we ever have any children. James has been away such a lot.'

Meg's cheeks took on a slight blush and Gladys couldn't help but notice the catch in her voice.

'You are still young my dear, there's plenty of time to have little ones once you have settled into your new life.'

'Yes of course. You are right, there's plenty of time yet. Now what can I do to help?'

James and Meg shared one of the children's rooms leaving the three young ones to bunk in together. Though well behaved the children were well used to being able to run freely about the farm and were seldom censured to be quiet, as city children would have been, and three of them in one small bedroom did create quite a din. Not that Meg complained, it really did remind her of home.

James spent the next two days with Henry discussing his plans for getting supplies into the valley to build a hut and stock sheds. Henry's brother, Daniel was waiting to take James order as soon as he was ready. Henry advised James what to look for when selecting a site and the type of buildings that would best suit the conditions of the area. You will need a steep pitched roof James, which will allow the snow to slide off and also give you some room in the rafters for storage. I would also advise a sturdy verandah so that you are not snowed in and can at least open your door during heavy snow falls. Nothing is worse than being trapped inside a small building for days and even weeks on end.'

'Sounds like you have had such an experience Henry.'

'I have James, I have, and it will haunt me for the rest of my life,' he laughed. 'Three of us were shepherding a few years ago up in the high country. We'd spent the night in one of the corrugated huts up there, very basic and not a lot of room. In one way that was a good thing as we were able to keep relatively warm but in another way being cooped up with two other smelly blokes was not a pleasant experience.'

'What happened?' asked James, his curiosity piqued.

'We stopped there because it had started to snow and got too heavy for us to make our way down before dark. Fortunately, we'd stacked plenty of firewood inside, so we were able to keep the fire going and we scrapped snow through a hole in the wall to keep us going in water. Our rations were not substantial so we ate sparsely not knowing how long we would be there.'

'So how long were you trapped there?' asked James

'Seven nightmarish days. The playing cards that had been left in the hut were almost worn out, as were our tempers. Of course, we had to toilet in the hut in a bucket and that was getting mighty rank as you can well imagine.'

James shuddered at the thought.

'Every day we would keep shoving at the door to see if the snow had stopped or was melting. We considered taking it off its hinges at one stage but decided we didn't want to fill the hut up with snow, so we kept pushing. Eventually we were able to push open a gap big enough to let a little daylight in above the door where the top of the snow came to. We pushed at the top layer of snow with the fire shovel until we were able to create a shelf low enough for us to empty out the bucket. The snow was packed solid and had been frozen over so it was very hard to make any headway, but we did finally manage to create a gap big enough for us to climb out and up on to the top of the snow drift. Of course, our horses were nowhere to be seen. Turns out they made their way safely back down to the farm on their own. We started to make our way down on foot. It wasn't snowing, in fact it was a glorious day. Then we spotted a group of men making their way up towards us on foot stomping tracks through the snow. We were all mighty pleased to see each other I can tell you. They had bottles of tea, and fresh sandwiches which have never tasted so good. Apparently, that was the first day that there had been no heavy rain or snow.'

31

James decided that was probably one story he would not relate to Meg; he didn't want to alarm her any more than was necessary at this stage.

December 1864
Stony Downs

James and Meg set out for Stony Downs at daybreak to go and see their newly acquired land and to find a suitable place to build their hut. And a hut is all it would be. Meg was under no illusion that it would be no more than 10 feet by 12 feet with one door and no windows.

'In time we will be able to build on to our homestead Meg, but you need to understand that we will be living a very simple life until then,' James had told her.

A lot of the money they had put aside had been spent on taking up the lease and the rest would be spent on supplies and the stock they would need to get started. Among the papers that James had brought back from the Land Office the day he announced the news to Meg about the lease holding, was a list of items they would need to set themselves up.

They could build on the number of ewes they planned to run on their 3000 acres but would have to wait and see how productive the land was first. They could only afford 1000 ewes at this stage at 30 shillings each and fifteen rams at £5 each. The two horses James and Meg purchased from Mr Phelps, along with a good solid dray came to £300. Their tools and supplies for the first 12 months amounted to £275 and they were to show that they had sufficient funds in a bank account to cover their expenses for the next three years. This amounted to £650 which appeared to be enough to satisfy the requirements of the Lease. Henry had offered them the use of his half-draught horses to pull the dray which they were told would be able to cope better with the river crossings and the mountainous terrain, so they gladly took up the offer.

James and Meg sat comfortably astride their familiar mounts. They travelled without speaking in the silence of the early dawn listening to the surrounding peace shattered only by the sweet sounds of the river as it trickled over its rounded stones. Shafts of daylight began to appear over the mountain tops to the East lightening the sky with the promise of a warm, blue sky day. They weaved their way up over and down the brown stubble covered hills to the river where they stopped and allowed the horses to drink before they picked their way along the stony riverbed to the next flat tussock area ahead of them. At one point they came to a narrow cutting at the base of two mountain ranges which was separated only by a rocky river bed.

'There will be places like this for much of the year that we will not be able to get through because the rivers will be running too high. You need to remember that my love. This terrain can be deadly, and we will need to treat it with great respect. Folks have told me dramatic stories of men who have come to grief in places such as this. I don't mean to frighten you, but you really must be aware of the climate hereabouts and the dangers that can befall you.'

'I understand James, I have been listening. It's not unlike the mountain areas Father and I used to ride around in the Highlands.'

'Yes, I guess there is a similarity, but you won't have had extremes of snow and heat as they have here. All I am saying Meg is that I want you to be very careful.'

'I really do understand James and I have listened to what others have told me about the mountains. They are stunning in their glory, but they can also be menacing in their fury. I have heard stories from the womenfolk too. Gladys has spoken to me at length about the many things I need to know.'

As the sun rose to the mid-heaven they pulled up and taking the sacks of food and supplies off the horses, tied the reins to thorny matagouri bushes and left them to graze. They built a small fire with some tussock, just enough to boil water for tea. They ate bread and cheese and cold mutton from the previous night's roast dinner and sat back for a time to enjoy the peace and tranquility of the valley.

'How long did you say it would take us to get there James?'

'I figured around two to three days if we don't dilly dally too long. It will be longer of course when we bring the wagon and stock through.'

'I'm looking forward to sleeping out under the stars with you, away from other people.'

James gave her a knowing smile and reaching over stroked her cheek with his finger.

'Me too my love,' he whispered huskily.

They tied their bundles behind the horses' saddles again and mounted, ready to continue their journey. The vast open valleys before them were divided by the generous expanse of the stony Lawrence River which at times reached from the base of one mountain range across to the one on the other side. At this time of the year small rivulets ran in ribbons down across the stony beds and it was not difficult to find a suitable crossing, but during the winter these rivulets joined up to become a raging torrent sometimes sending logs and debris screaming down the valleys at a frightening pace and with a deafening roar. In places the shallow water had become trapped in pools formed by rock formations created by the strong torrents which had run through this valley for longer than anyone knew. Shallow pools lay calm and peaceful, like mirrors, reflecting their stunning surroundings.

They found a suitable grassy knoll to set up for the night and set about making camp. James erected the V shaped tent which would be big enough for them to lie down in. He placed the three-pronged stays into the ground as far in as they would go then ran a piece of rope from the ground at one end, across the top of the stays and fastened it to the ground on the other side bracing the stays and the guide rope with rocks. He then placed a square of light canvas over the rope and fastened the sides down with rocks. This done he turned to setting up the fireplace. He formed a circle with more rocks that Meg had carried up from the river and laid some dry tussock in the middle. Making sure they had plenty of small bits of dry wood and twigs on hand, they set the tussock alight and as it took hold added more and more bits of wood until they were ready to drop a couple of larger pieces on top. They let these pieces burn down then placed their already blackened can full of cool river water over the embers to boil. They added a small handful of black tea leaves, allowed them to stew into a rich warming tea then sat back and enjoyed their brew with a couple of ships biscuits.

Once they had made themselves comfortable with tufts of grass padding to soften the stony ground beneath their weary bodies they slept well and awoke to a brightening sky indicating it was well into the morning.

'Oh, it appears we have overslept Meg. Best we get ourselves going. Let's stop a little further on for something to eat, shall we?' suggested James.

They packed their tent away, doused what embers were left of the fire, rolled up their bed rolls, saddled up the horses and got underway. They travelled quickly until the sun was starting to descend past its midday position. They were hungry and thirsty and took the time to make a small fire on which to boil some water for their tea. They ate more of the cheese and bread and drank their tea. They packed up and rode on again in silence, taking in their surroundings. As the day was drawing to a close James suggested they look for a suitable site to make camp for the night.

'Let's just get around this bend in the river and see if there is a suitable spot somewhere.'

As they rounded the bend, they were dismayed to see a large bank of dark and menacing clouds heading down the valley in their direction.

'Looks like we are in for a mighty deluge,' said James forlornly. 'Best we get set up as soon as possible before it reaches us. We need to find somewhere to shelter from the rain.'

They looked about them but could see nothing suitable within easy reach so decided to go back around the bend they had just come from. There they found a shallow hollow under a jutting rock where they hastily set up a shelter on the leeward side of the coming storm.

'What about the horses James, what should we do with them?'

'Not much we can do but set them loose and hope they don't get spooked or go too far if the storm brings thunder and lightning.'

The horses were restless as they were being unsaddled and as soon as their halters were off, they headed away up the hill.

'I guess they know where they need to be,' Meg was concerned, 'after all they are used to being out in all weathers aren't they?'

36

'Yes, I'm sure they will be just fine Meg, now come on let's get all this gear in under the rocks and cover it as best we can.'

They threw the canvas over the front of the rock placing large stones on top to hold it down against the wind that was starting to whisk up the valley towards them. They unrolled their blankets and taking out some bread and mutton, settled themselves down under the shelter of the rock for the night.

And what a night it was. First came the wind. It roared up the valley with such ferocity that James and Meg clung to each other in fright. They could hardly hear each other speak even at such close quarters. And then the rain came. It got heavier and heavier until it was coming down in sheets. Despite their best efforts the frightened pair were not able to stay dry. The storm kept up its might for several hours leaving Meg wondering if it was ever going to stop. And then, in the early hours just before daybreak, it stopped, and everything went very quiet. Meg and James, still huddled together, drifted off to sleep until they were rudely awakened by the horses snorting and neighing and nudging at their canvas covering. They gingerly poked their heads out and there they were, tossing their heads about and frolicking as if relieved they had survived the stormy night. James emerged from the cover first then turned to pull Meg to her feet. They stood slowly to full height stretching and flexing their tired cramped muscles. All about them the banks were running with small rivulets racing each other down to the river bed. The sun was just starting to appear over the mountain tops lighting the valley in a soft golden glow. There was nowhere dry enough to make a fire so Meg and James shook off as much water as they could from their bed rolls, dried the saddles as best they could and got themselves underway in search of a more suitable site to make camp and dry out. As the sun rose higher steam started rising off the horses' bodies.

'That was quite a storm,' remarked Meg. 'I can't believe how quickly the river has filled up with just that one burst of rain.'

'I guess that is what we will have to learn to live with now. From what I hear the wind can get pretty ferocious at times. There are those nor'westers we experienced in Christchurch, those wild, hot, dry winds that create dust storms and sometimes last for days.'

Meg shuddered. 'Let's hope that here at least we won't get the dust storms, they were dreadful, you could barely breath sometimes.'

'I've been told the sou'westers are the ones to look out for though, they bring the cold rain and snow.'

'I have been warned about that too,' added Meg, 'they tend to arrive without much warning unless you are constantly watching the skies. Bit like this one we just had.'

'That is something we will learn to do I expect, watch out for weather changes when we are working outside. Wait until winter when the snows come. I hear tell it can get quite deep and we could be trapped up here for several weeks.'

'Well then,' replied Meg philosophically, 'we shall just have to make sure we have plenty of food and firewood won't we.'

James laughed, 'Oh Meggy darling I do so love your strength and courage, you never cease to amaze me with what you take on and accomplish. Your family would be so proud of you. You must write and tell them of your exploits once we are settled.'

'Perhaps not James,' Meg was laughing, 'it might be best that they don't know too much lest they worry so.'

'Maybe you are right, write them and tell them as much as you think they might be comfortable with.'

They eventually came across an area further up the valley which had had a chance to dry out under the hot mid-morning sun. Here they were able to light a decent fire and dry themselves and their bed rolls and belongings out. They let the horses graze and once the fire died down to glowing embers, sat back and waited for the water to boil.

'James do you remember old Mrs Salinger from down the road back in Kent?'

'You mean that unusual lady with wild hair and eyes to match.'

Meg laughed, 'Yes that's the one. Well she is a herbalist, did you know that?'

'No, I did not. So why do you speak of her now?'

'Well, she taught me a lot about wild plants. We used to go walking up in the hills sometimes and she would show me what plants were edible and what ones were not. So, while we were in Christchurch I found a wee book of wild plants and took some notes. I'm not sure what I will find up here, but it might be useful to know such things.'

'So what brought that to mind now then?'

Meg looked down in to the tin cup containing her tea.

'This black tea is not much to my liking and I was just wondering if there was something else growing here that might make for a more pleasant brew.'

James threw back his head and roared with laughter. 'Meg you are such a tonic, you come out with the most amusing things sometimes.'

At the look of disappointment on Meg's face he quickly added, 'Thoughtful and intelligent things my love, but amusing just the same.'

The sun was well on its way towards the tops of the mountains in the west now so they stayed where they were for the night planning to make an early start next morning.

'We should be at Stony Downs by early tomorrow,' declared James.

'Stony Downs? Is that what you have named our run-holding?'

'Well I had to come up with something when I registered for it. It was the first thing that popped into my head.'

'I rather like it and it is most apt for this area, so I suppose Stony Downs it is then.'

They were up before sunrise the next morning eager to get underway. And true to his word they arrived at their run-holding before the sun was in the mid heaven.

'This is it Meg. As far as you can see to the East over there, up as far as that bend in the river to the West of us, this mountain range behind us right to the top and here where we are now are the boundaries of our property, 3000 hectares. Now all we need do is find a suitable site to build our home.'

He pulled a piece of paper out from one of the saddle-bags.

'Let's have another look at what the authorities suggest shall we, he smiled. 'And then we can make our own minds up as to whether we will follow their instructions or follow our own instincts.'

Meg read over his shoulder.

The site selected for a homestead should be near wood and water, where a sheltered spot can be fenced in for a garden. After the tents or whares have been put up, a sheep-yard must be constructed of wattle-hurdles or of sods.

'What's a faree,' asked Meg?'

James smiled at Meg's mispronunciation, 'It's the Maori word for a house or dwelling.'

'I see. So what else does it say on there?'

39

A wool-shed will afterwards have to be formed, and tarpaulins will be found useful to cover in the wool-shed, and for many other purposes; wool-sheds should be on a clear open space of clean grass, near to water and wood. A hurdle-yard should be kept specially for shearing. The permanent drafting-yard should be some way from the shearing-yard to avoid dust. After the rough work of the station is completed, a dipping-place with boiler should be made. Regard to natural boundaries of sea, swamp, cliff, or thick bush should be had in the selection of a new station.

'I suspect we will be busy for quite some time by the sound of this,' Meg said deep in thought.

'We won't need all of these things initially; we can take the sheep to Flaxbush Station for shearing and Henry said we could have the help of a couple of his workers when we need it. I thank God for that man Meg, I'm not sure how well we would do without his help.'

'And Gladys is such a lovely lady, she seems to know so much about so many things. I have learned a lot from her already,' Meg smiled.

'I too have learned so much from Henry. He is a wealth of knowledge. How blessed we are Meg to have come across such wonderful people.'

Once Meg and James were happy with the lie of the land and had come to an agreement on where their house should be built they spent a couple of days riding out around the property familiarising themselves with the terrain, the majestic mountains and the wide expanse of stony river beds which was now all a part of their run holding. There was plenty of flat tussock land between the house site and the river which would eventually be fenced, and a suitable site selected to build stock yards and a shearing shed. They chose to nestle the house on a grass covered knoll close to the foot of a rugged scrub covered mountain range. It was as far away from the river as they could get and surrounding them was a ready supply of firewood. The sheltered area between the house and the hillside behind it would be an ideal place to build the stables and sheds for the house cow and chickens that would eventually be brought in.

Meg's heart was fit to bursting as they rode along the river banks taking in the terrain of their new home. Despite it being summer the hills

40

were green with plants and grass, the thorny matagouri and tussock grass being the most predominant. The lower footings of the hills flowed down and ran out on to the river flats below creating a soft green carpet against the stark rugged blue mountain ranges above and all around them.

'Oh how I wish I could paint,' sighed Meg. 'I would love to be able to capture this and send it home to show my family.'

'There's no reason why you couldn't try to draw it my love, perhaps I will get you some paper and pencils for Christmas or your birthday.'

Meg smiled and blew him a kiss.

Meg and James saddled up reluctantly the next morning and rode back to Flaxbush Station to begin the next part of their mission. They had already fallen in love with Stony Downs and didn't want to leave just yet, but they knew there was much work to be done before winter set in and they were isolated by the raging rivers.

The House Site - January 1865

Soon after James and Meg returned to Flaxbush Station, James and two of the farmhands rode in to Christchurch to pick up the dray and load it with the building supplies that he needed. They were back within two weeks and after a two-night break at Flaxbush, headed out the following day to Stony Downs to get started on building the hut. It was to be one-room with a large covered verandah to give them shelter from the sun and snow. The pitch of the roof was steep and high enough for storage in the rafters and also to allow the snow to slide off in winter. The verandah area in the front would cover the width of the hut and the roof was also sloped so that the rain and snow would run off into a channel which would then be fed into barrels for their water supply. This would be a lot easier than having to cart the water in buckets from way down in the stream each day.

They would also build a futtah, a smaller hut high off the ground which would be used to store food supplies away from any animals. A long drop would be erected around the back of the house where it would be sheltered from the weather and beside it a low oblong shed which would serve as a stable for the horses at one end, a chicken coop at the other, with a small hole cut into the wall to let them come and go to their roosting boxes. The dog kennels would be set up in the middle. It would be walled in on three sides with the open side facing away from the prevailing wind giving the animals the shelter they would need in the winter and in stormy weather. On the sheltered side was a lean-to for the house cow. It was big enough for Bessy to lie down in and there was also room for Meg and James to sit on a stool and milk her of an evening. They had both been taught how to milk but Meg was far better at it than James and he would tend to leave it to Meg. Meg didn't mind, she rather enjoyed milking Bessy. She was very fond of the lovely patient old cow they had purchased off the Hopkins.

Over the next eight weeks James and the young men made two trips in and out of the valley before the buildings were finished. In the meantime, Meg enjoyed her time with Gladys and Henry at Flaxbush Station learning as much as she could about the life that lay ahead of her. They told her about the moods and weather patterns of the mountainous country they were entering into, they talked at length about mustering, shearing and lambing. James and Meg had come to an arrangement with the Hopkins with regards to manpower. The stock hands, Stephen and Marshall, were willing to ride into Stony Downs once a month, weather permitting, with mail and supplies and to help out with any stock work that needed to be done. In return James would make himself available for the seasonal musters and shearing at Flaxbush.

'I noticed you have a blacksmith shop,' Meg said to Henry one day. 'How often does the smithy turn up? I was thinking about the horses. No doubt with the rugged and stony terrain they need regular shoeing.'

'Yes they do, but unfortunately we haven't had a smithy here for some time, there seems to be a shortage of them at the moment.'

'Well,' said Meg hesitantly, 'I have learned to make horseshoes and with some help from one of the hands I could shoe your horses for you.'

Henry looked and Gladys and they both started laughing. Meg blushed and became somewhat embarrassed. Gladys saw her reddening cheeks.

'Oh Meg, we are not laughing *at* you, we are just surprise and absolutely delighted that you have learned these skills and we would be eternally grateful to you. You are a quick learner and we have been impressed with your varied talents, it's just that this was the last thing we expected to hear.'

Once the laughter died down Henry took Meg by the hand, pulled her to her feet and said, 'Right then young lady, let's put you to work. I have two horses here in the paddock desperately in need of new shoes. Gladys do you think you could rustle up some old clothes for Meg, we can't have her playing around in the smithy in these clothes.'

And that's where James found her on his return from building their new home two months later. 'So, this is what you get up to the minute my back is turned,' he laughed.

'James, you're back. Is it finished? Are we ready to go?'

'Yes my love, it is finished and yes we can go as soon as the sheep arrive. Henry tells me they should be here within the next couple of days. They will need a break for a couple of days before we take them any further and then we will need to push on so we can get them settled and fattened up before tupping time.'

'How many head will we have?' asked Meg

'I've bought 1,000 ewes and 2 rams. I was told 2 per hectare is the guideline but it does depend on what feed is available. Let's see how these ones go this season; I really can't afford to make any mistakes.'

In appreciation for all the kindness and support the Hopkins's had shown her, Meg had quietly been working on creating some items she thought Gladys and Henry might appreciate. When things were quiet and there was not a lot to do Meg would steal away to the smithy shed and get to work. She made two new pokers of different lengths for Gladys and two the same for her and James. Then she had several attempts at making trivets to rest hot pots on and finally succeeded in making three that she considered acceptable. She fashioned some new hooks to hang over the fire place, two for her new home and two for Gladys. She also made several hooks to attach to the walls of her new home, some to hang items on and some to support planks of wood for shelving. Gladys and Henry were delighted with their gifts and refused any offer of payment from Meg for the iron she had used to make her own items.

On March 22nd 1865, James and Meg loaded up a their dray with enough supplies for the next 12 months plus Meg's chest of linen and bedding, four chairs, a sturdy wooden table, a three legged stool for milking, further building and timber supplies a wooden bucket for water and a couple of other items Gladys felt they might need and had managed to squeeze into the corners of the well packed dray. Four of Henry's half Clydesdales would pull the dray. Henry would follow them over in a few days to have a look at the hut and bring the horses back.

The box with the chickens was tied firmly into one corner on the outer edge of the dray and Bessy the cow was tethered to the back, Jasper and Gus were tethered one on each side. Meg got the giggles as she climbed up on the dray to sit beside James.

'What is tickling your fancy young lady?' he couldn't help laughing with her.

'Do you see how bizarre we look James? The wagon is loaded up so high, the chickens are cackling away in the box, Bessy is tugging at her halter and the horses are none too pleased about being tethered either.'

James had to admit it did seem rather funny. They pulled out of the yard and started up the hill on their journey which at best would probably take four to five days. After the first hour of restlessness the animals finally settled down and ambled along concentrating on negotiating the uneven terrain.

James and Meg waved to the Hopkins family until they were out of sight.

'I will miss them,' she sighed.

'Yes, they are a lovely family. I do appreciate everything they have done for us. I just pray we can return their kindness one day. But from now on my love we will be at the mercy of these great mountains and whatever they might deem to throw at us.'

'That sounds so morbid and frightening.'

'Sorry Meg, I guess I am feeling a little trepidatious. This is a big step for us? Are you not just a little afraid and uncertain too?'

'Maybe just a little,' she confessed, 'but it is over-ridden with excitement James. We cannot look forward with dread and fear, we must have faith and trust in God and know that we will rise to whatever challenges beset us. We talked about this before we left England remember?'

James reached across and took Meg's hand.

'Of course, you are right Meg; we must be strong and have faith. We only have each other now and I have every faith in you. You have proven to me time and again since we have been in this country that you are a very strong and capable woman. I suspect you will be stronger in the face of adversity than I will ever be. I will be looking to you to keep me strong. Can you do that for me Meg? Is that asking too much?'

Meg was shocked to see this weakness in James. He had always held himself up to be the strong, supportive decisive one in their marriage and now here he was leaning on her for support. She rose to the challenge.

'Of course I will James, I love you and I know that whatever comes our way we will meet it head on, together. Now enough of this talk, let's just enjoy the ride home.

The two young farm hands who had helped James build the hut were driving the flock of sheep to Stony Downs. They had started out the day before and James expected to catch them up on the second day. He hoped the weather would hold so they wouldn't have too much trouble getting the sheep across the river.

'When the rivers run high or fast after heavy downpours or melting snow, it is nigh on impossible to get the sheep to cross,' Henry Hopkins had told James and Meg one evening as they sat around the dining room table. 'Once the first one takes the plunge the rest will generally follow but just getting that first one to go can be quite a challenge. I have a couple of hand reared sheep that I use as leaders which is most advantageous. Once the wool is wet it can weigh the sheep down and if the water is too deep and they can't get their footing they could be washed down stream to their peril. Once they have experienced a difficult crossing they become very wary of doing it again.'

James and Meg stopped at midday for a meal break. James helped Meg down off the wagon. They uncoupled the horses and let them forage for whatever sustenance they could find and set a place to light a fire and boil the tea. Gladys Hopkins had sent them off with a very well stocked basket of home-baked goods, enough to last them for several days.

'Well we won't starve,' laughed Meg as she lifted the lid of the basket that James had retrieved from the wagon for her. 'There's enough food in here to feed an army.'

'Once we catch up with Stephen and Marshall I doubt it will last for long,' James replied.

'What are they like, the two men?' asked Meg. 'You have worked with them for several weeks, but I have hardly spoken to them.'

47

'They are good chaps,' he said, 'hard working and reliable. I have no doubt they will become a valuable part of our lives as time goes on. People rely heavily on each other in remote places like this. I know when I have been out surveying and come across a farmhouse seemingly in the middle of nowhere high up in the hills, they greet me like a long lost friend. Once they know I am not an escaped convict or some such first,' he laughed. 'They seem to thrive on news from the outside world and to have someone new to talk to. Many a time I have been offered a bed for the night just so they can keep talking with me.'

'I never knew that James, you never mentioned it before,' Meg smiled at the thought.

The next day Meg and James caught up to Stephen and Marshall and the mob of sheep. They had made good time and had little or no trouble keeping the stock together.

'They aren't a bad mob Mr Morley,' said Stephen, the older of the two men. Your two dogs here are working well.'

'Good,' said James. Mr Hopkins has been teaching me how to train them and work them. I am not what you would call an animal person really. Mrs Morley here is the one for animals. They seem to be drawn to her and she to them, isn't that so my love?'

'Yes, but then I have worked with stock and had animals around me all my life. There was always a cat or two and a dog running around the yard at home and my father and I shared a love of horses. Did James tell you I used to ride in the Scottish Highlands with me Da for a few years?'

Stephen's face showed surprise and respect for this side of Meg. He knew her skills in the blacksmith shop but had not known of her ability working with stock.

'Well then, you are a fortunate man Mr Morley to be having a wife with such abilities as these. I don't doubt you would be the envy of many a run-holder.'

'I believe you might be right there Stephen.' Although James was a little embarrassed, he was also immensely proud of Meg.

Meg cleared away the remnants of their lunch and turned to Stephen.

'Mr Sangster, I would be obliged if I could change places with young Marshall and ride with you so that I might learn more about the way you work the dogs if that is acceptable. If my services as a farm hand are going to be required, then it would be best I get in as much practice as possible.'

Stephen glanced across at James looking for approval. James nodded trying to hide the smile tugging at the corners of his mouth.

'Yes, that's a capital idea.' James knew that Meg had been learning to work the dogs while he was away. She hadn't mentioned it herself but one of the Hopkins children had let it slip.

'Mrs Morley is clever with the dogs isn't she Mr Morley,' young Jenny had said. 'I watch her with Papa and they do what she tells them. I never heard a lady whistle like she does neither.'

'Whistle? You've heard Mrs Morley whistle?'

'To the dogs when she's working them, yes sir, she's very good at it too.'

James was shocked but highly amused. Meg had quietly amassed a number of skills since arriving in New Zealand, not that she always told him about them. She tended to find new things to try while he was away. He wondered if she thought he might disapprove. But disapprove he did not, in fact he was rather pleased.

James turned to Meg and said, 'Off you go then my dear. Let's see what Mr Sangster can teach you between now and the time we get home.'

He was curious to see what she would do.

Meg walked over to Marshall's horse, tucked her skirts up into the belt around her waist and deftly hoisted herself into the saddle.

'Humph, not as comfortable as my saddle,' she complained light heartedly, 'but it will just have to do.'

With that she and Stephen rode off to round up the sheep who were foraging down by the river. The dogs followed them. Two of them belonged to James and Meg, the other four belonged to Marshall and Stephen. Meg put her bottom lip between her teeth and whistled to their two dogs. They obeyed her immediately and started working their way around the flock. Stephen stopped dead in his tracks, his mouth hanging open in shock.

'Where did you learn to whistle like that?'

'Me Da taught me,' she laughed, and off she went to follow along behind her dogs as they worked the stock.

James couldn't help himself. He threw back is head and roared with laughter. He had finished packing up the dray and was sitting on the seat beside Marshall watching. Even though he knew Meg could whistle, she had never done it in front of him. Nor had she told him she could work the dogs.

'She's a bit of a dark horse that one,' smiled Marshall, although he was none too pleased to be relegated to the seat of the dray. He knew he was in for an uncomfortable bumpy ride.

Once the sheep settled into a comfortable steady amble, Meg looked around at the stunning beauty of the mountains rising up above them on either side of the valley. The river beds held a little more water than they did when she first came through in January. They picked their way across the stones as best they could and climbed up onto the grassy knolls whenever they were able. At night they would camp beside the river on a grassy patch and light a fire. The temperature dropped markedly as soon as the sun tipped over the mountain tops to slide down to the unseen horizon on the West Coast, but they enjoyed sleeping out under the stars beside the fire. The pinks and blues of the night sky never ceased to put an appreciative smile on Meg's face.

'I love the colours painted on the sky during sunsets and sunrises,' she remarked one evening while they were sitting around the campfire. 'Even in the Highlands I don't think I have ever seen skies as beautiful as these. The air was still with not a cloud in the sky as the first star appeared.

'When do you think we will reach the house?' Meg asked James 'I'm longing to see it.'

"I figure we will be there by early afternoon tomorrow all going well.'

True to his word, they rounded the bend of the river not long after their midday break the next day. Meg, still riding Marshall's horse much to his disgust, helped Stephen herd the sheep up onto the flat tussock covered plain that spread out in front of the hut. As soon as they were settled Meg rode over to the dray where James was waiting. She climbed down off Marshall's horse and handed him the reins then climbed up onto the dray. James lifted Meg down off the dray once the horses were pulled up outside the hut and carried her to the door. She didn't kick and squeal like he thought she might. She nuzzled her head into his neck and whispered, 'James this is wonderful, I love it.'

He carried her across the threshold, kissed her on the lips and set her down.

'Welcome home Mrs Morley.' Meg's body ached from days of riding and sleeping on the hard ground, but she was happy. James saw the look on her face and breathed a sigh of relief.

'You do like it then?'

'Our new home? Oh yes James I like it very much.'

Meg walked around inside the hut inspecting it closely. It was bereft of any linen and utensils, but Meg had brought those with her and was eager to unpack them and put them in place. She had been planning for this for the past two years. There was a wooden bed built into the corner of the room at one end and at the other end a large open fireplace made of river stones packed with clay around the bottom and surrounded with corrugated iron at the top.

'James this fireplace is beautifully done. I wasn't expecting anything quite like this.'

'Henry's brother, Daniel Hopkins, showed me how they are building chimneys in the city with bricks and suggested I might like to try doing the same thing with the river stones. Not sure if the mix is strong enough to hold them together but I guess all we can do is wait and see.'

'I am impressed. You have done a wonderful job; it feels cosy and the wall lining will stop the draught coming in between the timber walls. How clever.'

James beamed with satisfaction. He wasn't sure what Meg would think of the hut, but it seemed he had worried over nothing. Finishing off the internal inspection Meg tucked her arm into James's and said, 'Come on let's take a look outside.'

They walked around the building inspecting the foundations, the iron roof and the verandah, which Meg was especially pleased about.

'It will be lovely to sit out here of an evening and enjoy that wonderful view,' she smiled broadly as she leant on the railing looking towards the mountain ranges on the other side of the river. They walked around to the back of the house.

'I am pleased to see that the long-drop is not too far from the house. I don't fancy having to traipse too far when it snows.'

'When it snows we will use the po my love,' laughed James.

'Oh. You have built a futtah. Marvelous.'

51

'Yes, we had some timber left over and Stephen came up with the idea. He helped build the Hopkins's one back at Flaxbush and they find it most useful.'

'And I do like the shed James, I am pleased to know that the animals will be well sheltered against the weather. I would hate to lose any of them, they are becoming part of the family.'

'Let's not get too carried away Meg, they are only animals after all.'

'I know but we would be so lost without them wouldn't we.' James had to admit she was right, again.

'Let's unload the wagon and get some of the stores packed away in the futtah.'

Meg was relieved. She felt she had been holding her breath all this time in anticipation of seeing her new home. She was unsure of what to expect but now that she was here and satisfied with what she had seen she relaxed and allowed the excitement to take over. They unpacked the dray stowing everything against the walls of the hut until Meg had the chance to put them all in place.

First things first, she set the fire with the dried tussock grass and small sticks the men had gathered and left in the box they had made to sit against the wall alongside the fireplace. It had a lid across the top which would serve as a seat. Once the fire took hold, Meg hung a metal pot full of fresh river water on the hook she had made. Once the first bubbles started to appear in the pot Meg opened up the wooden box of tea leaves and ceremoniously dropped a small handful into the pot.

'Our very first cuppa in our new home,' she turned to the others with a huge smile as they walked in the door looking for a welcome brew.

Stephen stood in the doorway with a billy-can full of creamy warm milk. Thought I'd milk Bessy for you, she was almost bursting at the seams,' he laughed.

'Marvelous, thank you and do come in and sit down. James, where are the chairs?'

'Just out here on the verandah, where do you want them?'

'Bring the table in and let's set it up in the middle of the room and put the chairs around it.

Meg clapped her hands with delight when the table and chairs were all set up and the two men had seated themselves at the table. She went over to her trunk and opening the lid took out a red checked table cloth she had been embroidering. She shook it out and threw it across the table taking care to make sure it was sitting perfectly square. In the basket of food they had been delving into on their travels she took out four tin mugs and a cake tin containing a cake that Gladys Hopkins had made for them. Placing it on a plate from the basket, Meg handed James a knife and said, 'Why don't you do the honors and cut the cake James.'

He cut four generous slices as Meg poured steaming tea into the mugs.

'A toast,' she said raising her mug. 'Here's to us and Stony Downs. May our life here be blessed and filled with wonder and adventure.'

'Here's to health, wealth and happiness,' chimed in James.

'Hear hear,' added Stephen and Marshall in unison.

After the horses had been tended to and put in their stable for the night and the dogs fed and settled into their kennels, the two men set up camp a short distance away from the house to give Meg and James a little privacy on their first night in their new home. Meg had served up a meal of cold mutton, cheese and bread after which the men had bid the couple good night and left them to settle in. Meg got James to help her unpack the bedding so they could set up their bed. The mattress was rolled out on to the wooden frame and the sheets and blankets made up on top. Then Meg very carefully and slowly pulled out a package from the bottom of the trunk.

'What have you got there Meg?'

'I made this while you were away surveying, when we lived in Christchurch, and I have been keeping it hidden until this moment.'

Her eyes filled with tears.

'Mother gave me squares of material she had been saving over the years. Each time one of our pieces of clothing were no longer wearable she would cut out a square or two from the best part of the garment, wash it and press it and put it away. When we left England, she gave me the parcel and suggested I might like to make a quilt with the pieces of fabric so that I would be reminded of home when I went to bed at night.'

She gave way to a flood of tears as she gently unfolded the beautiful quilt and laid it on the bed. The colours dancing before her eyes.

'One day I shall tell you where every little piece came from,' she sniffed, 'but not tonight.'

James pulled her into his arms and held her close until her sobs gave way to sniffles.

'My poor darling, do you miss home so much? Was I wrong to bring you all the way out here to the middle of nowhere?'

'No, of course not James, please don't think that. I am tired and a little overwhelmed, but these are bitter sweet tears. Yes of course I miss my family, but I am also excited to be starting our new life together. It is what we have dreamed of and talked about for the past five years. And now here we are at last.'

Stony Downs - March 1865

The next morning Meg and James woke up to a perfect clear blue-sky day. They had slept in longer than they planned. James was well aware that he had taken up much of the farmhands' time over the past few months and he was anxious that they get back to Flaxbush Station as soon as possible as there was plenty of work there for them at this time of the year. James made an agreement with Henry to be available for the musters and at shearing time. Henry also asked if James would consider surveying his property. Due to the remote terrain of the property the information Henry had gleaned from the Land Office was incomplete and did not give him as much information as he needed to stock the land effectively. James was delighted, it would give him an opportunity to survey his own property as well. Another part of the agreement that James and Meg were grateful for was that Henry would free up one of the farmhands to ride over to Stony Downs once a month to check in and make sure everything was going well.

'You can let the lad know if there is anything you need and he can bring it out to you the following month and also help you with anything you can't manage on your own. If you have any mail to post

55

give it to him, we will send it off with our own and bring back any for you.' Henry had told James and Meg at the time.

While Meg stood beside the fire stirring the porridge, which was bubbling away in her brand new black iron cooking pot, the men sat at the table poring over a crude map.

'Now I would suggest you keep the mob here along this flat area until there is a good snow cap on the mountain top then let them go. They will stay below the snow line. That valley is pretty thick with matagouri and Spaniard grass, so I doubt they will be able to get through it to the other side. They will most likely spread themselves out from here to here and down as far as here. Bring them down to the lower slopes again before they start lambing,' Stephen said, stabbing his finger at various places on the map. 'Marshall and I will come back for the spring muster around early November. All you have to do in the meantime is ride the boundaries on a regular basis to make sure the sheep are not losing condition and wandering too far afield. Fencing will be your next priority James.'

They packed away the map so Meg could place the plates and spoons on the table. She served up the porridge and once the tea had brewed she poured them all a cup and sat down.

Stephen turned to address Meg. 'I don't know if James has told you Meg but where this hut is situated will mean you will be in the dark for several weeks during mid-winter. The sun won't reach into this valley at all during that time. I don't mean to alarm you, I just thought you should be prepared. It is not pleasant, but it is only for a relatively short time.'

Meg glanced across the table at James, concern on her face.

'Did you know about this before you built here? She asked.

'Stephen and I talked about it before we decided to build here, but the truth is Meg we didn't have a lot of options. The lie of the land here is perfect for everything else we need. We would have to build close to the river in order not to be in darkness for a few weeks once a year and that is simply not a safe or wise thing to do.'

Meg looked at the two men for a few moments before she spoke.

'Well, that's that then I suppose,' she muttered. 'The alternative, being drowned by a raging river, is more untenable than being immersed in the cold and dark for several weeks.' She watched their faces as they

56

waited with bated breath for an angry outburst or worse still, tears, but instead Meg just smiled. 'Oh come on you lot, it's not the end of the world, is it. I'm sure I will be able to cope with it all. I am pleased we bought a good supply of candles James. Is that why you bought more that you thought we might need?'

James was relieved. 'Actually no, I was just being over cautious, I don't like being in the dark myself,' he laughed. 'I meant to tell you when we came back from building the hut, Meg, but there was so much else going on it just slipped my mind. Are you really not too upset about this?'

'I will confess it is a little daunting but I'm sure we will manage. There will always be challenges of one sort or another won't there.'

As soon as they finished eating, the men excused themselves and went out to saddle up their horses. Meg and James thanked them profusely for all the hard work they had done and all the help and advice they had been given and said they would look forward to seeing them again soon. The men rode off waving their last goodbyes as they rounded the bend in the river, two silhouettes in the distance. Once they were out of sight James looked at Meg and smiled.

'Well my dear, here we are at last, the life we have been waiting for.'

Meg hugged her husband then turned to go inside to make the necessary preparations for a mutton stew with carrots and potatoes. James unpacked the rest of the supplies and tools and put them in their allotted places.

The next morning after breakfast James and Meg took the horses and dogs down to the river for a drink and dipped their tin cups in the cool sweet water. They sat on the banks of the river for a while soaking up their new surroundings. The peace and tranquillity was occasionally broken by the cry of a Kea as it flew overhead inquisitively, or the bleating of a sheep. Meg turned around to look back over her shoulder at the house. She had to agree that it was an ideal spot to build the hut, despite the fact that it would not get any sun for several weeks in winter. Their home, as Meg now preferred to call it, was situated just below a grass and tussock covered mountain range with a large flat area spreading out in front of it which ran right down to the river. Much of the area was covered in matagouri, not an attractive plant by any means. Meg thought it looked like an angry bush and although he laughed at this comment,

James had to agree. Matagouri was not one of his favourite plants, it tore at his clothing when he was out surveying. The sheep would nibble at its green leaves if they got hungry enough and while the bushes were covered in angry looking thorns, they did offer shelter for the sheep, especially in the winter. The plant Meg disliked the most was the Spaniard grass. It had long spear-shaped leaves with needle sharp ends that cut the flesh of any animal or person walking too close. Horses would often suffer from nasty cuts on their lower legs. The dogs seemed to be able to avoid the beastly plants, but Meg and James had both been cut and pricked by these plants several times already.

'Can we burn these plants off around the house without burning it down do you think James. I really don't like them.'

'I don't think anyone does like them, except maybe the sheep,' he laughed. 'But yes, in answer to your question we will pick a nice calm day and set a fire break right around the house and get rid of the stuff. I want to set this area up for when we put up yards and a shearing stand anyway. It would be good to get some decent grass growing if we can.'

Meg picked up a stick and started to idly poke at rocks in the water. The dogs came up to her looking for some reassurance and a bit of attention now that there were no other dogs around to keep them occupied. Meg loved to play with them, but James was not so sure it was a good idea.

'They are working dogs Meg, not domestic animals.'

'But they will be living with us and in winter I will be bringing them inside where it's warm.'

'No you won't, they will be staying outside in their kennels and they will live outside. They will be well sheltered in the shed.' Meg opened her mouth to object.

'No Meg, I have spoken and that is all there is to the matter. I will not have dogs in the house.'

Meg was upset both at James' decision and also at the way he had spoken to her. She could get her own way most of the time but every now and then, if James felt strongly enough about something, he would put his foot down. This was clearly one of those times.

The next few weeks flew by as Meg set up house and James busied himself with building a bench, a mantelpiece above the fire-place, shelves both inside and on the outside of the house and creating a fenced off area so Meg could get her vegetable garden going. James also hung a rope around the bed so Meg could tie a curtain to it and close the bed off from the rest of the room. When a visitor needed a bed, they could set one up in the corner of the room beside the fireplace and still have their privacy. Crockery and utensils were placed on the bench while tins and pots and boxes of food which didn't need to be in the futtah were placed underneath. On the mantel Meg placed a tin of matches, a framed wedding photo and two family photos, one of James, his brother and their parents and one of her family all dressed in their Sunday best. She also placed two matching horse ornaments one at each end of the mantelpiece. She had been given these by her parents when she was thirteen years old and she had treasured them ever since.

The day that Stephen returned for the first of their monthly visits Meg was out collecting wild flowers. He had spotted her up the hill as he came up the valley and called out. She came running down to meet him.

'Stephen, how lovely to see you, how are you?' she asked breathlessly.

'I am well Mrs Morley, how about you? You are looking very healthy and rosy cheeked if I might say.'

'You might say,' she laughed, 'and yes James and I are perfectly happy and healthy in our new home. Come and see how much we have done already.'

Stephen was impressed with the way Meg had managed to turn a basic hut into a warm and inviting home.

'Well this does look grand Mrs Morley, I am impressed. And Mr Morley, I see your building skills are improving,' he laughed.

James laughed too and said, 'Look Stephen, I've told you before please call us James and Meg. I think we know each other well enough to do that now, don't we?'

Stephen nodded his head a little shyly, 'Right you are then...James.'

'So, what's been happening back at Flaxbush, what have they been doing?' James asked, indicating for Stephen to take a seat at the table.

'Well we've turned the rams out with the ewes. We've sown the oat paddocks and we dug up that patch of potatoes, got a mighty fine crop

59

this year too. I've bought a bag for you with Mr and Mrs H's best regards.'

'Capital Stephen, capital. We won't be planting ours until June, so these are most welcome. You be sure and thank the Hopkins's for us.'

The next morning Stephen rode out with James to check on the stock.

'They all look to be doing well Mr...umm James.'

'I thought they were too, glad to hear you agree.'

'Are you folk all sorted for supplies then? Nothing you might be needing next time I come?'

'I'm all good thanks Stephen but best we check with Meg.'

'I've finished reading one of the books Mrs Hopkins gave me, perhaps you could take it back and swap it for another one for me please Stephen, that would be most appreciated, and I have a letter to post please,' was Meg's response to Stephen's enquiry.

'Glad to help,' he smiled back at her doffing his hat.

'Does Mr Hopkins want me to give him a hand with the autumn muster Stephen?'

'We did talk about it, but Mr H thinks it would be best if you settle in here for a bit before you leave Meg on her own.'

'That's very thoughtful of him, thank you. But tell him I will be ready to help with the shearing and dipping as soon as he has need of me.'

Stephen stayed a second night but rose early so as not to disturb James and Meg, quietly saddled up and rode off back to Flaxbush. The skies lightened as he rode up the valley but ahead of him, heading in his direction he spotted a familiar looking dark bank of cloud. He pushed his horse on as quickly as he could to find shelter before the rain started to come down, as he knew it would. He was quite adept at reading the weather having lived and worked in the mountains for several years. He knew it would be cold and the rain would fall in sheets like a waterfall.

James came up from the river with a bucket of water. There hadn't been enough rain to fill their water barrels as yet.

'Looks like we won't have to fetch water for much longer,' he told Meg. 'There's a mighty sou'wester heading this way, and fast. The water barrels will be full in no time.'

Meg went out to check on the animals. They had already made their own way to the shed to get settled before the storm came in. She was impressed that they were able to sense changes in the weather, sometimes long before she and James did.

It started to rain lightly at first getting heavier and heavier until it fell in sheets. The sound of the wind roaring up the valley and the noise of the rain on the tin roof was frightening. Meg and James settled themselves beside the fire to wait out the fury raging outside, cringing whenever they heard sounds of destruction. Slowly the house started to fill with smoke as the ferocity of the wind forced it back down the tin chimney. The corrugated iron rattled furiously as it braced itself against the onslaught of tiny stones and pieces of wood and debris pounding against it. James quickly poked at the fire until it died down to embers so as not to create any more smoke. It got so cold they crawled into their bed, snuggling up together for warmth and comfort. The storm rattled on right through the day and into the night and then, just as suddenly as it had started, the wind died down and everything went quiet. There was barely a sound as James climbed out of bed to tend to the fire.

'It's gone from one extreme to another,' commented Meg sitting up watching the fire roar into life again. She was glad of the extra warmth as the temperature had dropped markedly. Wrapping a shawl around her shoulders she opened the door to look outside. The dogs jumped out of their kennels and shook themselves seeming none the worse for the storm and started barking. Meg pulled on her boots and ran around the back to check on the animals. She knelt down and gave the dogs a hug and ruffled their fur. She rubbed the noses of the horses and spoke softly to them, running her hand over them to make sure they hadn't been struck by any flying debris. They were a little skittish at first but settled down under her soothing touch. The chickens were still cackling with distress, but Meg knew they would eventually settle down. Bessy was lying down in her stall chewing her cud and appeared nonplussed about the whole affair.

'I suspect you have been through many of these storms old girl and not always had shelter either,' she spoke softly and scratched Bessy between the ears. Bessy's ears twitched but she didn't move away. Satisfied that the shed was still intact and the animals were unharmed Meg went back inside to check on the mutton stew which was now starting to bubble away again with the renewed heat beneath it.

'There's hardly a puddle out there James, it's almost as if it has all been sucked down into the dry earth.'

'I'm not surprised Meg, it's been very dry here with not much rain up until now and here we are running headlong into March. If we get another couple of good rainfalls we might get enough grass to keep the sheep going for a while but they will be struggling to find food before too long.'

After they had eaten and Meg had finished washing up the dishes in the tin pan she used as a wash basin, she dried her hands, took off her apron and peeped out the door to see if the dogs were still sitting under the verandah by the door.

'Come along me hearties,' she said to the dogs, 'best be getting you back into your beds now.' She took an old piece of sacking and rubbed the moisture out of their fur as best she could. 'Can't have you getting sick now can we, we need you lovely boys.'

'They are dogs Meg; they don't need molly coddling for goodness sake.'

Meg chose to ignore the rebuff. She loved the dogs and that would not change no matter what James said or did.

The next morning was picture perfect. Meg gasped in pure delight when she opened the door. They had slept in until well after daybreak not wanting to leave the warmth and comfort of their bed.

'Oh James, isn't this the most beautiful sight you have ever seen? I love it when the rain has washed everything clean, the air has such a fresh rich smell too it, mmm,' she sighed taking in a deep breath.

They hurried through their breakfast routine so they could get out and go for a walk and inspect their surroundings for damage. Meg added scrambled eggs to the menu for a bit of extra sustenance. They re-checked the shed and the futtah closely.

Meg leant against the wall of the house and watched James as he scraped off his overnight beard with his razor and strop.

'You built these sheds remarkably well James, they are holding together nicely,' said Meg proudly. 'You are so clever. Looks like you will have to rebuild the garden fence though. And there's the dray lying upside down over there. I do hope it is not too badly damaged.'

'The chimney seems to have held up well against the wind last night, so I am wondering if it might be better to build a stone wall around the garden instead of replacing the wooden one,' James pondered as he rinsed his face in cold water from the tin basin on the wooden bench in front of him wiping himself dry on the towel Meg held out for him. She giggled as he reached out and putting his hand behind her head pulled her towards him so he could rub his newly shaved face against hers.

'I don't mind if you want to keep your beard James. I almost don't recognize you when you come back from surveying with your big bushy face, but it doesn't bother me. In fact, I quite like it.'

'That's good to know my love but I must admit I prefer to be clean shaven in the summer months, I might let it grow back in winter again though.'

'Rebuilding will give us something to do I suppose,' sighed Meg, continuing on their conversation. 'Lugging all those stones up from the river is going to be hard work.'

'I've thought of that,' smiled James, 'I will make up a sled of some kind so we can get the horses to drag the stones up rather than carry them.'

'What a clever man you are. Maybe we could try using the dray?'

They checked the outside of the house carefully and were relieved to find it had stood up well in its first stand against the weather. Once they put everything back where it belonged and had re-hung the tools on the hooks on the back wall they went for a walk, the dogs bounding excitedly along beside them. They let the horses out of their stalls and left them to wander freely to forage. James watched Meg's face as they walked along in silence. She was enraptured by the beauty of her surroundings. She stretched her arms out wide and danced around in a circle.

'I can't believe this is all ours James. I imagine this must be what Heaven is like, don't you agree?' James pulled her into a strong embrace and kissed her.

'It warms my heart greatly to see you so happy Meg. As I've said to you before, I have often wondered if I did the right thing by bringing you here but seeing you here, like this, it puts my mind at ease, it truly does.'

Every day Meg would remark on the beauty of her landscape. She always found something to marvel over. Even when they were hard at work outside, she would lift her head and smile ignoring the aches and pains gnawing away at her tired body.

Their life settled into a comfortable daily routine of washing, cooking, dishes, sourcing firewood, milking the cow, collecting the eggs,

63

checking the stock, gathering water, collecting river stones for the fences, killing a sheep when they needed meat for themselves and the dogs, and getting the garden ready for planting in the spring. In the evenings they loved to sit out under the verandah and watch the stars appear. When it cooled down, they would move inside by the fire and read, sometimes Meg would do some mending and sometimes they would simply sit staring into the fire just talking.

Sometimes on a clear day they would walk across the river together with James' gun and go looking for rabbits to add a bit of variety to their mutton diet. Meg eventually persuaded James to teach her how to use his rifle.

'It is not something to be trifled with Meg, you must treat it with great respect.'

He taught her how to clean and load it with powder and shot and how to aim at her target. Unsurprisingly he found she had a sharp eye and more often than not her shots would hit their intended target.

Across the far side of the river a little further up was a large stand of trees and native bush which housed a number of beautiful song birds and a few wild animals. Unfortunately, it was so far from the house that the only time they could hear the birds was on a very still evening.

'Do you think we could plant a stand of native trees close to the house so we could attract more birds James?' Meg had asked as they sat listening and trying to identify the bird songs.

'We have all those trees on the hill behind us but there's no reason we couldn't perhaps plant some natives around the place,' he agreed.

Their days were governed by the rising and setting of the sun with their midday meal being taken when the sun was high in the sky. They had no calendars, just a record of the days as recorded in Meg's journals. They got up with the dawn and went to bed when it was completely dark with the fire being their only source of light. Meg had the wax candles, but she would only use them sparingly when they needed extra light.

In April Stephen and Marshall came back with some building materials and between the four of them they managed to put up a crude shearing stand which could be covered with a heavy canvas roof when the shearers arrived. They then made fences forming two paddocks on the flat grassy areas beside the shearing stand. The rest of the fencing would be done the following summer as time permitted. This would be the men's last visit before the spring muster. They were lucky to have gotten through to Stony Downs this time as there had been quite a bit of rain in recent weeks and the rivers were starting to flow steadily creating crossing hazards, even for the experienced riders.

'You two sure you will be okay here on your own for the next few months? Don't know how long it will be before we can get back in. And we don't how long it will be before you can get out, for that matter. Mrs H has sent some more books and there is some material to make a couple of dresses for the Hopkins girls. Mrs H said you knew all about it Meg.'

'I do Stephen, Gladys sent a note with you last time asking if I would consider making the girls some dresses and I am pleased the fabrics are here.'

Meg had opened the box Stephen brought with him from the Hopkins and was delighted to see lace and ribbons among the folds of pretty fabrics, cotton reels and other sewing notions. She hadn't made dresses for young girls since before she left England when she used to help her mother sew garments for her siblings.

'I will be well occupied I am sure. Oh, and thank you for the extra tallow candles they will be very much appreciated.'

'You're welcome, I made them myself. I thought they might help get you through the dark days. I haven't experienced the like myself, but I am sure it will be a challenging time. Best of luck and we will see you both as soon as the rivers drop enough for us to cross.'

By early June the air was crisp and cool, and the days were getting shorter. A white blanket of snow was starting to settle on the mountain tops and creep down towards the river's edge. The shallow pools of water that had become trapped along the rocky river bed were often frozen over. Meg loved to jump on the puddles and break the ice, the dogs would yip and bark and join in the fun with her, scratching at the ice along the edges. Meg loved to run out onto bigger pieces of ice and watch the dogs run after her sliding and skating comically as they tried to regain their footing. James would stand to one side laughing and shaking his head at their silly antics.

One evening as they settled by the fire Meg noticed that it was unusually quiet.

'Something feels different James.'

She got up from her chair and opened the door a crack. At first she couldn't see anything so she took a candle and held it out the door. She let out a squeal of delight. James followed her to the door and looked out over her shoulder. Snow was falling steadily and was beginning to settle on the ground. Meg went back inside, took the lamp off the wall and lighting it took it out and hung it on the outside hook so they could see a little further out in front of the verandah. She took their jackets off the hook beside the door and handing James his coat, donned her own.

'What do we need these for? Where do you think we are going, it's dark and it's snowing?'

'I know, isn't it wonderful. I love the snow, come on let's go out in it.'

'I'm sure you are quite mad my dear,' he laughed as he donned his coat and followed her out into the night.

They made snowballs and threw them at each other. They ran about falling headlong into the snow. Meg let the dogs out of their kennels and the delighted pair ran about and jumped all over them joining in the fun and making them laugh. Eventually they were all quite wet and cold.

'Okay everyone, I think it's time we went inside before we catch our death of cold,' ordered James.

Meg saluted him, 'Aye aye Cap'n. But we must bring the boys in to dry them out before they go back out to the kennels, pleeeeeez.' she begged.

James knew the folly of leaving the dogs outside in their wet state and so reluctantly agreed. They sat obediently by the fire as Meg dried them with a soft rag and let them stretch out in front of the fire to dry off.

'I swear I can hear them purring,' laughed James. 'But this is a one-off, do you hear me?'

Meg nodded and looked away so he couldn't see her smile.

Winter had settled in with a vengeance by mid-July and the sun didn't shine on them for several weeks. When the sun did manage to break through on a clear crisp blue sky day, they only had daylight for a short time as the sun travelled quickly between mountain tops. Even Meg found it difficult to remain positive during those sunless days. The snow would pile up outside and they would have to dig a pathway to get to the animals.

66

Meg and James missed Stephen's monthly visits, but they knew he would be back again in the spring once the rivers were passable. There were one or two places along the riverbeds between the two stations that were completely impassable when the river was running swift and high. They would be cut off completely with no way out. This fact concerned James more than it did Meg.

'Does it not concern you that we can be trapped here for weeks Meg,' he asked her one cold and dismal evening. 'What if something was to happen to one of us. There is no way of letting anyone know. What if you were with child and needed help?'

'James, stop. You are worrying about things that might never happen. We need to hang on to our faith, we must, otherwise we might as well give up and go back home. I know these days and nights are testing us, but we must hang on and remain positive otherwise we will never survive out here. We knew this life was going to be a challenge, we talked about it endlessly,' she sighed in frustration. 'Please, it is only for a few short weeks of the year, the rest of the time here is well worth the sacrifice don't you think?'

'Yes, you are right,' sighed James, 'I guess I am feeling a bit melancholy tonight. But speaking of children, I wonder why we haven't been blessed with them yet. Do you ever think about it?'

'I think about it often,' sighed Meg sadly. 'I don't know why I am not with child. It's not as if we haven't tried is it?' she smiled shyly glancing at him beneath her eyelashes, cheeks reddening.

'Maybe next time we go to Christchurch we can visit the Doctor,' he suggested hesitantly.

'Yes,' she sighed, 'that might be a good idea.'

The subject was dropped and wouldn't be brought up again for some time.

Spring 1865

Spring came at last. It was late September; the days grew longer and brighter as the sun shone warmly down the valley. It had been a long cold dreary winter but now the snow was thawing, tumbling down the mountains in avalanches racing to reach the creek beds at their base. The rivers roared with the added volumes of water racing hell for leather downstream as if it was running late for a very important meeting. At times the river spanned a mile wide from bank to bank. It would tumble over the rocks in great torrents to where the gap between the base of two mountain ranges would meet forcing the water to navigate a narrow gap with such force and ferocity the noise was deafening. Slowly, day by day, week by week the water level dropped to where it was eventually passable in places. Spring flowers bloomed again along the river banks. Alpine plants shook off their winter coats and emerged renewed and bursting with colour. The air was still cool and crisp in the mornings and it smelled fresh and seemed to pulsate with the new season's growth. The sun was brighter and rose earlier in the mornings pouring more hours of daylight down into the once darkened valley. After the stark white of snow, it was pleasing to the eye to see the green starting to appear on the hillsides and plains around them.

Meg and James were anxious to check on the stock as soon as they felt it was safe to leave the confines of their immediate surrounds.

'They will be starting to lamb soon,' James said to Meg one morning. 'Now that most of the snow has melted, we must get up there as soon as possible.'

They picked a calm clear morning packed up their saddle bags and took a bed roll each, preparing to camp out overnight if need be. They took rope, sharp knives, sacks and whatever else they thought they might need. Meg fed the chickens and collected the eggs. She milked Bessy and put some of the warm milk into a bottle to take with them for their tea. The dogs had been let off when James went to let the horses out of the stable. Meg whistled to them as she climbed up on to Jasper's saddle and reached for the reins. Giving him a pat on the neck she made a soft clucking noise and the horse moved off down towards the river. James rode up alongside her. They went at a steady pace stopping briefly for a light meal of bread, cheese and milk rather than lighting a fire for their tea.

They reached the first of the flock by late afternoon and dropping off their bed rolls and provisions at a suitable camp site, rode around as many of the sheep as they could find. They checked their condition and to see if they looked as though they were close to lambing. Their presence startled some of the sheep which got up and ran in the opposite direction. The dogs were whistled back in behind the horses so as not to disturb the sheep any further.

'Looks like we have a couple of lambs already James. They look quite healthy too.'

Meg got down off her horse and walked slowly across to where a tiny lamb was feeding hungrily from its mother, it's tail wriggling so much it was almost losing its balance. The ewe started to walk away so Meg stopped and sat down. James came up quietly and joined her. They both sat studying the sheep they could see from their vantage point. After a while James stood up.

'I am well pleased Meg; they do look fit and healthy. This looks to be about half the flock, we will have to search for the rest. It's a lovely settled day and we've found a good spot to camp, let's set up before it gets dark then we can use this as a base.'

They set the stones up to make a fire. James pulled a fallen log over by the fire for them to sit on. They rode around for a couple of hours in search of more sheep and spotting some higher up on the mountainside further along the ranges they opted to return to their camp and set out to round them up first thing in the morning. As soon as they got back to camp Meg started preparing something for them to eat while James collected tussock and dry wood to get the fire going. After dinner they rolled out their bed rolls and once it got dark lay down beside the fire and watched the stars together.

'This is absolute bliss James; it takes me back to the nights I spent camping out with Da.'

'Yes, I always love sleeping under the stars too when I am out surveying. Unless it looks like rain or it's particularly breezy, I often don't bother putting up any shelter. You know, I think I sleep better in the outdoors under the stars than I do in a soft warm bed,' he chuckled. 'Must be something about the fresh air I guess.' Meg nodded in agreement.

They rose at sun-up the next morning and after a quick breakfast, saddled up and rode off to round up the rest of the flock. They had to climb further than they expected but eventually they reached the stock. These ones didn't look to be in as good condition and there were no lambs yet.

'Why did they not stay down on the flats?' Meg was frustrated.

'Who can say what goes on in a sheep's head, I doubt sometimes they have a brain at all,' replied James.

He let out a groan and pointed over to the valley. Meg turned around to see what was causing his distress. She could see a dead sheep over by the edge of the valley. They rode over to get a closer look and found that it had been dead for some time. Down in the valley they could see three more decaying carcasses.

'Oh James, I wonder what happened.'

'They either went down there for feed and couldn't get back up or they have lost their footing and rolled down. When they are heavy with lamb they can get cast quite easily and not be able to right themselves again. But then you already know about that.'

'I do, yes. They may also have been seeking shelter from the weather. We really must get that fencing under way as soon as we can.'

'Yes, that is something I will be talking with Henry about when we see them in December.'

71

'In order to pay the lease this year Meg, we need as many lambs as possible. Let's hope for a good season and that the lambs fetch a good price at the sales. Henry said the prices were quite high last year.

A flash of something caught Meg's eye and she looked up to see what it was.

'Oh James, that bird, how beautiful it is. Look at the way it glides through the air. Do you know what it is?'

'That is one I do know Meg, it's a Falcon, one of the raptor family. I have often seen them during my survey work and find them fascinating to watch as they hover looking for their prey. They swoop down striking like lightning bolts. You see them fly up with their poor prey squirming in their talons.'

Meg shuddered at the thought. She had seen similar birds of prey in the Highlands.

They were a fair way up the hillside now and, as she looked across to the mountains on the other side, she was able to see more clearly the loose flows of rocks which formed great rifts down the sides of the mountains.

'What causes all those rock falls James. They look like grey rivers from here?'

'It's their formation and the severity of the weather that play a large part. The mountains came up quite rapidly by all accounts and couple that with extreme temperatures from freezing to thawing and then add in high rainfalls this is what happens. Come, I'll take you up here a bit further and you can stand on top of your very first scree flow.'

'Scree?' What a strange name for it.

'Most of the rock is called greywacke but the rock flows which come down the sides of the mountains and form the rocky river beds down below are often referred to as scree flows. In some places you will find schist which is flat and comes in a variety of colours due to the minerals it is made up of. It glitters in water especially with the sun shining on it, quite an attractive rock I think you will find my dear. Because it is a flat rock it is useful for building walls and buildings. If we find enough big pieces around here, we could use them to put along the top of your garden walls.'

Meg was fascinated. She dismounted and walked across the tongue of the wide expanse of scree they were now standing on. My word it must be difficult for horses to walk on,' she remarked.

72

'Yes, I think most people walk their horses across such flows. Right then, geology lesson over, it's time we headed back to camp. Remind me to keep an eye out for some schist.'

Stephen was the first visitor to arrive on Stony Downs after the winter thaw. It was late September and the raging rivers had eased enough to allow him to attempt a crossing. It had taken him a day longer than anticipated as he had to travel back and forth along the river banks looking for suitable crossings. His horse, Genuine, was a pretty gutsy stallion and less fearful of the rivers than most. When asked about the horse's name Stephen had answered that when they first got him as a foal one of the farmhands had muttered, 'That damned thing is a genuine pain in the arse, won't do a damn thing we ask of it.'

That's when Stephen had stepped in. He took the young horse in hand and with patience and kindness had eventually won its trust. They had been inseparable working partners ever since.

Stephen trusted Genuine to choose most of the crossings but on occasion Stephen opted to test the waters on foot and lead him across. He loved and valued his horse too much to ever want to risk losing him in a mis-judged river crossing.

Meg's heart skipped a beat when she spotted Stephen.

'James,' she called 'James we have a visitor. Stephen has come.'

James shook his hand warmly; Meg resisted the urge to hug him such was her delight at seeing him. Little did she know that Stephen's heart was dancing around in his chest at the sight of her too.

They spent a productive few days under Stephen's guidance as they made plans for the upcoming muster and shearing season. In the evenings they sat outside under the verandah and shared their life history and experiences. Stephen told a colourful tale of his life and had Meg and James in fits of laughter at the things he got up to when he was a young lad.

He was the son of a convict who had been sent to prison in Australia for stealing a sheep to feed his starving family back home in England. He served his time and as soon as he was released he made his way to the nearest pub where he met up with a colourful ex-convict named Agnes. They married and had four children, Stephen being the youngest. It wasn't a stable family life, Stephen's father often spent time in prison for stealing and his mother was not exactly what you would call motherly. Stephen left home at 14 and found passage as a cabin boy on one of the ships heading for New Zealand. He didn't much care where he ended up, he just wanted to go anywhere, far away from his unstable family life. He was a hard worker and had no trouble finding work when he first arrived. He met the previous owner of Flaxbush Station at a stock sale in Christchurch and got talking about the horses they were checking out in the yards. Alexander Formsby took a liking to Stephen and offered him a job right there on the spot. Stephen accepted and when Henry took over Flaxbush Station he was more than happy to retain Stephen as his head stockman such was the recommendation from Alexander Formsby.

Stephen had spent the last fifteen years of his life at Flaxbush and had no intention of leaving, he loved the land and the work and the people. This was his home now. He'd met up with young women when he was in town, but he couldn't see himself settling down with a wife and family. Maybe he just hadn't met the right woman yet, James had suggested.

'You may be right James,' he'd answered thoughtfully, flicking a quick glance at Meg. 'Would be nice to find someone as clever as your Meg here, she's worth her weight in gold don't you think?'

James smiled at Meg and took her hand. 'That she is Stephen, that she is. I am a very lucky man.'

Stephen stayed for two nights sleeping outside under the stars beside the shed where, he insisted, he was most comfortable. When he left, Meg and James set about doing the things Stephen had suggested they get done before the shearers arrived. Mending and building fences would be their first priority.

Stephen, Marshall and two shearers arrived to help muster and shear the following month. They would be needed back at Flaxbush to shear around 10,000 sheep late November, so Meg and James decided they would try their hand at doing their own weaning, docking and drenching themselves once the shearing was over.

Marshall offered to stay and help with Henry Hopkins's blessing. James immediately accepted much to Meg's relief. She knew James could be a bit stubborn at times, but this would have been a big job for just the two of them and their primitive facilities.

It was a stunning hot day with a little bit of haze drifting overhead as they saddled up and attached their saddle bags full of provisions ready to head out for the spring muster. The two shearers stayed behind to set up the shearing stands, attaching the heavy tarpaulin across the top to give them protection from the weather as they bent over the sheep. Meg was excited beyond measure to be mustering their very own stock on their very own land. She beamed from ear to ear the whole morning.

'Meg, what are you smiling about?' laughed James. 'You have been grinning like a Cheshire cat all morning.'

'I can't help it James, this brings back memories of my mustering days with Da. I did so love those times and here I am doing it again. All my favourite things rolled in together, the dogs, the horses, the perfect weather, our very own land and the prospect of riding up into the mountains to bring down our very own flock of sheep.'

The look on James face made her laugh. 'Oh, and you too of course, my love,' she could hardly contain herself.

James smiled weakly back at her, content to let her indulge in whatever fantasies that pleased her. All he could see was a couple of hard days ride ahead of him followed by several days of even harder work.

Stephen took the highest peak on one side, Marshall went across the valley to make sure no stock had gone through to the other side, he would then come back through the valley itself to flush out any ewes hiding away in the undergrowth. James headed out to the left of where they expected most of the stock to be while Meg worked her way down on the right-hand side. Every now and then she would stop and take a look around at the scenery. Far out in front of her were the higher pastures where the stock would be brought back to after shearing. The valley down to her left was flanked on both sides by high mountain ranges, standing proudly under their snowy caps. They ran off into the distance joined by the rocky Lawrence river running down through the middle of them. To her right the horizon was blocked in the middle distance by a mountain range that divided the river in two sending one river cascading out to the west, the other river turning back heading south. The southern fork was the only route they knew to get them back to the Canterbury Plains, via Flaxbush Station. Meg had studied several maps and was sure that if she climbed up to the top of the mountain range opposite, she would be able to see Christchurch and the sea. She promised herself that when she was doing a boundary run before the end of summer, she would climb up and see.

A whistle in the distance and the bleating of sheep brought her back to reality. Stephen had spotted some sheep way above him and had sent his dogs up to bring them down. Meg set to work; the muster had begun.

Just on dusk everyone except Stephen had arrived back at camp, their sheep all gathered together on the grassy flats by the river. They seemed content to stay there foraging around amongst the flax and tussock.

'I suggest you burn off that scrub in the valley and let some grass come through Mr Morley,' said Marshall as he took a welcome mug of tea from Meg. 'It's a bit of a drawback as it is, the sheep get lost in there and get caught up in the brambles and they die. I found about ten I reckon.'

'Yes, capital idea Marshall, I shall do that.'

He was not happy about losing another 10 ewes.

The camp fire had died down to hot embers with a pot of Meg's delicious stew bubbling over it by the time Stephen appeared. He was carrying a lamb across his lap.

'Had a stubborn old ewe wouldn't move until I spotted her lamb. Looks like the mite has a broken leg, she didn't want to leave it,' explained Stephen once he got his sheep and the lamb settled with the others. 'Did a quick count, don't think we got them all yet. Looks like we could be short about 200.'

'James nodded. Guess we will have to go back again tomorrow then.'

'You get this lot moving in the morning and I can look for the rest. At least you can get the shearing underway in the meantime.'

'I won't be much use at the shearing shed until the fleeces start coming off so perhaps I could help you?' Meg looked across at James for approval.

He thought about it for a moment. 'I guess it will only take a few hours won't it.'

'Yes, I expect so; it just depends on where the blighters are.'

James nodded but didn't say anything more.

'You are comfortable with me staying behind aren't you James?' Meg asked as they settled down to sleep.

'It's usually me heading off surveying and leaving you behind, seems a bit odd the other way around I must admit,' he smiled. 'I am just not used to you being so independent Meg, you are a strong and capable young woman, I need to get used to that.'

They spooned together and slept soundly until the first golden rays of the new day woke them.

While Meg packed up the breakfast things Stephen helped Marshall and James get the sheep rounded up and on their way up the river bed where they would cross back to the other side and walk up the grassy flats back towards the house paddocks where the shearers were waiting.

Marshall carried the lamb with the broken leg across his saddle. As soon as they were off Stephen and Meg mounted their horses, whistled their dogs, who were wondering why they weren't allowed to follow the others, and turned their mounts back up towards the mountains to search for the missing ewes. They rode side by side in silence, watching for stock. They dismounted as they neared the top of the range to allow their horses to navigate the scree slopes as best they could.

'Surely they wouldn't come this far up, would they?' queried Meg. 'There's barely anything for them to eat.'

'Actually, you would be surprised what they can forage for up here.'

He knelt down and drawing a couple of rocks aside revealed moss and alpine flowers. When you get down and really have a look it is surprising just how many plants there are growing above the tree line. I know there are not many stands of trees hereabouts, but you know what I mean,' Stephen smiled as he held out a cheerfully coloured alpine flower to Meg.

'There's a nice stand of native trees further up the valley towards the fork in the river. I must go and have a closer look one day.'

'Yes, I know where you mean. I haven't been there for a while. Have you seen the opal lake?'

'Opal Lake? No. I didn't know there was a lake around here. Where is it?' Meg was intrigued, an Opal Lake sounded wonderful.

'It's in the Lawrence Glacier. It's further up past that stand of bush.'

'I've never been further than here,' said Meg. 'What is it like further up?'

'Wild and untamed,' laughed Stephen. 'You could make your way through to Canterbury up the Rakaia River that way but there is a very narrow pass where you have to clamber over rocks, and it is quite a trek over rivers and mountains. Best done on foot; not an easy route.'

They continued on with their search and just as they were about to give up and go further afield one of the dogs started barking. They scrambled up to the top of the range and there at the top on a flat tussock area were the missing sheep. The dogs immediately leapt into action and began to head around the perimeter of the flock while Stephen and Meg stationed themselves to channel the sheep down the mountain side in a single file. It worked perfectly, with Meg and Stephen eventually able to walk behind the mob, the dogs on either side keeping them in line.

While they were riding down Meg looked around and marvelled at the sight. Behind her were several mountain ranges layered one behind the other. Some were shaded a deeper blue than the others and some snowy white mountain tops were being kissed by the sun so that they stood out stark and bright against a deep blue background.

'That's part of the Southern Alps over there with snow on the top,' called Stephen. 'Stunning don't you think? They run right down the western side of the island.'

'I thought we might see the sea from up here,' responded Meg.

'You mean the Christchurch side? No, but you might from the mountains opposite.'

'I thought that might be the case, I plan to head up there sometime to have a look.'

'You just be careful if you go riding around here by yourself Meg, it can be treacherous to the uninitiated and the weather can change very quickly as you well know. Speaking of which, look there, down the valley, I don't like the look of that cloud bank heading this way,' he seemed a little concerned. 'Let's get this lot down as quickly as we can. We need to get them across the river before it starts raining.'

Meg and Stephen pushed the sheep harder than they intended to but they both knew that time was of the essence. Finally, they got the mob down to the river flats. Stephen immediately started moving them up the river to where they could cross to the other side.

'I'll follow on behind with my dogs Stephen, and bring up the stragglers, you push on ahead.'

78

Meg dropped back behind the mob and whistled to her dogs to join her. Now that the sheep were down on the flat land and on the move they would follow one another, all she had to do was to keep the slower ones moving. She was hungry but knew she wouldn't have time to eat until the sheep were safely across the river. She was about to reach into her saddle bags to see if she could find something to nibble on when she felt the first drop of rain. She dismounted and untied the oilskin coat which was always tied to the back of her saddle. She shook it out picking up the hat she had forgotten was rolled up inside. She donned both hat and coat and threw herself back up into the saddle. She could see Stephen way up in the distance. He was almost at the river crossing. Relieved she set out to catch up with the rest of the mob and pushed them on as quickly as she could without scattering them.

The clouds rolled in quicker than she expected and before long the rain was coming down heavily. She snuggled into her coat, put her head down against the strong sou-wester wind and held on tight to her hat. She allowed the horse to walk on without direction, trusting that it would follow the dogs and the other mob of sheep.

The sound of water roaring close by brought her head up. Water was flowing all around them, they had ventured too close to the river. The horse became unsettled and started to balk. Meg tried to urge him on, but he was having none of it. She dismounted discarding her hat and tucking it firmly under the saddle. She grabbed the reins and with head down walked closer to the edge of the river where she hoped they would be able to cross. The water was flowing fast but it wasn't too deep yet. The horse reared giving Meg a fright, but she hung on to the reins and pulling the horse's head down reached out and stroked his neck speaking and clucking softly to him as she gently led him through the water. The horse relaxed a little and allowed Meg to lead him, but he leapt out of the water and up the bank as soon as she got him close to the edge. The reins were wrenched out of Meg's hands and she was thrown back in to the water. She managed to pull herself across the rocks, regain her footing and drop herself down on to the grass bank to catch her breath. She looked around anxiously for Jasper and was relieved to see him standing a little way off, head down and back to the wind. Meg got up and walked slowly over to him.

'It's alright Jasper, you will be alright my boy. You are going to have to get used to this you know.' She slowly reached out and took hold of the reins. She rubbed the horse's nose and nuzzled into his neck. 'Come on boy, let's go.' She tugged gently on the reins and walked with Jasper until he was settled again.

The rain was still pouring down in torrents, but the sheep had thankfully kept moving and were leaping and bounding across the river under the urging of the dogs and following Stephen's flock. Stephen was now on the other side of the river guiding his sheep into the paddocks. She hoped he hadn't seen her fall into the water. Or James, for that matter. She didn't want either of them worrying about her being out on her own.

When she arrived at the house James was pacing around under the verandah, angry and disappointed.

'This damned rain is going to put us back several days while we wait for the sheep to dry out.'

'Shouldn't be more than a day or so.' Stephen was not unduly concerned. 'In the meantime, there is plenty of work we can help you with I'm sure.'

Meg was thrilled at the delay because she got the waist height wall built around under her verandah roof which would give them a little more shelter from the weather and a dry area in which to store their firewood and utensils.

They also carefully burnt off some of the tussock in front of the house so James could finally sow the grass seed Stephen had brought over the last time he visited. James had stored it in the shed waiting for the right time to sow. Meg would finally have a green front lawn. Once the patch had burnt out and the ground had cooled the men erected a wood fence around the small area that would make a frame for Meg to create her much longed for garden. She was planning on bringing some seeds and plants back from Christchurch in December. She was anxious to get her vegetable garden growing. The ground would be turned and left fallow until planting time. Cloches would be needed to keep the hens from scratching the seedlings out of the ground. James had added that to his list of things to do.

Finally, after three days of warm sunshine, Stephen deemed the sheep dry enough to shear. The two shearers set to work with great gusto. It took two weeks to get the job done, each shearer handling around 30 to 35 sheep per day. When they needed a break Stephen and Marshall grabbed up the shears to help out. They weren't as slick and skilled as the professional shearers, but they did help. James studied the procedure closely and near the end of the last day with only six sheep left in the pen one of the shearers offered to let James try his hand.

'Do you think I might try too?' asked Meg.

The shearer was not sure about this idea, she was a mere 'woman' after all, and women did not shear sheep. They were permitted to gather and sort fleeces as Meg had done with great agility. This had earned their respect, but shearing was a man's work. The shearer glanced across at James to seek his approval. James nodded his agreement and after trying his hand at the first two sheep stepped aside and let Meg up on the platform. Her hands hardly spanned the grips of the scissors-like shears, but she was determined to try. She tucked her skirts between her legs, straddled the sheep as she was instructed and proceeded to work the shears as best she could. She got a fit of the giggles at one point as she struggled with the shears but eventually she managed to get the sheep shorn.

'Not a bad effort Meg,' smiled Stephen in approval. 'Now try another one and see how you go.'

Meg sheared three more sheep and by the last one had mastered it reasonably well. She made a mental note to see if she could pick up a smaller pair of shears in Christchurch so she could join in next season. Her back ached with just those few sheep but she was well pleased with her efforts. James was quiet and a little stand-offish, but Meg refused to let his mood bring her down. He was jealous, something she was just starting to notice about him, but she wasn't about to be any less than what she was just because he didn't like it.

The sheep were turned out into grassy paddocks close to the house so they could be brought back in after Christmas to separate the lambs from the ewes and then the lambs would be sorted, with some going back into the flock while the others would be driven to market. The ewes had all been doused with an arsenic mixture to ward off lice and disease and the lambs had had their tails cut off and the males castrated. This was the part Meg hated but she knew it had to be done and did her best to hold herself together at the sight of the poor wee mites scurrying about in pain wondering what had happened to them.

The shearers had gone back to Flaxbush Station to get on with the shearing there while Stephen and Marshall stayed behind to help James and Meg with the drenching. Finally, it was all over and after a hearty meal, lots of chatter and laughter the men settled down for their last night at Stony Downs. Early next morning they had a light breakfast and saddled up ready to head for Flaxbush Station, James included.

'We won't keep him too long Meg,' said Stephen as he said his goodbyes. 'It's a pity you couldn't come with us, but I understand you need to stay here and look after the animals.'

'I am sure I will be just fine Stephen, thank you for your concern.'

She was looking forward to having some time to herself. She kissed James fondly and smiled as she waved him off. She loved him very much, but he was becoming restless and moody lately creating a difficult air between them. When she had questioned him about it, he had shrugged it off, but she suspected he missed being out on the ranges doing what he loved most, surveying. When the time was right she was going to talk to him about it. Meanwhile she was free to take Jasper and her dogs Sally and Buster out for long rides on her own without being answerable to James.

While she was on her own, Meg enjoyed many a long day in the saddle checking the stock and exploring the boundaries of their run-holding. Not that she would confess any of this to James. She decided the less he knew about how far she rode the better, she didn't want him to worry about her unduly.

James returned from Flaxbush on a hot, dry day, salty sweat running down his brow stinging his eyes. The shearing was finally over for another season and hay making was about to begin on Flaxbush Station. James had offered to stay but Henry had suggested James go back to Stony Downs and return for Christmas. They could stay on for a week or two then to help pick up the hay. It would have been cut, turned, dried and baled and they would welcome all hands to pick up the bales and stack them in the hay shed.

The offer was extended to them both to join the family for Christmas. There would be quite a gathering of friends and extended members of the Hopkins family. Tents would be erected outside for the children. The woolshed would be turned in to makeshift accommodation for the younger members of the family and others, if they chose, could sleep out under the stars. Meg was delighted when James told her the news.

'What fun,' exclaimed Meg. 'I have missed family gatherings, this will be a wonderful way to spend Christmas, don't you think?'

'You know I am not a great one for Christmas Meg. We never really celebrated it at home. My brother and I received a gift each from my parents and that was about it.'

'Well it's time for a change then isn't it,' responded Meg determinedly. 'We will go and you, Mr Morley, will have a very good time.'

'Oh, will I now.' James swung her up into the air. 'I have missed you these past couple of weeks Meg, I really have.'

'Good, because I have missed you too.' Shyly she pulled him over to the bed. 'Would you like to show me how much you have missed me James.'

'I would Mrs Morley, I would.'

Christchurch – November 1865

Meg was so excited she couldn't sleep. She had not been off the station for almost a year and was looking forward to seeing Gladys and the Hopkins family again and was even more excited to be going shopping in Christchurch. This time she was better prepared and had quite a list of the things she needed.

Cotton dresses and cotton fabric, muslin was of no benefit to their farming lifestyle.

Petticoats, the two she had were discoloured and getting rather tattered; as were her two work dresses.

Vegetable and flower seeds.

Small shears for shearing

Utensils and instruction booklets for making butter and cheese

Sturdy work boots

Wool socks

Food supplies

Books – exchange with Gladys

Powder and Ammunition

Oats for horses

Bales of hay for animal beds – purchase from Flaxbush

James checked over Meg's list crossing off the shears and adding his own requirements.

'You won't need shears Meg; you don't need to be doing any shearing for goodness sake.'

Meg bit her tongue but resolved that one way or another she would purchase her shears and conceal them from James. She was relieved that he had not crossed her boots and dresses off the list, but she knew too that he still expected her to work alongside him so he must have decided these were necessary items.

James had warned their financial situation would be tight, at least until they could get their lambs to market in March, but he would try the Bank for a bridging loan in the meantime.

'Meg, I know how hard you have worked this past year and I would like to make it up to you by giving you an allowance to purchase some niceties for yourself. Of course they will need to be suited to our lifestyle, but I am sure you have in mind some purchases you might like to make.'

'That is so thoughtful of you James, thank you,' Meg's eyes filled with tears. 'I love it here and I really don't mind the hard work, in fact I rather enjoy it,' she smiled.

James pulled her into his arms so that she couldn't see the look on his face. He had become more and more restless within himself. He hadn't adapted to the farming life as well as Meg had. He often missed the freedom and excitement of discovering new unexplored land when he was out surveying, especially among the mountain ranges. This farming life was becoming a bit of a bore to him. However, he would persevere and see if he could get some surveying work during the times he knew Meg could cope with the running of the farm. He knew she was well capable, and he felt it would help to settle this restlessness he was unable to shake off. He was also grateful for the help offered by Henry and the farm hands whenever he was away.

Christchurch had grown in the year since Meg and James last visited. Meg was surprised to see so many new stores opened up on the main street. There was even a brand new women's apparel store offering dresses, hats, gloves, shoes, coats, trousers and even a department of haberdashery. Meg and James booked into the new hotel and sank themselves into their first night of luxury in a very long time. Meg drew a

86

bath adding scented oils from the coloured glass bottles sitting on the bathroom window sill. James went into town and left her in peace returning a short time later with a pretty but practical gown for her to wear out to dinner that evening. Meg stepped out of the tub, dried herself off and dabbed exquisite smelling talc on her body. She wrapped the towel around her and went into the bedroom just in time to see James spreading the gown gently on the bed.

Meg flew into his arms forgetting to hold the towel. He pulled her to him and gently laid her down on the bed pushing the gown aside. He made love to her the way he used to do in the early days of their marriage. Something he hadn't done in a long while. Meg was breathless and pink cheeked, revelling in this unexpected surge of passion from her husband.

'You smell divinely delicious my love,' he sighed as he rolled, spent, on to his back.

'Well, I must take some of these toilettes back home then if this is the reaction they evoke.' They both laughed and cuddled up together to enjoy the afterglow of their lovemaking.

Meg looked a picture on James' arm that evening as they walked in to the best restaurant in town. It was furnished with dark stained wood booths with deep burgundy patterned cushions on the bottoms and the backs of the seats. The burgundy velvet drapes hung majestically from floor to ceiling tied back with matching tasselled ties to reveal white lace curtains. Crystal chandeliers and mirrors completed the effect which succeeded in taking Megs breath away. She stood in awe as James registered them in for dinner with the maître d'. They savoured the much longed for delicacies that city people take for granted.

'You know, I think this food tastes all the better for not having had such fare for so long don't you think?' Meg asked James as she placed another forkful of delicious salmon into her mouth.

'I agree. It will take us a while to settle back in to plain fare again I'm sure.'

They slept like they hadn't slept in years in their soft feather down bed. Meg was reluctant to get up the next morning until she remembered she had shopping to do.

'Shall we go our separate ways and do our shopping today James or do you want to see what I am buying?'

'I'm sure I can trust you not to over-indulge my darling. Come with me to the bank and I will furnish you with funds both for the household and the allowance I promised you. You deserve to treat yourself.'

Meg hadn't been this excited for such a long time. She kissed James as they came out of the bank and almost danced down the steps to begin her shopping spree.

'Get an errand boy to take your purchases back to the hotel for you Meg,' James called after her.

She spun around waving her acknowledgement and gave him a beaming smile. It did James' heart good to see her so happy. He had been feeling guilty over his sullen moods of late. He turned on his heel and headed directly over to see his former boss in the Surveyors office. Shopping for supplies was the last thing in his mind.

Meg danced down the street with a smile on her face causing the men to smile and tip their hats at her and the women to glance sideways with disdain, or was it jealousy. She walked past windows bedecked in wonderful displays until she came to a perfumery. This was where she would indulge herself using the allowance James had given her.

After a delightful twenty minutes of trying perfume and smelling talcum powders and soaps she finally chose two cakes of lavender soap, which she would only use on special occasions, and two more as a gift for Gladys. She added a round pack of talcum with a soft puff applicator which she would also only use on special occasions.

The sales lady had been intrigued with Meg and her story. The young woman's lifestyle seemed incredibly hard to someone who had grown up in the city. Before the sales lady wrapped Meg's parcel, she asked her to wait for a moment and disappeared through a side door to an office. She came out beaming and reaching under the counter produced a small glass bottle of lavender perfume.

'I told the manager about your run-holding and what a marvellously strong woman you are to be living such an isolated and difficult life. We would both like you to accept this small gift from us.'

Meg was quite taken aback.

'I..I don't know what to say. How kind of you, thank you so very much.' Her eyes filled with tears. She was feeling most humbled.

The lady pushed the beautifully wrapped parcel across the counter and put her hand on top of Meg's.

'Just you enjoy your wares my dear and enjoy the rest of your day.'

'I will, I most certainly will.'

Meg felt as if she was walking on air, the smile still plastered across her face as if she had just found a fortune. The rest of her purchases were fun and exciting, but nothing could match the time she spent in the perfumery. When at last she arrived back at the hotel she was exhausted. She'd stopped for a sandwich and a cup of tea at lunchtime and had not seen hide nor hare of James.

She was expecting to find James sitting in their hotel room waiting, and cross, as it was almost time for dinner. She flung the door open with a big smile, but the room was empty. The purchases an errand boy had brought back to the room for her were stacked neatly in the corner but there was no sign that James had even been back since this morning. Relieved Meg quickly freshened up using her new perfume and changed into her new gown. Now it was she who sat patiently waiting for him and getting a little cross as the time rolled by.

It was well after dark when he finally made an appearance. He stumbled in the door with a silly grin on his face. He was drunk. Meg was shocked. She had never seen James drunk. Even at the odd party they had attended together he had always held himself in check, but now here he was stumbling around the room grinning at her. She wasn't quite sure how to react. He looked at her sheepishly.

'Shhhhoorry my loovly, I'sh a bit late,' he hiccupped.

Meg laughed. He looked so ridiculously funny that she couldn't help herself. She took him by the arm and sat him down on the edge of the bed where he promptly fell backwards and started to snore. Smiling she bent down and took off his shoes, swung his legs up onto the bed and drew a blanket over him. Figuring he would probably not wake until morning she went downstairs to dine alone. To her amazement Stephen was sitting in the lobby of the hotel.

'Meg,' he rose out of his chair, hand extended. 'What a lovely surprise, are you and James staying here?'

'Yes, and you?'

'No, I was supposed to meet an old friend for dinner, but he is running late.'

Just then the desk clerk came over with a note for Stephen. He read it then slipped it into his pocket.

'Is James on his way down?'

'No, he came home a short time ago rather inebriated and has passed out snoring quite loudly on the bed.'

Stephen offered his arm to Meg saying, 'Looks like we are both on our own tonight, would you care to dine with me?'

'I'd be delighted,' she said taking his arm as they headed towards the hotel dining room.

When Meg crept in to her room much later that evening she was relieved to see that James hadn't stirred. He would never know about this day; the lovely chat she had with her old friend the smithy, the pleasant evening she shared with Stephen and of course the wonderful shopping spree. She wanted to keep these special memories to herself.

Meg and James loaded the dray with Meg's purchases next morning. James hadn't bought a single thing. They drove down to the merchant store and tied the horses to the hitching rail outside while they went in to get their food supplies. They made their purchases and as the men carried them out and loaded them onto the dray Meg checked them off on her list.

6 x bags of flour, check.

4 x wooden boxes of tea, check

3 x tins of baking powder, check

3 wooden buckets of sugar, check

3 bags salt, check

3 bags washing soda, check

Matches? 'James, we don't appear to have matches.'

James went back inside and came out with several tins of matches in a paper bag.

Potatoes, both eating and seed potatoes, check

Carrots, check

Seeds? She walked around to the other side of the dray and checked the names on the bags of seeds with what was on her list: carrots, cabbage, pumpkin, turnips, beans, check

Herb seeds: Lavender, Mint, Rosemary, Sage, check

Once they were loaded up and ready to go Meg turned to James.

'I have a little of my allowance left, I wondered if we could stop and get an apple tree and a couple of rose bushes.'

90

'Well if you're sure you can get them to grow in our climate Meg. Otherwise it's a waste of money.'

'I know the roses love the cold, Gladys has several healthy ones in her garden, and they have a large healthy apple tree in their orchard. How wonderful would it be to grow our own apples James?'

'Very well then. As a matter of fact, I was considering picking up some willow sticks to plant along the edge of the river close to the house and maybe some poplars.'

Meg beamed. 'It would be lovely to have some trees growing around us wouldn't it. That Hawthorn hedge you planted when we first got there is starting to grow well too; it will be an ideal buffer against the sou-westers when it grows a little taller.'

They found a man growing and selling plants on the outskirts of town. They chose the hardiest variety of apple and two sweet smelling, rambling rose bushes, one pink and the other yellow. Meg checked with the orchardist about the wisdom of growing fruit in the mountains. He chose the apple variety he thought would grow best, given the conditions, and then asked if she would be prepared to trial an apricot and a lemon tree for him and let him know how they fared. Meg was thrilled to bits.

'Of course, we would love to, wouldn't we James. Just tell me where the best place is to plant them. Thank you very much.'

Meg's head was buzzing with plans and ideas as they drove out of town. So it appeared was James.' not that Meg noticed for a while. She assumed he was more than likely suffering from a terrible headache brought on by his over indulgence in alcohol the previous day, but he had said nothing about it and she hadn't asked.

They stopped for lunch at Lake Clearwater bringing back memories of their first ever trip into the region. James became more relaxed and his mood lightened as they set a fire to make a cup of tea.

'Meg, I'm sorry I have been moody of late.'

'What is it James? I know something has been troubling you for some time. Tell me. Maybe I can help.'

'There's nothing you can do my love. It has nothing to do with you, it's something within me.'

'Are you ill, is that it?' Meg was suddenly concerned. How would she cope if James became ill? But he laughed.

'No, no, nothing like that. Look if I tell you please don't get cross.'

'I'm worried now James. I promise, I won't get cross, what is it?'

'I miss surveying. I want to go back to my surveying work. I am just not the farmer you are Meg. You put me to shame sometimes.'

Meg's heart sank. 'You want to give up our farm?'

'No!' James was on his feet and pulled her up and hugged her tight. 'No of course not, I know how much you love it there. No what I was thinking was perhaps we could do both. There are going to be times when there is not a lot for me to do on the farm and if Stephen and Marshall aren't available, perhaps we could take on a farm cadet. I could do some surveying and bring in some more money so we can extend our run-holding and our sheep numbers.'

Meg was stunned. She hadn't been expecting this. She pulled away from James arms and turned away walking slowly down to the water's edge. James let her go. He wanted to give her time to think it over.

Eventually Meg walked back and sat down beside James taking the hot tea he offered her.

'Well, once again Mr Morley you have stopped me in my tracks. I am relieved that it is only the fact that you are missing your old occupation that has been bothering you but why did you not discuss it with me sooner?'

'I did intend to, but I didn't know how you would react.'

'Well, I am amenable to the idea. What I want to know now though is what happened last night; I have never seen you drunk before.'

'Well,' he cast his eyes down sheepishly, 'one thing led to another. I met up with some old workmates in the Bully Arms and, well, you saw the result. We got to swapping surveying stories and I guess I was just envious. The more they talked the more I drank. Do you think it will be too much Meg? Do you think you would be alright on your own if I was to go away now and then?'

'James, you have been going off mustering and helping the Hopkins for a week or so at a time already and I cope very well. I am not afraid to be on my own if that is what bothers you. Maybe we could share a farm cadet with the Hopkins'. I'm not sure I would need a cadet full time; it would mean another mouth to feed and I suppose we would have to pay him a wage.'

'Let's talk about that later. Right now we had better get ourselves back on the road. The Hopkins are expecting us for dinner tonight are they not?'

'They are indeed, and I have bought a tin of sweets for the children and some perfumed soap for Gladys, I hope they like them.'

'I'm sure they will.' He smiled warmly at Meg and kissed her on the cheek. 'You are such a special person my Meggie love. Thank you.'

Meg was relieved to see James back to his old self again. They chatted all the way to Flaxbush and were in high spirits when they pulled into the yard.

The children came running out to greet them followed by Henry who un-hitched the horses then helped James push the dray into the shed for the night. The oldest Hopkins child, Howard, washed the horses and brushed them down giving them a feed of oats. Meg, clutching her beautifully wrapped parcels walked up the steps to sit on the verandah where Gladys had set out glasses and a bottle of whiskey for the men and a bottle of elderberry wine for her and Meg. The children were allowed lemonade, a treat on special occasions. Once they were seated and everyone had their drinks, Meg produced the gifts. The youngest child, Clementine was allowed to open the children's gift. They were thrilled when they saw it was sweets, a rare delicacy for them living so far away from town.

'Can we have one now Mummy, please, please, please?' begged Clementine.

'Just one for now. It will be dinner time soon and I don't want you to spoil your appetite.'

The children dived into the tin to pick out a sweet each.

When Glady's opened her parcel containing her oil of roses soap she was absolutely delighted.

'Oh Meg, how lovely, thank you. It will be a nice change from carbolic and washing soda,' she laughed.

Meg looked around to make sure the men weren't listening and said, 'Gladys, if that soap has the same effect on Henry as it did on James then you had better be prepared to get that baby cradle out again.'

Gladys roared with laughter. 'Oh Meg, you are such a card.'

Lowering her voice, she leant close to Meg. 'So, did you go and see the Doctor dear?'

'I did. I didn't say anything to James, but I did have a talk with the Doctor. He said there didn't seem to be any reason why I couldn't have a baby and that sometimes the man's sperm count could be low. He just said to just give it time, that we have had a big upheaval and lifestyle change and to not be in such a rush as we are both still young.'

'Sage advice my dear, sage advice. Right, now come along let's go and see what is happening in the kitchen shall we.'

It was a long and pleasant evening. There was plenty to talk about. So much so that after dinner Henry and James took their drinks out to the verandah while Gladys and Meg did the dishes and got the children to bed. Finally, they sat at the kitchen table with a cup of sweet tea and Meg told Gladys about her shopping trip. She had been bursting to tell someone about all the things she'd bought, and Gladys was the perfect listener.

'Did you manage to get the mail posted for us?'

'Yes, yes it was the first thing we did when we arrived in town. I have sent a very long letter to my family back in England. I just hope I haven't said anything that may cause them to worry. I have to be careful what I say in case it upsets them.'

'I understand, I felt the same way with my parents at first but over the years they have gotten used to hearing about our trials and tribulations. Was there any mail for you?'

Meg smiled as tears welled up in her pretty blue eyes. 'Yes, there was a packet waiting for me. None for James, sadly enough. I haven't opened it yet; I will do that once we have settled back down after all this excitement.'

James and Henry spent the following day discussing the sheep sales and making plans to get their lambs to market. It was to be a joint effort for which James was very grateful.

They rose early the next morning, keen to get home now and get their plants in the ground and James had a special surprise for Meg. They retrieved the dray from the shed and hitched up the horses. Meg went off to get their two collie dogs who had been looked after by the Hopkins's while they were away. They jumped all over Meg with such delight they almost knocked her over. She laughed and crouched down to give them both big hugs resulting in wet licks all over her face. She didn't mind, she loved these bouncing, energetic black and white bundles of joy, they were substitutes for her not having children to love. While she was pre-occupied with the dogs, Henry took James aside.

'Here is the parcel you ordered from my brother, James. He dropped it off on his last visit.'

It was well wrapped, and they tied it firmly on to the dray packing some of the softer packages around it. Meg climbed aboard the dray not noticing the package.

'You will most likely pass Marshall on the way back. He was looking forward to being in sole charge for a change instead of always taking orders,' smiled Henry.

'Well, we are very grateful Henry. Please let me know what I can do for you in return.'

'My boy Howard will be finishing school this year. He is well versed in farming. How would you feel about taking him on as a cadet for a while?'

James looked across at Meg and grinned.

'As a matter of fact, Henry, Meg and I were discussing that very thing the other day. I want to go and do some more surveying work and rather than leave Meg on her own I suggested we might engage a cadet.

'Marvellous, let's talk more about it when we get together for Christmas. You are still planning on coming back for Christmas, aren't you?'

'You bet we are. We'll get all these supplies sorted and get the plants in the ground and we'll bring the dray back ready for picking up the hay.'

Henry doffed his hat to Meg. 'Travel well then and we will see you soon.'

They didn't see Marshall on their way home, instead they found him waiting for them with the fire going and a delicious smelling stew bubbling away over the flames.

'Welcome home,' he grinned stepping out from under the verandah to meet them. Did you have a nice time in Christchurch?'

'We did, Marshall, we had a marvellous time,' enthused Meg. 'Thank you so much for taking care of things here while we were away. How did you get on?'

'I must admit I have loved every minute Mrs M, being me own boss and all. Quite a treat it was,' he was beaming from ear to ear.

95

'Something smells delicious, what are you cooking? There was not much left in the cupboards when we left.'

'I killed one of the fat lambs for you, it's hanging out the back in the futtah,' he replied proudly.

'But there's something else I can smell, what else have you added?'

'Oh, that would be the wild thyme, I guess. Me Mum used to use it in her cooking.'

'Wild thyme? Really? I didn't know there was any growing here.'

'I found a patch in amongst the rocks up on the hill behind the house here. I will show you if you like.'

'Come on you two, we can't stand around here chattering on about wild plants all day,' huffed James as he carried sacks of food around the back of the house to the futtah. Marshall, there is a parcel I will need your help with,' he called over his shoulder.

'Sure Mr M.'

Meg noticed the parcel James must have been talking about when she retrieved her plants from the dray. She placed the plants carefully on the ground against the house under the verandah roof with a mental note to give them some water as soon as they had unpacked the dray. She gathered up all her new purchases and went inside to put them in a box under the bed. She would bring them out and open them one day when she was alone.

Marshall had been busy doing odd jobs around the place while they were away. He had extended the chook run and put up a more solid fence around Meg's garden to replace the one which had been destroyed in the storm.

'Marshall this is wonderful, thank you. Look James, isn't that just the finest garden fence you ever saw.'

James smiled indulgently.

'I hope you don't mind Mr M,' Marshall said apologetically. 'I just wanted to help is all.'

'Marshall, I am grateful, thank you. I just have not had the time to do as much as I would have liked so your help is appreciated,' he said as magnanimously as he could. 'As a matter of fact, I have one more job I would appreciate your help with if you don't mind. It will mean staying over another night though.'

96

Marshall beamed, 'Of course Mr M, I'd be happy to. What is it you are wanting to do?'

James walked over to the dray and began untying the large carefully packed parcel. Meg watched with interest.

'What on earth is that James? I don't remember seeing that being put on the dray.'

'That's because you were too busy playing with the dogs Meg,' he smiled. 'This, my love,' he said as he heaved it up and got Marshall to help him carry it under the verandah, 'is your new window. Happy birthday Meg.'

Meg stood gaping at James with her mouth open. She looked so comical it made James and Marshall laugh.

'I swear James Morley you are going to be the death of me with all these surprises. Not that I'm complaining mind you. This is so exciting. Is this what you want Marshall to help you with? Are you going to do this tomorrow?'

'We are Meg. While Marshall is here, I will utilize his expertise and we will cut a hole in the wall and put in a window for you. You just have to decide where you want it.'

'I already know exactly where I want it,' Meg was almost crying with excitement, 'Here, right above the bench so I can look out to the river.'

There was a lot of upheaval the next morning as the cupboards under the bench and the utensils above the bench were removed to make way for the window. A new home would be found for the utensils, Meg had no qualms about that.

There was a lot of discussion over dinner the night before about the best way to tackle the job so as soon as breakfast was over next morning they were on the job knowing exactly what they needed to do. They measured up the window and marked up the wall where it would go. It had to be a snug fit to withstand strong winds and storms. James was reassured that Marshall had inserted a window in one of the shearers huts on the mountain the previous year so at least one of them knew what they were doing.

'What can I do to help?' asked Meg.

'Mrs M we will need some clay to pack around the edges to block up the gaps if you would like to fetch some for us and perhaps work with it to make it pliable.'

97

Meg took the spade down from the hook behind the house, picked up an old sack and went off to get some clay. They worked away all morning until the moment came to place the window in the hole in the wall. The glass was sectioned into four small panes which were enclosed in a strong, white, painted wooden casing. It took three of them to lift it into place. At last the job was done. Marshall set about pushing the clay into all the gaps on both sides to prevent any draughts. Meg stood inside looking out of her new window, tears rolling down her cheeks. James put his arm around Meg's shoulders.

'Meg what is it? Do you not like it?'

'I love it James, I am so happy. These are happy tears,' she smiled up at him. 'Thank you for this, you have no idea what a difference it makes.'

'I think I do Meg, I think I do.' He leant down and kissed the top of her head.

Marshall left early the next morning to get back to Flaxbush to once again become an employee instead of the 'master'.

'Any time you want someone to take care of your farm Mr M, Mrs M, I'm your man,' he said as he mounted his horse.

'Marshall, thank you, you have been a godsend to us. I very much appreciate all you have done, especially with the window. Please apologise to Henry for the delay in your return,' replied James.

'I suspect he already knows why I haven't returned,' he laughed. 'Bye for now, see you at Christmas.'

'Meg, how about you pack me some lunch. Think I might go and check the stock. I expect you will be busy putting things to rights in the house for a while.'

'I would love to come too but yes you are right, I would like to get things back in order, but I will come next time.'

James rode off leaving Meg to reorganize her kitchen. She put all the utensils and pots back under the bench and put away the fresh food stocks, glancing out of her new window every few minutes. It surprised her how much light the window let in, they would not need to use their wax candles and lamps as much now. Meg loved to see her cupboards full of supplies again and her mind raced with ideas for dinner that night.

Gladys had given her some fresh fruit from the orchard and their sweet aromas filled the house. Meg was happy, she started to sing, something she hadn't done in a very long time. She was still humming away to herself when James returned home. He stood outside the door for a moment and picking up on the tune she was humming, started to whistle along with her. She swung around smiling. This was the happiest she had been for some time, James was relieved. He was feeling much happier himself.

Christmas 1865

Meg was teaching herself to make butter and cream from Bessie's beautiful fresh milk. After several failed attempts, she finally achieved a reasonable result much to James delight.

'Marvellous Meg,' he commented when she presented him with fresh bread smeared with lashings of butter one afternoon. 'Where did you learn to make butter like this? I am most impressed.' He bit into the bread again and let out a satisfied sigh.

'Gladys gave me her old churn and paddles when we came back from Christchurch and she showed me what to do. I have also made some cream, look.'

James was thrilled. 'This will make such a difference to our meals Meg.'

Meg smiled with satisfaction, 'Yes there is so much more I can do now, with fresh eggs and butter.'

She walked over to a shelf, took down a round cake tin and carefully removed the lid. I made this to take to the Hopkins's for Christmas.'

'I wish you hadn't shown me that Meg, it looks delicious. Can you not make another one?'

'I could, but I am mindful of our supplies.'

'Hang the supplies Meg. If need be, I will make another run through to Christchurch,' he laughed, 'now cut that cake and let's be having ourselves a wee feast.'

Meg planted the rambling rose bushes on the sheltered side of the house hoping they would grow up the walls. James helped her plant the fruit trees and build a fence around them to stop any animals from nibbling at them. The herb seeds were planted along the garden fences to form a border for the vegetable plants once they started to grow. It had been a busy few weeks for both of them as they made improvements to the property. The next project on the list was to build a room on to the back of the house for the farmhands when they came to help out and also for young Howard Hopkins when he came to work for them as a cadet.

Christmas at Flaxbush was a grand affair. In all there were thirty adults and children and although it appeared to be utter bedlam, everybody worked in together and things ran rather smoothly when it came to meal times and getting children off to bed. Not that they got much sleep at all, they spent many hours laughing and talking into the night while the adults sat around on the verandah and did the same.

The day before Christmas as the womenfolk were busy preparing for the Christmas feast, there was a knock on the homestead door. Gladys wiped her hands on her apron and went to see who it was. There standing in the open doorway was a tall handsome man, someone she had never seen before. She wondered if he might have been a long-lost relation she had yet to meet.

'Can I help you young man?' she asked pleasantly.

'I'm looking for a Meg Morley, I understand she lives here-abouts.'

'Meg? Oh Meg, yes, yes, she does. In fact, she's right here. Meg, there's someone here to see you,' Gladys called over her shoulder.

'Me?' Meg called back, 'Who on earth would come all this way to see....' she stopped in her tracks when she reached the door and saw who was standing there. She burst into tears and with a loud wail threw herself into the arms of the handsome stranger much to the bemusement of the ladies who had gathered behind her. Meg clung around his neck sobbing as if her heart would break.

'Bradley. Oh my heavens, Bradley. What on earth are you doing here? When did you come? How did you find me?' she sobbed. The young man held her tight stroking her back.

'Best go get James,' Gladys whispered to her sister-in-law. Meg pulled herself away from Bradley so she could examine his face.

'It really is you isn't it? It really is you?' she cried.

'Yes Meggie, it really is me,' he smiled, tears were rolling down his cheeks too.

'Meg, please, put us out of our misery, who is this fine young man?'

Meg turned around to address the small group of women and children gathering around them.

'This,' she waved her arm proudly at the young man, 'is my beloved brother Bradley, all the way from England.'

Once the jubilation and celebration of Bradley's arrival settled down Meg took him aside so she could finally talk to him alone.

'Is everything alright at home Bradley?' she asked. "Are you here to bring me bad news?'

'No, no Meg, that is not the case at all. In fact, everyone is fit and well at home. No, I've been saving up my earnings and decided I would like to come out and find you and see if there was work here for me too. You painted such a picture of this country Meg; I just had to come and see for myself.'

'I am so happy you did Bradley; this will be the best Christmas ever.'

And it was. Meg couldn't remember a happier celebration than this Christmas with her brother. Even James was happy to see him.

'I am well pleased to see Bradley, Meg. I do hope he finds work that will keep him here for a while so we can see more of him.'

'I would like that too,' she sighed as she drifted off to sleep.

Bradley found a space in the woolshed to settle down for the night. He had been welcomed into the fold and was looking forward to the Christmas feast the next day. Stephen had taken a liking to the young man and made sure he was settled and comfortable.

The Christmas feast was a sight to behold. Wooden trestle tables covered with white linen table cloths had been set up under the trees in the orchard. Everyone had brought their best crockery and cutlery with

103

them, all well packed and carefully transported for the occasion. Even crystal glasses reflecting the sun sparkled brightly on the beautifully set tables.

'Crystal glasses? Well I never,' exclaimed Meg. 'Margaret, how on earth did you get them here in one piece, they look so precious.'

'They are mostly wedding gifts Meg. We rarely use them at home, so I was happy to pack them in a trunk and bring them here. It's gratifying to see them in use.'

The children had been out gathering wild flowers and these were stuffed into glass jars and placed on the tables as centrepieces. Boxes and planks were set up on either side of the trestle tables to serve as seating. Finally, the Christmas luncheon was ready and with great fanfare and laughter the pork roast was brought out followed by two very large stuffed turkeys, six chickens and a roast leg of mutton.

The men had spent the morning spit roasting the pork and mutton over an open fire and were proud of their efforts. Then came the bowls of vegetables; boiled potatoes with homemade butter and parsley tossed through them, fresh peas that had been shucked out of their shells by the children that morning, fresh picked beans, pumpkin, a variety of pickles and sauces brought by the visitors, breads, cheeses and beer also brought by the visitors. Fresh squeezed lemonade was provided for the women and children and platters of fresh fruit and cream set aside for dessert. It was a jolly occasion with lots of loud chatter and laughter. Everyone seemed to be talking at once, when they weren't eating.

When the sun began to go down the atmosphere became quiet and peaceful. A few murmured voices could be heard here and there, the dishes had all been cleared from an evening meal of leftovers, the children were all fast asleep in their beds and some of the adults were dozing in their chairs. Meg and Bradley stole off to a place where they could be alone to talk some more.

'Bradley, you have no idea how happy I am to see you. I doubted I would ever see any of my family again.'

Tears welled up in her eyes and Bradley reached out and gently stroked her cheek to wipe them away.

'We've all missed you Meg, Mum and Dad especially, but we are all so very proud of you. This was a very brave thing you did, coming all the way across the ocean to start a new life. So, tell me honestly, are you happy with your life Meg?'

104

'I am Bradley, I truly am. I won't lie, it hasn't always been easy but then anything worth doing is not always easy is it.'

'No, I suppose not,' he agreed.

'What are your plans Bradley? Will you come and stay with us a while?'

'I would like that very much. I do need to find work, but I want to spend some time with you and James first. I didn't come all this way just to work, I came here to see you too.'

James wandered a little unsteadily over to see them. He had been drinking most of the day and was quite inebriated.

'James, Bradley would like to stay with us for a while before he leaves to find work.'

'Are you willing to do some work for us Bradley?' he slurred.

'Yes of course. You know I'm not a free-loader James.'

'Good, that's settled then. I have work for you in return for board and keep and I can pay you a small sum as well once the lambs have been sold. I need a room built on to the house and the lambs will need to be rounded up and sorted for the sales. We will be driving them through to here and running all the lambs together through to the sales in Christchurch in March. Can you stay that long?'

'Yes, yes of course, I would love to help out, thank you James.'

Bradley held his hand out and they shook on the deal.

Bradley enjoyed being out and about in the country air, on horseback, but he wasn't sure that this was the life for him long term and when it came time to take the sheep up the river and on through to Flaxbush, he was ready to travel further afield and see what else New Zealand had to offer. He had come straight from the boat in Lyttleton to Christchurch, found out where Meg and James were from the Lands and Survey office and headed straight out to see them. He'd fallen in love with the land and the mountain ranges just as Meg had done. He could see for himself what she had tried to describe in her letters home.

James and Henry reaped a tidy profit from their lambs at the sales. Prices were good and the lambs were fat and healthy.

'Your lambs did better than I expected James. There must be more feed on your property than I thought. I must come and have another look sometime soon. Perhaps you could increase your stock numbers?'

'Yes, I was thinking that too Henry. As a matter of fact, I was just talking to Jack Sanders over there. Word is there is another abandoned run in the Arrowsmith area. He's suggested I go and check it out at the Land Office, thinks it might border Stony Downs.'

'Capital, James, capital. Look, I'll come with you if you like, see if it might be worth pursuing.'

'Thanks Henry I would appreciate your input.'

'Yes, that run-holding at Arrowsmith has indeed been abandoned,' informed the clerk at the Land Office

'Do you know why?' asked Henry.

'From what I can gather they didn't have the capital to buy the stock they needed to keep the place profitable. They couldn't make the lease payments.'

'How many hectares is the lease may I ask?' James was studying the map.

'About 3,000 hectares.'

'What do you think Henry? Looks like it is right on my boundary doesn't it?'

'Which boundary might that be sir?' asked the Land Office Clerk.

'Stony Downs.'

'Well then yes you are right sir, this property is right on your boundary. It has been accessed through here by the former run-holders but there's no reason why you can't access it from your own property here,' he said, pointing at the river flats and passes on the map.

'Put my name on it will you please. I will come back before you close to let you know one way or another.'

'Right you are sir.'

James and Henry walked out of the office into the late summer heat, beads of perspiration immediately forming on their brows after the coolness of the Land Office.

'What do you think Henry? Do you think it would work? It would mean I would need to buy another 3,000 head of stock wouldn't it?'

'I think it could work well James. You don't have to buy any more stock right away, rather than sell your lambs next year you could use them to stock the Arrowsmith run.'

'Best I find Meg and let her know what I plan to do then.'

James found Meg and Gladys in the lady's haberdashery. He caught her eye and summoned her outside, he didn't feel comfortable in a lady's store.

'James, what is it? Is everything alright?'

'Yes, yes of course. Well, it's just that …'

'James what is it?'

'Meg, we did well in the lamb sales today and there is an opportunity to take a lease on a run-holding that borders Stony Downs. I need to make a decision today, once word gets out there will be a rush on for it.'

'Are you asking me or telling me James?'

'I'm asking you, I guess. If I am to go away surveying, I need to know that you will be able to cope on your own with the extra block of land. Could you Meg? Could you cope?'

Meg was thoughtful for a moment.

'I guess, if we took on a cadet full time and I had help from the Hopkins's when I needed it I could do it, yes.' James pulled her to him and kissed her soundly on the lips.

'I love you Mrs Morley,' he said as he backed away before turning and walking briskly back up the street to the Land Office. Meg, blushing, looked around to see if anyone was watching and went back into the haberdashery.

'Is everything alright Meg?' asked Gladys. 'You look quite flushed.'

To celebrate the deal done in the Land Office, Henry, Gladys, James, Meg and Bradley met up in the local hotel for dinner.

'Here's to the newly formed Stony and Arrowsmith Downs run-holding,' proclaimed James as he stood and raised his glass in celebration.

'Here's to a profitable future,' replied Henry.

There was plenty for the Hopkins and the Morley's to talk about over dinner but while they waited for desert Meg turned to Bradley.

'So what have you decided to do Bradley? Are you coming back with us for a while?'

Bradley smiled apologetically.

'Sorry Meg, I have enjoyed my time with you, it has been wonderful, but I need to go and find something else. It has been a pleasure meeting you Gladys, Henry,' he said as he acknowledged the

Hopkins and I have certainly gained a lot of experience from working with you James, but it is time for me to move on now. Meg, I will be back, I promise you that.'

'But what will you do, where will you go?'

Meg was heartbroken. She had hoped he would stay a bit longer.

'Well,' Bradley glanced down sheepishly, 'I have been talking with a chap today about the gold strikes. He was here during the Clutha gold rush but is heading now over to the West Coast. I thought I might go with him and see what it's all about.'

'Gold? I thought the gold rush was over,' remarked Henry.

'In some places yes but there is talk of more yet to be found on the West Coast. I just thought I would go and see for myself. Satisfy my curiosity. This is not something I would have thought about back home but here, in this country, why not try something new?'

That night in the hotel where they all stayed, the men remained downstairs in the lounge with their glasses of port while Meg and Gladys went upstairs to their beds.

'Tell me more about the gold diggings Bradley,' James was curious.

'Not much to tell really, I only heard about it today. Seems there has been some pretty good strikes in the past few years but with so many people coming in from all over the place to try their luck most of them have dried up. Jimmy, the chap I was talking to today seems to think that there might still be some more opportunities on the West Coast though and was happy to take me along with him. Said it was always good to travel in pairs with someone you can trust. It sounds like the gold camps are not the friendliest of places.'

James sat back thoughtfully. 'Not thinking of giving up farming and going in search of gold too are you James?'

'No, but I am curious. Be sure to come back and tell us how you get on Bradley.'

'I will, maybe I could come back for Christmas again next year.'

'Yes, please do that. You will always have a home with us, you know that. When do you plan on leaving?'

'Tomorrow morning. I will have breakfast with you before I go. Give me a chance to say goodbye to Meg.'

'She will miss you; you know.'

'Yes, I will miss her too.'

Meg and the Cadet - 1866

In April, a week before they were due to start crutching on Stony Downs, Henry, Stephen and Marshall arrived to join Meg and James on an excursion to check out the newly acquired Arrowsmith run. They figured it would take the best part of four, maybe five days so they would need to carry all the supplies they would need to last them. The poplars and willows were turning golden yellow; autumn was on its way.

'Probably not the best time of year to be riding the boundaries,' commented Henry, 'but the weather has been settled enough lately and if we are to go by my entries in last year's diary it should last until late May.'

They packed wet weather gear and warm clothing tightly wrapped up with their blankets and bedrolls. Their food supplies were packed into flour sacks and tied to the horses' saddles, sharing the load between all five horses. Meg had cooked a large piece of mutton which was well wrapped and put into one sack. In the other sacks she packed cheeses that she had proudly made, bread, cake and tea.

Henry brought a couple of sacks of lemons, apples and apricots from their orchard, so Meg added some fruit to the bags as well. They set off with Meg and James' two dogs and Henry and Stephen's four dogs all happily running along behind the horses.

It took them almost three days to get to the new run holding. They found a suitable camp site and set up for the first night. The next morning was clear and blue so they decided to climb the mountain range in order to get an over view of the land. James was in his element, his surveying skills coming to the fore.

'I surveyed that area over there when we were still in Christchurch,' he said proudly. He pointed out a mountain range to Meg.

'I would have seen this property from there. Little did I know that one day I would be leasing it. It's quite possible that we will find a pile of rocks on the top of this range left there by another surveyor. I heard of a chap by the name of Jollie who worked around this area for a while.'

They rode their horses as far up as they could then left them tied up where there was a bit of food for them to forage. The hillside was covered in trees and scrub, it was tough going. Marshall and Stephen went ahead with a sharp blade each and cut a track for the others to follow.

'Might need to do a bit of burning off up here James. Let some grass come through.'

'Yes, I was thinking that myself Henry. This is not good for sheep. Meg, how are you getting on. Do you want to wait here for us?'

'No, I'm alright. I will keep going a bit longer.'

About half way up the hill the bush stopped and gave way to loose shingle and rock.

'We will need to be very careful on this stuff,' warned James. 'I've come a bit of a cropper on this kind of ground before. Started to slide near the top and didn't stop until I reached the trees one time. Gave myself a bit of a fright. Once you start to slide it's difficult to stop unless you can brace yourself against a rock.'

'You didn't tell me that James.' scolded Meg.

'Did no harm my love, didn't see the point in fussing over nothing,' smiled James.

They scrambled their way to the top, lying down on soft moss to catch their breath.

'I didn't expect there to be anything up here but rocks and snow,' remarked Meg.

'No, it's surprising what grows up here isn't it,' replied Henry.

They stood and looked around, stunned into silence by the majestic expanse of mountain ranges before them.

Meg's soft voice broke the silence. 'This is absolutely stunning. James, let's build a house up here,' she laughed. 'One would never tire of the views.'

'In winter, my love, you would be totally covered with snow, there wouldn't be any views. Besides, all you would see is snow and you would probably get snow blindness.'

'You are such a spoil sport,' she punched James playfully on the arm.

'Ah, just as I expected, look, here's a surveyor's mark,' said James pointing to a large pile of rocks. He retrieved his looking glass from the bundle tied to his back. 'And across there is another marker. Here Meg, come take a look.'

James stood behind Meg leaning over her shoulder as she focused the telescope, pointing her in the right direction. 'Can you see that pile of rocks on the top of that mountain there?'

'Oh yes. Is that what you call a trig?'

'It is, yes. Now if you swing around here to your right you will see our river, the Lawrence, and further around way over in the distance is a tributary that runs down to the Hakatere. That's the one that runs up to Flaxbush. Come back this way to your left, can you see a lake in the distance?'

'Yes, yes I see it, the sun is shining on it.'

'That is Lake Heron.'

He turned around.

'If we were up a bit higher, on that Southern Alpine Range behind us we would be able to see the West Coast of the island and the ocean. Do you chaps want to have a look?'

'Yes,' they chorused, and lined up to take their turn.

'You've never really spoken about your surveying work James. I've never really known what you chaps do and what it's like for you being out in all weathers measuring land. What's it like?' Stephen asked.

James sat down on one of the rocks, the others standing or sitting around to listen.

'We use a theodolite and chains to do our measuring. We create a landmark and use that as our line of sight. I didn't want to carry all my

111

gear with me this time, but you are welcome to come out with me sometime and I can show you how it all works.'

'You're on James, I'd love to,' said Henry.

'Me too,' chimed in Stephen. 'Do you get lonely? What's it like, being out on your own I mean?'

'A lot of the time surveyors work in pairs. It depends what the terrain is like whether I take someone with me or not. If it's a simple job I can do it myself, but it is much easier when there is someone else with you. There is a chap in Christchurch I have worked with on many occasions, we get along well enough.'

'I guess you must camp out a lot then,' said Marshall.

'Yes. You become very good at setting up camp, lighting camp fires and packing it all up again. I have been caught in a few downpours and been chilled to the bone, but I've never been caught in snow thank goodness.'

'Speaking of the cold we better push on. Once that sun goes down the temperatures will drop markedly,' said Henry. 'I am surprised there is not more snow on the tops of the Southern Alpine Range. I expected it to be a lot further down than it is,' he said.

The group slipped and slid their way down the shingle slope grabbing hold of rocks to steady themselves. Finally, they got to the tree line and retraced their steps through the path they created on the way up. The horses were standing quietly waiting for them. They rode back to the camp and settled in for the night.

The next morning they packed up and moved off further down along the grassy slopes of the river to the far boundary. They set up camp again and decided to ride out for a while before dark. As they pulled up at the base of the bush line there was a tremendous racket coming from the bush. The dogs were barking madly and there was a blood curdling scream, one that Meg had never heard the likes of before. It chilled her to the bone.

'My God, what on earth is that,' she cried.

'Wild boar I suspect,' exclaimed Henry as he leapt off his horse and grabbed his gun.

'Stephen you come with me, the rest of you stay here and have your guns at the ready in case it comes charging out,' instructed Henry.

Meg was nervous. She didn't have a gun, James had it. All she had was a sharp knife she kept in a pouch behind her saddle. She reached for it now, her hands shaking. They had been out pig hunting before but all they ever got was rabbit. She had never seen a wild boar up close.

Suddenly a black beast with white tusks curled up on either side of its nose ran straight towards them from the bush. The horses screamed and reared. James and Marshall managed to stay on their horses, but Meg was tossed to the ground losing her grip on the knife. She cried out as pain ripped through her hip. She rolled over on to her stomach and grabbed for the knife. She looked up and saw that the boar was almost upon her, it looked enormous and menacing. James raised his rifle but hesitated to shoot in case he hit Meg. Marshall tried a shot but missed. As the boar advanced on Meg she rolled over on to her back and held the knife upright. The boar came over her head and as it jumped across her body she thrust the knife up with all the strength she could muster. There was another piercing scream and blood started squirting everywhere. The boar landed on Megs legs kicking and screaming. Marshall fired a shot to its head and it went limp.

Meg sat up and tried to pull herself out, howling and kicking at the beast trying the get her legs free. But the beast was too heavy and she had to wait until Marshall and James lifted it off. She was trembling from head to foot, gasping for air. James knelt down beside her and took her in his arms.

'Meg, my beautiful Meg, are you alright my darling?' He was terrified she might be badly injured.

'I, I... I think so.' she sobbed. 'I, aaagh, that hurts,' she cried out as James ran his hand over her legs.

He stripped off his jacket and lay Meg back down on the ground. 'Lie down Meg, I am going to check you over. Just tell me where it hurts alright?'

'Yes, mmm, aaagh yes that hurts. Stop, stop,' she screamed, 'Ouch that really hurts.'

'What do you think James?' Henry was leaning over concentrating on Meg.

'I would say she has a badly bruised hip and the weight of that boar may have fractured her leg. Can you wiggle your toes Meg?'

'Yes, but it hurts like hell.'

'Good your leg is not broken at least. Let's just see if we can sit you up.'

Meg groaned as James and Henry gently pulled her into a sitting position. Henry supported her back while James checked her head to make sure she didn't have any lumps or abrasions.

'Are you feeling faint?'

Meg shook her head.

'What about your back, is there any pain in your back?' Henry was asking.

'No, no, just mainly in my hip and my legs.'

'Right,' said Henry, 'let's set up camp here and make the poor girl a cup of tea.'

They all sat in silence for a while catching their breath and calming down from their adrenalin rush. Then, despite the pain, Meg started to giggle. The men looked at her, not sure if this was laughter brought on by drinking too much brandy or if it was hysteria.

'Are you alright Meg? This isn't very funny.'

Meg laughed out loud.

'It is really. Here you are, four strong men with guns and it took a woman lying on her back on the ground to bring down the mighty beast.'

She was laughing heartily now and after a moment the men joined in.

'Meg, you are absolutely right. You are a bloody legend if you will excuse my language,' laughed Henry. They turned and looked at the boar lying bleeding with the knife still stuck in its belly. The dogs were trying to get a closer look but were shooed away.

'James, you and I are on dinner duty tonight. We will be having roast pork I think,' laughed Henry, 'You didn't happen to bring any brandy with you I suppose?'

'No, sometimes I do when I am out surveying but not this time sadly.'

'I carry a little bottle of laudanum with me for emergencies. I don't like to use it unnecessarily but, in this case, I wondered if a wee drop might ease the pain and help you get a good night's sleep Meg. It's entirely up to you.'

'Thank you Stephen, I guess a small measure might be helpful if I am to ride back tomorrow.'

'That was one heck of a feat you pulled off there young lady,' laughed Henry, 'where on earth did you learn to do that?'

114

'I saw a man being attacked by a wild animal once, back in the Highlands. One of the shepherds had to stick a knife in the animal's stomach when it lunged for him. His gun jammed so he threw it away and drew his knife out of his belt and waited until the animal came at him. It was the most terrifying thing I had ever seen but I guess the memory of it saved my life.'

'I will have nightmares from watching you lying on the ground with that boar bearing down on you Meg, I swear I will,' groaned James.

'Me too,' agreed Stephen. 'How are you feeling now Meg, is the pain lessening at all?'

'Yes, it is a bit; I am feeling a little better now that I've had a chance to calm down. Not sure how I will go riding a horse tomorrow, but I guess we will find out.'

They made Meg as comfortable as possible using leaves and moss to pack up a soft base for her to lie on. She was in a lot of pain, but she was also enjoying the attention she was receiving from her companions. She ran her hands over her body herself to check for any blood or broken bones and felt confident enough that there were none they hadn't already been identified but she suspected there would be some mighty black bruises appearing before too long.

The roast pork was delicious, certainly a welcome change from mutton. They sat back with their hot cups of tea and finally started to talk about the day's events as the dogs continued to gnaw contentedly away on their pork bones.

Clouds were starting to build up when they awoke next morning. Marshall gathered some wood and re-set the fire while Stephen rummaged through the sacks of food to prepare breakfast. James and Henry were nowhere to be seen.

'I didn't hear them ride off?' Meg said to Stephen.

'No, you were out to it Meg, that laudanum worked its magic. They managed to creep out quietly without disturbing you.'

'Where have they gone?'

'James thought he spotted a building on the other side of the river close to the eastern boundary. He and Henry have gone to check it out and see if it's on Arrowsmith land. It could well have belonged to the previous occupants.'

115

Meg raised herself up gingerly. Her legs ached and felt stiff but once she started to move them about the pain eased and she was able to stand. Stephen rushed forward to help her up.

'How are you feeling this morning Meg? You gave us all a heck of a fright last night.'

Meg smiled up at him.

'I'm alright Stephen, just a little stiff and bruised but otherwise I'm fine.'

She pulled up her skirts to reveal nasty red and black bruises and abrasions on her legs.

'Hmmm, best we wash those abrasions,' remarked Stephen. 'Don't want them becoming infected.'

He went off down to the river to get some water and when it had been heated he carefully washed her wounds.

'We should have done this last night.'

'I doubt I would have let anyone near my legs last night,' she sighed, 'they were far too sore.'

James and Henry were gone for several hours. Stephen had gone off after breakfast to find them, leaving Marshall to clean up and pack everything away ready to load on to the horses when they returned.

Meg watched the three men making their way back across the stony creek bed, the dogs tagging along behind.

'Did you find it?' asked Meg as soon as they dismounted.

'Yes, there is a dwelling of sorts. Very basic but it appears sturdy enough. It will serve as a base for when we come down to this part of the run. We could leave it set up so that we didn't have to carry so much with us,' informed James. 'There are some good grassy slopes up the side of the ranges just beyond those rolling hills in the foreground. I must admit, it looks better than I expected. Meg, how are you feeling this morning?'

'Much better. I should be able to ride. The bruising is on the shins mostly so it should be comfortable enough to sit on my horse.'

'Good. Marshall, I want you to ride back home with Meg. Stephen, Henry and I will finish the boundary run. We should be with you in two to three days.'

Meg started to protest.

'No Meg, I want you to go home and rest. Please. You will have plenty of time to see the rest of the place when we are checking stock.'

Meg was disappointed but she knew there was no point in aggravating her wounds. There was work to be done and she would need to be fit and well for that. They divided up enough food for Meg and Marshall for a few days and repacked. James knelt down and put his hands out for Meg to put her foot on to help her mount her horse. Marshall watched, he would probably have to do that when it was just him and Meg. She winced as she carefully dragged her leg across the patient horse and gently lowered herself onto the saddle before letting out a sigh of relief.

'I think I'm going to be alright. I feel a bit stiff but for now I am all good.'

'Excellent. You two head off then. We will wait here to see that you are going alright then we will head off too.' James issued the instruction.

Meg's shins were throbbing by the time they made camp that night, but she didn't want to say anything to Marshall. He was a dear young man but a bit shy with women, so she didn't want to worry him unduly.

'I don't like the look of that weather Marshall,' she said as they ate their supper.

'No, I don't either Mrs M. Looks to me like it will be raining before long. Just as well we have that rock shelf there to shelter under.'

'Yes, I think we should pack everything up and get ourselves organized. The weather here is unpredictable as you well know, it could be upon us before we know.'

They pushed their supplies and swags as far as they could under the rocky overhang jutting out from the side of a bank then settled down and made themselves as comfortable as possible, their wet weather gear ready to pull over them when the rain came. And it did, just after nightfall. It started with just a few heavy warning drops that got heavier and heavier until it was coming down in torrents. Water flowed down the hill and ran off the top and sides of their shelter in rivulets.

'I feel like we are under a waterfall,' Meg yelled to Marshall above the roar of the building wind and driving rain.

It rained all night and all the next day. As soon as it was daylight Meg and Marshall rummaged around in the bags and had a quick snack of bread and cheese before donning their wet weather coats and hats. The horses were not keen to be moving but with encouragement from Meg

117

they finally settled enough for them to mount up. The two riders tied their supplies to their bodies under their coats in an attempt to keep the food dry. They would be riding for most of the day to reach the house and would need more food.

Meg didn't mind the rain, she had ridden through plenty of rain storms in the Highlands but this rain today was icy cold, the wind bitter. Marshall looked worried.

'Mrs M, I think we might be heading for snow,' he yelled across at her as they carefully negotiated their way along the slippery water sodden banks beside the river. The water was starting to form into one big river, flowing swiftly and stretching almost from bank to bank. The noise was deafening. Meg could see Marshall was trying to say something to her. She strained to hear him but all she caught was the word 'snow'. Her heart raced. She hoped they would reach home before it started.

'What about the others?' she screamed back at Marshall. 'Do you think they will be able to find shelter? What if they get stranded?'

Marshall brought his horse right up close to Meg's and leant across so he could yell in her ear.

'Don't worry Mrs M, they have plenty of experience between them and there is that hut they found. My guess is they will have headed back to that when they saw the storm coming. They will be fine, and they have enough food for a few more days yet.'

Meg nodded, agreeing that he was probably right. They were about five miles from home when the rain eased off, the temperature dropped, and the first snowflakes started to fall. By the time they reached the house it was falling steadily. They rode straight in under the shelter of the stables and dismounted. They unsaddled the horses and fed them some oats. Meg fetched the eggs from the hen house while Marshall quickly milked Bessy. She was ready and waiting with a very full udder and was pleased to at last be relieved of some of her milk. Meg ducked in under the verandah and hastily doffed her coat and hat. She was frozen, the temperature continued to fall, she needed to get the fire started. By the time Marshall appeared with a bucket of warm milk Meg had the fire roaring and was preparing a hot meal for them both. They had a drink of warm milk which helped to stave off their hunger.

'I think it's best you stay in here with me tonight Marshall. Who knows how much snow we will get and I don't want you freezing to death in the room out the back. Henry would never forgive me,' she laughed.

She knew Marshall would feel a bit uncomfortable, so she tried to make light of the matter. 'You can sleep here by the fire if you like.'

When Meg woke in the morning there was an eerie stillness in the air. She got out of bed, pulled her shawl around her shoulders and went to look out the window. Her gasp woke Marshall up.

'What? What is it Mrs M?' he sat up with a start.

'Come and look, the snow has settled, it must be over twelve inches deep. Doesn't it look so pretty though.'

Marshall stood beside her looking out the window.

'Enjoy it for now Mrs M, most of it will be gone by tonight.'

And he was right. The sun came out and the beautiful white landscape melted into a soggy mush. The river was flowing strongly with little rapids forming here and there as it tumbled across stones which had been dry for much of the summer.

'I do hope the others were able to find suitable shelter for the night,' muttered Meg, 'it was bitterly cold.'

'I'm sure they will be just fine Mrs M, as I said they had the hut at Arrowsmith to go to.'

It was an anxious wait before Meg spotted the riders in the distance three days later.

'They're here Marshall, I can see them,' she called, relief flooding through her.

The riders finally reached the house, tired but seemingly hale and hearty.

'Did you find shelter during the snow storm?' was her first question.

'Yes, we managed to make it back to the hut and get a fire going. Had a bit of trouble getting back across the creek though, almost lost a couple of the dogs,' said James as he slid off his horse.

Meg glanced around anxiously.

'It's alright Meg; we managed to drag them out before they got injured.'

She went over to her two beloved dogs and checked them over. They welcomed her attention with soppy wet tongues, and she laughed as she buried her head in their black and white furry necks.

'I wish you wouldn't do that Meg, they are working dogs for goodness sake,' admonished James.

119

Meg chose to ignore his words.

'Come on in all of you, I have a nice warm fire going and a stew on the go. How about some fresh scones and cream, and a nice cup of tea in the meantime?'

There were no refusals of that offer.

'Did you check the lambs on the way through? It was raining so hard Marshall and I just pushed on for home, we didn't stop to see if they were alright,' Meg asked James.

'Yes, we moved them up away from the river and brought them further down this way for the night. We will go back for them in the morning.'

The weather cleared and stayed fine for the two days it took to remove the dags from the sheep.

'You've got some good healthy stock there James. If you can afford to reduce the number of lambs for next year's sales you could put some of them on the Arrowsmith run,' suggested Henry.

'Yes, I plan on doing some more surveying work this year, that income will help compensate for the reduced lamb pay-out. At least it will cover the two leases. We would like to take young Howard on as a cadet if he is still interested. Meg will need a hand while I am away.'

'Yes, Howard is dead keen to come and work for you. He's a good lad, a bit wet behind the ears but a quick learner. He can ride back with you after we finish our crutching at Flaxbush if you like.'

Howard proved to be good company for Meg during the long weeks James was away surveying. He was quiet and shy at first, but they soon got used to each other. They would take turns at reading to each other from the Bible of an evening. The Hopkins were Catholics and would host the Bishop a few times a year when was in the area. People came from right around the district to attend the services he provided. Even though she was Anglican, Meg enjoyed the Bishops visits. She was in the habit of reading a chapter from the Bible every night before going to sleep. James was not overly religious but would attend the services at Flaxbush without complaint. He did it for Meg, he knew she appreciated it. Meg was thrilled when Howard found the courage to start discussing passages that left him confused as to their meaning.

Life on Stony Downs ran smoothly under Meg and Howard's watch. They regularly did the boundary run and when the weather looked stable enough, they rode on down to spend a night or two at the Arrowsmith hut. Meg was disappointed when she first saw it. It was a simple dwelling, made with wattle and clay and sporting a thatched roof of pampas grass. The roof inside had the remains of an old canvas tent lining still hanging from it. The chimney was in need of repair, shafts of daylight streamed in from several quarters.

'How on earth did they keep warm in winter?' Meg pondered.

'Perhaps it was only used in the summer and for mustering,' Howard offered.

'Perhaps you are right,' she agreed. She walked around the hut gathering long pieces of tussock grass to form a crude brush to clean out the hut. If they were going to stay there for the night it would need to be cleaner than it was.

'Howard, go gather some wood and get a fire going would you please?'

'Sure thing Mrs M.'

Meg swept the dust and cobwebs out of the hut before bringing their supplies in. There were beds along two walls, wide enough for two people to bunk head to tail if need be. She put their bedrolls on the beds and wiping down the table and chairs with her skirt, set the table for their meal. It would be sparse; they chose not to bring any more than the basics.

'This is nice isn't it?' Meg said to Howard as they sat in front of the roaring fire.

'Yes, I quite enjoy staying in the shepherds' huts. It's a lot more peaceful than home,' he smiled shyly. I would rather sleep out under the stars than inside though. Mum sometimes lets us sleep on the verandah at night by ourselves, that's fun.'

Meg smiled thinking back on her own childhood. Sleeping outside was unheard of.

She planned to stay two nights in the hut with the intention of firing some of the bush area James had talked to her about. It was on the opposite side of the river and about a mile further on from the hut. They were to set it going then come back to the hut and do some exploring in and around the bush at the base of the mountain up behind the hut. Meg was in two minds about burning off the trees and scrub. While she thrilled

121

at the sight of a fire racing up a hillside devouring everything in its path, she despaired of injuring or killing the birds and animals. She just hoped they would get out of the way in time.

They set out early in the morning and picked a suitable spot to start the fire. They gathered dried tussock to make a torch which they would light and then touch to dried bushes to get the fire started. It would take on a life of its own once it got started and all they could do was get well out of the way and watch. They started in the middle of the patch they wanted to burn and walked off in opposite directions until Meg gave the signal to stop. They both stood back and once the fire took hold they mounted their horses and rode back across the river. They sat on the other side for a while and watched as the fire raced quickly up the hill engulfing everything in its path.

'Fire is quite destructive isn't it Howard?' she mused.

'Yes,' he nodded. He didn't much like the fires. He witnessed one get out of control a couple of years back. It destroyed a house and almost killed one of the workers. Fire frightened him but he had never said anything to anyone about it.

'Right, that looks like it's going well, shall we go and have a look around? I would quite like to have a look over there amongst the trees.'

They rode together in silence until they got close to the trees. The grass was long and lush so Meg dismounted and tied her horse to a fallen log, leaving it to graze while they searched the bush on foot. Just before they entered the dark mysterious bush Meg stopped and listened.

'Can you hear that Howard? It's a buzzing sound. Surely there's no bees here, would there be?'

'Might be,' he pondered. 'We had a wild bee hive on our place once but Dad got rid of it in case we got stung. It was in the orchard and a bit too close to the house.'

Meg followed the sound and to her delight spotted the hive.

'Fresh honey, how wonderful. Do you know how to get the honey out Howard?'

He shook his head. 'Not really, I learned a bit about it in school. You have to make a fire underneath to make smoke which makes them drowsy and then you can reach in and break off a piece of honey comb.'

'Let's give it a try, shall we?' Meg was excited, she loved honey and would love to take some back home.

122

With Howard's help she placed a small pile of stones on the ground underneath the hive and placed dried tussock and dead leaves on top, just enough to make a bit of smoke. It worked a treat. Once the smoke wafted up to the hive and the bees became lethargic she carefully reached in and snapped off a piece of the gold honey comb. She put it in her mouth her eyes lighting up in ecstasy as the sticky golden substance ran down her arm. She broke a piece off and gave it to Howard who sucked on it hungrily and licked his lips.

'Mmmm that tastes pretty darn good,' he smiled. 'Ooops, best move away a bit, the bees are coming back to life,' he laughed.

'I will bring something back tomorrow to put the honey comb into so we can take some home.'

Meg's mind was spinning with ideas for using the honey, in cups of tea and in her baking.

'With the lemons you brought me from your orchard Howard we could make lemon curd. I just love lemon curd, don't you? We used to make it back home.'

'Yes, Mother made some with the honey from the hive after Dad got rid of the bees, but we haven't had any since. I like it too.'

They went back to where the horses were grazing and decided to go into the bush on foot. The undergrowth was thick in places, so they had to pick their way carefully among the ferns, shrubs, insect riddled fallen trees and low-slung branches. The ground beneath their feet was soft and spongy with damp moss, the air had an acrid damp earthy smell, but Meg loved it. Best of all was the sound of the birds. She had brought her bird book with her and was ready to identify any that would stop long enough for her to get a good look at. The first one was a curious Wood Pigeon.

'I know that one,' she pointed it out to Howard. 'No doubt you do too.'

'Wood Pigeon.'

'Yes, you are right. I understand the Maori people say they make for good eating. Looks too beautiful to eat don't you think. Oh, look there,' she whispered, 'see, that? It has two little red bits hanging down from the sides of its mouth.'

She retrieved the bird book from her pocket.

'It's a Saddleback,' she whispered, 'pretty isn't it.'

Howard nodded but kept quiet, not wanting to frighten the bird away. They sat quietly on a fallen log for some time just watching and waiting for the birds to appear. The birds, in turn, seemed to be interested in the two intruders themselves and came fairly close to sit on low branches as both species eyed each other.

'It's getting cold, best we head back to the hut and check on that fire,' Meg said after they had been sitting for a while.

It was getting dark now and the fire was nothing more than a smoking hillside, but the edges still held an orange glow which stayed lit up into the night. '

We did that Howard, you and me. We did that,' smiled Meg gleefully. 'Gives you a sense of power don't you think?'

Howard chuckled, 'Never thought of it like that, yes I guess it does a bit.'

Winter - 1866

James returned in late July after a four-month stint surveying. He had promised Meg he would be home in time for lambing and mustering. Meg was thrilled to see him; she had missed him more than she thought she would. Howard was to be relieved of his duties and sent back to Flaxbush. He was a bit disappointed James was back, he had enjoyed his time with Meg. She was fun to be with and she had taught him more about reading and English history than he'd ever learnt in school.

The first morning James and Meg were alone together they lay in each other's arms after making love, enjoying the closeness.

'I met up with Bradley, Meg. He sends his fondest regards to you.'

Meg sat up in bed. 'You did? You saw Bradley? How is he, what is he doing?'

'Well, he's done very well for himself you will be pleased to hear. He has been living with his friend Terry in a tent in a place called Kaniere; not far from Hokitika. Apparently they found some large nuggets in a previously worked over area. They are not sure if they were missed or whether they were brought down the river in recent heavy rains.

Bradley was talking about giving up looking for more gold and setting up shop in Hokitika though. I don't think he likes living rough.'

Meg laughed, 'No he was always fond of his creature comforts. What sort of shop? Does this mean he doesn't want to go back to England?' Meg's face lit up at the thought.

'He was talking about a general merchant store. There is a small one in the town and he said he would like to buy it and expand it. He has some useful supply contacts back in England and has met up with a couple of chaps from Australia who are interested in supplying him with goods as well.'

'Mama and Da will be so proud of him. This will mean that we can go and visit him and he can come visit us maybe once or twice a year. Oh James, that is wonderful news. But where did you meet up with him?'

'I did some work in Christchurch for a week or two and was then asked if I would go down to Dunedin. I joined another three chaps down there and we headed up the West Coast. We worked our way up for almost three months surveying until we came to Hokitika. That's where I saw him, he was in a hotel drinking with his friends. I could hardly believe my eyes. And neither could he I might add, his eyes nearly popped right out of his head,' laughed James. 'He is looking forward to coming back for Christmas again this year to spend some more time with you.'

Meg was delighted that her brother might be staying in New Zealand. She leapt out of bed, drawing her shawl around her for warmth. The days were cooler now, winter was setting in.

'Let's spend the day outside today James and make the most of this beautiful sunny day. The daylight hours are getting shorter and soon we will be going into those dreadful dreary weeks with no sunshine at all. I'm not looking forward to that again.'

'Well young lady, we will just have to come up with ways of getting ourselves through that time then won't we,' Meg blushed at the glint in his eye and the innuendo in his smile.

'You really have missed me haven't you my darling,' she smiled as she pulled him out of bed.

Over the next few weeks Meg delighted James with her new recipes. He was stunned when she produced some honey for his fresh baked scones his first morning home.

'Honey? Where on earth did you find honey? It's from a wild hive isn't it?'

'Yes, there is one behind the hut at Arrowsmith. Howard and I found it when we went down to do the firing.'

'This is heavenly Meggie, well done,' he said licking his fingers.

Within a few weeks the snow was lying thick on the ground and would stay that way until the spring thaw but that didn't stop Meg and James venturing out when they could. They would check on the sheep now residing on the lower pastures at the base of the ranges. It was a relatively easy ride on horseback but the dogs would get tired from having to jump their way through the snow. A lot of the time James and Meg would take a soggy dog each and carry them across their laps until they got to the river's edge where there was less snow and more solid footing for the dogs. Much to James amusement Meg had made booties from a sheep skin that she and Howard had dried and treated in the summer when they had killed a sheep for the larder. Meg wanted to learn to tan the lamb and sheep skins and was pleased to discover that Howard had learned the skill from one of the farmhands working for his father. They didn't have the right ingredients to make the leather supple, but they were able to salt it, dry it and work it into a reasonable pelt. Howard promised to bring some alum, saltpetre and bran with him when he came back which would make a solution to treat the pelt and make it supple and more useable. The pelt could then be turned into jackets, slippers, muffs, hats, bed covers or warm rugs. Meg had cut small rounds of the leather and chewed on them to soften them and then running a string thread through holes at the top was able to fashion a boot of sorts to protect the dogs' feet. The dogs were prone to stone cuts and frost bite and she hated seeing them limping and in pain.

Too soon the dark days came and they were housebound a lot of the time when the weather was cold and bleak. They had to make sure they had plenty of firewood stacked under the verandah during these times in case the snow got too deep for them to get out to the sheds at the back of the house. If the weather was particularly nasty James would allow the dogs to stay under the verandah or sleep by the fire when it got too far below freezing. He had lined the walls of the shed with sacks and canvas as best he could to give some protection to Bessy and the horses.

He padded the hen house up with dry straw and made sure that all the animals had plenty of dry feed when they couldn't get out to forage for themselves.

As the dismal weeks of gloom dragged on James and Meg got tired of each other's company. They had read all the books Gladys had lent them at Christmas. They played cards until they were fed up with them. They made a point of going outside each day just to get some fresh air and a break from each other. They would go off in opposite directions most of the time just to be on their own but when the day wasn't too bleak they would ride together to check on the sheep. The lack of Vitamin D from the sun was causing them to become weak and short tempered. They would argue over silly little things. Meg was becoming weepy and nauseous.

Finally, when they were at the end of their tether a ray of sunshine crept its way through one of the small panes of the window. Meg just looked at it for a while as it played on a tin mug sitting on the bench beneath the window. When it dawned on her that the sun was finally breaking through, she raced to the door and threw it open. She ran out into the snow and holding her arms out wide, shut her eyes, and tilted her head up to feel the warmth of the sun on her face for the first time in weeks.

From that day on the sun stayed longer and longer until it was around long enough to start melting the snow. James and Meg's spirits lifted considerably over the next few days although Meg continued to feel unwell in the mornings. It was mid-September and lambing was due to start, if it hadn't already. With the ram being out with the ewes all the time there was no accurate way of knowing when the ewes had got in lamb. Their spirits lifted even more when, on their first lambing beat, they found that lambing was well under way and new born lambs were bounding around everywhere.

'Aren't they the cutest wee things,' mused Meg. 'This is my favourite time of the year I think, seeing all these beautiful little creatures so full of life and fun. They make me smile.'

'Well I'm glad something makes you smile Meg. You have been rather grumpy of late.'

Meg was shocked. 'James, what a dreadful thing to say. You haven't exactly been easy to get along with yourself.'

She started to cry and immediately James regretted his harsh words.

'I'm sorry Meg. Please, don't cry. I guess these past few weeks have taken more of a toll on me than I realized. I shouldn't have said that. I know you have been feeling unwell lately, I am worried about you.'

Meg sniffled and wiped her nose on her sleeve. 'I don't know what's wrong with me but let's just see if we can do our best to pick ourselves up. I will try hard not to be grumpy with you if you will try hard not to get grumpy with me.'

James smiled, 'Yes, I will try my love, but you must let me know if you begin to feel any worse or you develop any pain.' His attention turned back to the lambs careening around the paddocks and leaping over rocks.

'They love to stand on top of things,' smiled Meg, 'I remember them doing that back in the Highlands. I used to sit and watch them for hours.'

'Well, you can sit and watch them for hours if you like but I suspect I will have to come back with a pick axe to chip the ice off you if you do. Come on let's get off the horses for a while and go for a walk. We can check them more closely if we are on foot. Best bring the bags with us in case we need to do any deliveries.'

As the temperatures slowly rose, the melted snow ran down the hillsides pouring into the already fast flowing rivers below swelling them to capacity and breaching their banks. It made for tricky crossing on horseback and impossible on foot. A lot of horses were shy of fast flowing water and not without cause. If they lost their footing they could be washed down stream. Sometimes they could regain their footing when they reached a shallow patch, other times they would drown or get caught up in fallen trees and debris and die a painful death, their riders sometimes succumbing to a similar fate. James had witnessed such an instance once and vowed he would never push his horses into that situation. When they couldn't cross the river safely to check on the stock, he would sit up on the hillside directly opposite and study them through his eye glass, not that there was anything he could do if any of the stock were in trouble.

Finally, it was almost Christmas again and Meg watched and waited eagerly for Bradley to arrive. This year the Hopkins's were coming to Stony Downs for their Christmas feast. They were planning to arrive a week or so after Christmas so that the Hopkins's could have their Christmas Day with friends and family who were coming to stay. Meg had been busy with preparations for weeks but was thoroughly enjoying herself. She was in high spirits for more than just the fact that it was Christmas and Bradley was coming to visit. Meg was with child at last. She had put her morning sickness and lack of monthly cycles down to the long dark days of mid-winter but now she knew for certain and planned to tell James on Christmas morning. It would be her Christmas gift to him, one she knew could never be surpassed by any other gift on earth.

Bradley duly arrived two days before Christmas and the festivities began in earnest. He had picked up the mail from the Post Office and carried the letters and a large package with him all the way to Stony Downs. There were letters from home for all of them, James included.

'Shall we open the parcel today or wait for Christmas morning?' she asked James.

'I think we should wait, what do you think Bradley?'

'I'm not sure my sister can wait James; she looks like she's fit to burst.'

'Oh you two, stop teasing,' laughed Meg.

Christmas morning arrived and Meg was up with the birds. She hardly slept a wink all night she was so excited, not just about the parcel but about sharing her news with James. It was hard keeping it a secret but she wanted to wait until Christmas morning.

They set up the large stone fireplace outside which was often used during the peak summer months as it was far too hot to cook inside the small hut. Meg went out with a pot of water to get it boiling for their tea. She put the large wrought iron pan on the side to heat and went in to make pancakes. She had fresh lemons, cream and honey to put on them. Meg and James so enjoyed the honey that Meg had found behind the Arrowsmith hut that they had gone back for more and had the combs stored in large tins in the futtah.

James was the next to wake up and get out of bed, Bradley was sleeping in the room out the back and hadn't shown his face yet.

'Good morning sleepy head,' she kissed James on the cheek. 'Merry Christmas.'

'And a Merry Christmas to you to my love,' he mumbled sleepily.

'Before Bradley gets up, I want to tell you something. It is my gift to you.'

'That's intriguing, what do you want to tell me?'

'You are going to be a father James. I am with child.'

The look on James face made Meg's heart leap with joy. His eyes filled with tears, his mouth hung open, he was absolutely speechless.

'You, you're.... really? Oh, my beautiful Meggie, really?' He drew her down to sit beside him on the bed, cradled her in his arms and cried. 'I can't believe it. Are you sure? How many months?'

'Four, I think. It must have happened when we had nothing better to do during those dark weeks of winter.'

James chortled with laughter, 'Well something good came out of that time at least. Something very good. Are you well Meg? I know you were sick for a while, but I thought you were depressed from being cooped up inside for so long. It was the morning sickness all along then?'

'Yes, it would appear so,' giggled Meg.

They sat quietly together until they heard the door of the back room open.

'Sounds like Bradley is up. Shall we tell him the news?'

'Let's tell him together over breakfast,' Meg suggested.

Bradley was over the moon with the news. I'm to be an uncle then? That is grand news, well done Meg. So, what took you so long?'

'The doctor didn't really know,' Meg replied shyly.

'Maybe you just didn't try hard enough,' he threw a big grin at James.

'Cheeky blighter,' laughed James. Meg blushed and got up to make some more tea.

'Now then I'm not waiting any longer, let's open this parcel from home,' demanded Bradley.

Meg carefully opened the parcel and there, inside, was the most beautiful cream hand spun, knitted blanket. It was so deliciously soft Meg buried her face in it. When she came up for air the tears were streaming down her face. She let out a sob.

'It smells like Mama,' she cried.

Even Bradley welled up and had to look away. He quickly opened his own letter to distract himself but that didn't help. The sight of his mother's hand writing undid him completely. Giving in to his emotions he went and sat down beside Meg; put his arm around her shoulders and drawing her to him cried right along with her. James stared at them, smiling.

'Goodness me, what is it with you Winstanley's,' he laughed. 'Are you happy or sad?'

'I'm happy,' Meg smiled at him through her tears. 'What about you my dear brother, are you happy?'

'Yes,' he choked, 'yes I am. Perhaps a bit homesick but definitely happy.'

He hugged Meg then went back to his letter.

'What about you James, are you happy?'

'How could I not be Meg; I am going to be a father. I wish I could see the looks on my parents faces when they read my next letter informing them they are going to be grandparents.'

'I expect they will be delighted.'

'Yes, maybe they will be, it will be interesting to read their reply won't it?'

Meg could feel there was something wrapped up in the blanket. She carefully unfolded it to reveal several beautifully wrapped packages with hand written name cards.

'Bradley, James, here's a parcel for each of you, and it looks like several for me. Aren't I the spoilt one? I wonder what's in this one?'

She opened the large envelope to reveal several newspapers.

'Jolly good show,' said James, 'I haven't read a good English newspaper since we left home,' and he promptly settled down to read one while Bradley picked up another.

Meg unwrapped the rest of her parcels to reveal Lavender soap and a handkerchief embroidered with lavender flowers from her sisters. A delightful painting from one brother, and a small notebook from the other. The last package was well wrapped and revealed a cream, bone handled, hair brush wrapped in a hand knitted woollen hat and a matching pair of gloves. Meg felt humbled by the thoughtful gifts. She hadn't been expecting anything more than perhaps a card full of Christmas wishes. This was a wonderful surprise. She looked up to see what Bradley and James had in their parcels. They both got hand knitted woollen socks, a handkerchief each with their initials embroidered on them and a tortoise-shell comb.

The three of them sat in silence for a while reading the papers and exchanging letters before sitting back to discuss the contents.

132

The Hopkins family arrived the following week carrying sacks and boxes of food stuffs, enough to feed a small army. Stephen was with them, he had nowhere else to go having arrived in New Zealand on his own and never married.

Tents were set up out back for the children, Stephen would share the room out the back with Bradley, Gladys and Henry would sleep in Meg and James' bed, Meg and James chose to sleep under the stars on makeshift straw mattresses. Everyone was excited to hear Meg's news and talked about the impending arrival over tea and cake. Gladys and Henry brought left over cold meats and fare from their Christmas feasts and fresh fruits from the orchard. Meg's garden produced enough potatoes and fresh beans for them all. She proudly took Gladys over to her garden to show them how it was progressing, the two girls tagging along behind.

'Meg this looks wonderful,' remarked Gladys, 'you obviously have green fingers.'

'How did you get green fingers Meg,' asked Clementine glancing at Meg's hands.

The women both laughed. 'It's just an expression Clemie. When someone is good at gardening you say they have green fingers. My word look at those herb plants, they are flourishing here aren't they. Come on girls you can pick the beans while Meg and I pull some carrots. I noticed you have already done the pumpkin.'

'Yes, I got James to chop it up for me. He has suddenly become over protective lately.'

'Of course he has, you are carrying his child. He might become a bit smothering but be indulgent Meg, it will pass soon enough, just enjoy the attention while it lasts. Come on girls, we haven't got all day.'

The women prepared the vegetables and hung the pot over the fire to heat while the men set up an improvised outdoor table and seating. Gladys brought out her long white linen table cloth, silver cutlery and glassware.

'Good heavens Gladys, you didn't have to cart those beautiful things all the way here.'

'It was no bother Meg, don't fuss yourself. It is our pleasure, truly.'

133

The weather was perfect and the atmosphere most convivial. The festivities lasted well into the night. As the men sat around the fire in the late evening smoking and drinking, Gladys took Meg aside and talked to her about the impending arrival of her baby.

'Do you know much about the birthing process Meg?'

'No not really,' Meg confessed. 'Mama did pop a small Doctor's booklet into my trunk before I left but to be honest, I found it more alarming than informative.'

'Might I suggest you come and stay with us a month or two before your due date. That way we can keep an eye on you and be on hand when the time comes. I have a neighbour friend not too far away we can call on if need be. I have helped deliver my share of babies and had my three of course so I am sure between us we will do just fine,' Gladys patted Megs hand comfortingly.

James agreed with the plan when it was presented to him. He hadn't given the matter much thought until then and realized that it would be foolish for Meg to have her first baby so far from medical assistance. He knew he would not be of much help to her, he had never had anything to do with children let alone babies and childbirth.

The storm of 1867

Happy New Year my lovely mother to be,' James kissed Meg soundly on the lips and drew her into to a warm embrace as they stood outside looking at the stars.

'And a Happy New Year to you Daddy to be,' giggled Meg. 'This time next year we will be three instead of just us two. Our baby will be about seven months old by then I should think.

'When we go to the lamb sales in Christchurch Meg, we will go to the Doctor and make sure everything is alright with you and the baby. Then I think you should stay with the Hopkins's until the baby comes.'

'I feel fine James, but yes I agree. I must see a Doctor and it would be comforting to be with Gladys when the time comes. I have every confidence in her, I know she will take good care of me.'

James kissed his wife on the top of her head.

'Right then, let's take a walk with the dogs shall we. You need to exercise, Gladys tells me,' he smiled down at Meg. 'Come on Buster, Sally,' he called to the dogs. 'You can come and get some exercise too.'

The dogs didn't need any encouragement. Being heading dogs they were always full of energy and ready for action.

After the busy Spring muster followed by the weaning, shearing and haymaking it was nice to take some time out before the lambs were drafted for market.

'I'm not sure I want to take any lambs to market this year Meg. I have earned enough from my surveying work to keep up with the lease payments this year. I have talked to Henry and he agrees, we could draft out the bigger, fatter lambs and I could take them down to Arrowsmith and see how they fare.'

Meg nodded in agreement.

'Yes, that area that Howard and I fired last year looks as though it has got some good grass growing on it now. It should keep them going for a while.'

It's a pity it's on the opposite side of the river though, it won't always be accessible when the river is running high.'

'We will just have to keep our fingers crossed and hope for the best then,' said Meg, in her usual philosophical way.

'Ever the optimist, aren't you Meggie,' James laughed.

It was another very good lambing season giving James around 1500 lambs to choose from to stock the Arrowsmith run. He planned to run a few of the older ewes with them as well.

'Not much good sending a bunch of youngsters off with no leadership and supervision,' he laughed.

'Yes, I can just imagine the mischief they would all get up to,' laughed Meg.

James wouldn't let Meg go with him to take the flock down to Arrowsmith.

'You need to stay here and rest up Meg.'

She reluctantly agreed. At six months she was starting to feel the weight of the baby, especially when she tried to mount her horse.

When they left for Flaxbush three weeks later Meg refused to ride on the dray.

'Meg, I really think you should. You might want to lie down in the back if you get tired.'

'James the dray is not overly comfortable, I would feel much better riding Jasper.'

James was annoyed, but he indulged Meg hoping that perhaps they could take a wagon from Flaxbush in to town. He would get Gladys on side and ask her to convince Meg to travel by wagon rather than on horseback. He didn't want to think about what might happen if she was to fall off her horse.

In the end Meg agreed to compromise and ride side-saddle.

James was grateful that Gladys agreed with him when it came time for them all to leave for Christchurch, following along behind the lambs that Stephen and Henry were taking to market.

'We will take it slowly and follow the lambs this year Meg. There is no hurry and we do want to get you there and back in one piece. We will leave in plenty of time to make the sales, we don't want the lambs to lose any condition.'

The weather was kind to them, and they enjoyed sitting around the camp fire on the three nights and four days it took them to get there. Howard came with them. He was heading off to further his studies in farm management. Henry was proud of his first born. He did not have much of an education himself, but Howard was proving to be a keen scholar with a quick mind. Meg would miss him, but she knew they wouldn't need any help this year; James made it clear he would be staying home and helping to raise his family.

'No more surveying for me Meg,' he had said.

The sales weren't as good as the previous year but enough to make Henry a tidy profit. Meg visited the doctor for a check-up and was given the all clear. The doctor did have one concern however and because of this he called Gladys Hopkins into his office. She had been sitting in the waiting room.

'I know this is not ethical, to speak of another patient, Mrs Hopkins but I need to know that I can count on you should Mrs Morley run into any difficulties. I understand you have made arrangements for her to stay with you when her time comes and that there is a midwife nearby.'

'Yes, we decided it would be best that she stay with us from now on rather than run the risk of being trapped by the rivers.'

'Good, good,' muttered the doctor as he wrote up his notes. 'Now I don't want to alarm you, but I am concerned that Mrs Morley's pelvic muscles may have become very tight from a lifetime of horse riding. I have seen this before with women who have ridden astride horses for several years. I would much rather have them riding side saddle if I had my way,' he looked up and caught Gladys's amused grin. 'I know, I am often accused of being an old-fashioned fool,' he laughed with her. 'I would like you to send for the midwife as soon as she starts going into labour. If there appears to be any serious concerns please send someone for me immediately, I would rather you called me, and everything be alright, than leave the poor girl in labour for days on end.'

Gladys was concerned but nodded her understanding.

'Yes, yes of course Doctor. I will keep a close eye on her. I have only ever helped to deliver two babies in recent years, I hope I can help bring this one into the world safely too.'

'I have every faith in you and your midwife neighbour Mrs Hopkins. I was there for the safe delivery of your own children; you have a level head and a strong disposition. I know I can count on you.'

'What did the Doctor say Gladys? Is everything alright?' Meg's eyes showed her concern as Gladys came out of the Doctor's office.

'Yes, everything is fine Meg, he just wanted to make sure I remembered how to deliver a baby,' she laughed putting Meg's mind at ease. 'Now come on let us go and have a nice cup of tea and a cream bun in that wee tea shop you like so much.'

Meg and Gladys clucked and oohed and aahed over the baby clothes they had purchased, buying way more than they knew she would need.

'I have plenty of hand me downs Meg, some of them have barely been used, the little blighters grow out of them so quickly. And, I didn't want to tell you yet, but I have been knitting up a storm and so have some of our friends and neighbours. There will be more than enough items of clothing for your wee babe, believe me.'

Meg's eyes welled up with tears.

'Really? They have all been knitting for my baby?'

'Yes Meg, and there are muslin wraps and nappies and all sorts of other things besides.'

'Gladys, thank you. This is so special, thank you. I don't know what else to say.'

'You don't have to say anything my dear. The knitters amongst us love to knit for a new born. We don't get many opportunities so we make the most of it when we can. Some of them are spinners and the garments they knit for their families are beautiful. I will show you when we get home.'

Meg settled in to Howard's old room at Flaxbush while James went on to Stony Downs to keep an eye on the farm. A rider would be sent to fetch him as her time drew closer. It was normally a two to three-day ride but if the rivers were low enough and he rode through the night, he could get to Flaxbush a lot quicker if he needed to.

It was eight weeks later when Meg felt a twinge in her lower back.

'Oh,' she gasped. She was sitting in the sun in the front room stitching a smock for the baby.

'Are you alright Meg?'

'Yes, I think so, just a twinge. I haven't been feeling so good these past couple of days.'

Gladys nodded. 'That's a sure sign that something is happening. Perhaps we should get Stephen or Marshall to go and fetch James.'

Marshall opted to go, enjoying the importance of the mission. Within hours Meg started to feel tightening pains in her lower stomach.

'I think it might be contractions Gladys,' she said. 'They tighten up and then ease off. They are quite painful.'

'Yes, my dear girl, it certainly sounds like contractions to me. We'd best get you into bed and get ourselves organized. I suspect this baby is about to make an entrance.'

Henry took the children to a neighbour's place and came back with the neighbour's wife and Mrs Stanton, the midwife. By the time they arrived Meg was well in to her labour, the contractions were coming every five minutes.

Day grew into night and then into the dawn of a new day with still no sign of the baby's head crowning. Gladys was becoming more and more concerned with each passing hour. The midwife took Gladys aside and spoke quietly to her.

'What do you make of it Georgette, what do you think the problem is?' asked Gladys

Mrs Stanton's eyes welled up with tears, she was relieved that she could talk to someone about her concerns, they were weighing heavily on her now.

'I can't hear the baby's heartbeat Gladys; we need to get that baby out and we need to do it now.'

'Right then, tell me what to do,' Gladys rolled up her sleeves ready for action.

Mrs Stanton was very commanding and had everyone jumping to her demands. Gladys gasped when she saw the midwife take an ugly metal contraption from her bag.

'These are forceps Gladys, obviously you have been lucky enough not to have had use of them before but believe me they have their uses.'

By the time the baby was delivered Marshall was back with James.

He stormed into the bedroom and stopped in his tracks.

'What is happening, why is there so much blood? Meg?'

He rushed over and knelt beside his wife's bed, reaching out and stroking her head.

'She is exhausted Mr Morley, the birth has been a difficult one, she needs rest now.'

'What about the baby?' he glanced anxiously around the room. Mrs Stanton beckoned him aside.

'I'm sorry Mr Morley but your son didn't survive the birth. We did everything we could.'

'A son?' cried James. 'We had a son, and he's dead? But how? Why? Everything was going so well.'

Gladys took James out to the kitchen.

'Listen James,' she said gently, 'sometimes these things happen and there's nothing we can do about it. I am deeply sorry for your loss, I truly am.'

'But what happened?'

'Meg is a very strong young woman. The Doctor was concerned that she had been riding horses most of her life and that her leg and pelvic muscles were very strong. As he feared, they just didn't give way enough for the baby to push through and by the time we were able to get him out it was too late.'

'You mean it was Meg's fault? Meg killed our baby because she rode horses?'

'No James, Meg did not kill the baby. For heaven's sake man get a grip on yourself. Next time things will be different.'

140

'Next time! Next time!' screamed James. 'There won't be a next time I can assure you.' He stormed out the door slamming it behind him. Henry went after him.

'Now calm down James, I know you are distraught but blaming Meg isn't going to do either of you any good. That poor lass needs you now more than ever. She has put up a valiant fight for days. She is exhausted and the loss of the baby is going to hit her pretty hard too.'

'If she hadn't been so bloody selfish and pig headed my son would be alive now. Instead, because of her my son is dead. I shall never forgive her for this. How can I. She murdered my son! You have no idea how much I longed to have a son to take over the farm. A son I could teach to...' he broke down and sobbed. All the pent-up frustrations and jealousy over watching Meg become a better farmer than he would ever be, came pouring out in a bitter tirade.

'James, there will be other sons. Just because this one didn't make it doesn't mean there won't be other children. You just have to be patient man.'

James wasn't listening; he was too wrapped up in his own pain.

'James, come inside and sit with Meg, she needs you now son,' continued Henry.

He took James arm, but James yanked it away.

'Leave me alone,' he spat. 'There will be no more children. How could I trust that woman to bring them into the world safely? She has ruined her body. She can't deliver a baby, so I won't put her through the trouble of trying again.'

The bitterness oozed out of James as he spat his words out.

'James,' Henry was grappling for words, 'James, lots of women carry babies to term and then lose them for a variety of reasons. It's not as uncommon as you might think; thousands of babies die every year. As tragic as that is, unfortunately it is just the way life goes sometimes.'

James was in no mood to listen to reason. He turned and made his way to the stables where he began to saddle up his horse again.

'Where are you going James? For God's sake man come inside. You need to calm down and go and see your wife. She needs you. Don't be selfish about this James. James!'

Henry reached out to James, but he pushed him aside, threw himself up into the saddle and rode off. Stephen had been watching the

141

whole thing from the shadows of the stable. He was furious beyond measure at James' reaction.

'Cowardly bastard,' he hissed. He watched as James rode out of sight and Henry walked dejectedly back to the house head down, shoulders slumped. He wasn't looking forward to telling Gladys and Meg that James had gone back to Stony Downs. He would not tell them about the conversation he had just had with James either, he would tell them James was concerned for his stock and had ridden back to check on them and that he would be back in a week or so. God, he hoped he was right.

Meg slept for twelve hours and awoke to find Gladys sitting beside her bed with a worried expression on her face.

'Gladys, whatever's the matter, where's the baby?'

Gladys began to weep. She had been weeping off and on since she saw the beautiful baby lying dead in the midwife's arms.

'Oh my poor darling Meg, I am so sorry but the baby didn't make it. The midwife did her best, but it was too late, the poor wee mite had given up the fight.'

Meg couldn't believe what she was hearing.

'No, that can't be right. No, you are lying. Bring me my baby, please Gladys bring me my baby,' she was becoming hysterical.

'Meg you need to calm down.'

The midwife heard Meg's cries and hurried into the room.

'Meg I am truly sorry my dear but there was nothing we could do; the baby just couldn't come out on its own and we were just too late getting him out before he gave up.'

'Him?' she whispered. 'It was a boy?'

'Yes. And he was a fine looking wee fellow too. I'm sorry Meg but this is going to take some time for you to come to terms with.'

'Where's James?' she asked looking around the room. Gladys and the midwife exchanged glances.

'What? Has something happened to James as well?'

'No Meg,' Gladys said quietly, 'He had to get back to the farm. He will be back in a week or so.'

Gladys was hoping Henry was right about that, she had seen the anger and disappointment on James's face when he was talking with the midwife after the birth.

142

Meg was disappointed, she needed James now. They needed each other. She broke down and melted into a flood of tears.

Stephen was angry. He was more than that, he was furious.

'How could James just leave like that, full of anger, without seeing Meg?'

He decided that he would be there for her as much as she needed. He had a soft spot for the lovely Meg, right from the first moment he saw her. If James wasn't going to be there for her then he damn well would be.

Stephen visited Meg every day sitting beside her bed chatting away about nothing and everything, but she barely responded. It broke his heart to see her this way. The bright, beautiful Meg he had grown to love was becoming a shell of her former self. Her zest for life seemed to have gone.

The Doctor visited as soon as he was able and told Gladys that Meg was improving physically but he was worried about her mental state. I would like to see her stay here for a few more weeks Gladys. I don't want her back in those mountains on her own until I feel she is well and truly ready, especially if James hasn't come to terms with his loss. Has he returned yet?'

'No, nobody has seen him. We were going to send one of the lads off to check on him, but we felt perhaps it was best to let him grieve in his own way. He knows where we are when he needs us.'

'Perhaps, perhaps,' the doctor was concerned. 'Still there's no telling how a man will react to losing a child, much like the mother. It is such a bitter blow that some of them never recover from, and that's why I am concerned about young Meg. Keep a close eye on her Gladys, you have done a marvellous job so far but if you have any concerns about her mental well-being please keep a note of her behaviour and let me know when I come back on my rounds next month. Did she get to see and hold her baby to say goodbye? And the burial, did she take part in that? I take it the wee bairn has been buried in your family plot?'

'Yes he has Doctor. We had a lovely little ceremony. We carried Meg out to the plot on a chair but she seemed distant, detached. I'm not sure that she really even knew what was going on. We tried to show her the baby but she was having none of it so no, she never got to see him or hold him.'

'Hmmm, let's hope this doesn't cause lasting damage for the poor girl.' The Doctor patted Gladys shoulder kindly, sympathetically and left.

James didn't return the following week. Stephen offered to ride out to Stony Downs to check on him, but he wasn't sure how he would react when he saw the man. As it turned out the night before he was due to leave there was a heavy downpour and the rivers flooded. It took several days for the rivers to subside enough to cross but by then Stephen was fully involved with preparations for the Autumn muster.

The Doctor declared Meg physically fit to travel back to her home when he returned three weeks later but he was still concerned about her mental state.

'How has she been Gladys?' asked the Doctor as they sat at the kitchen table sipping tea.

'To be honest with you Doctor I'm just not sure. She is very withdrawn a lot of the time but every now and then she perks up and seems to be her old self again.'

'When does that happen?'

'What do you mean?'

'What is happening when Meg perks up, something must be getting through to her?'

'Or someone,' smiled Gladys. 'Now that you mention it, it is generally when Stephen is around. I hadn't really linked the two together before now but yes when I come to think of it, Stephen seems to be the one person she is responding to the most.'

'Marvellous, then his visits should be encouraged, provided they are not inappropriate of course.' The Doctor blushed. 'With the absence of her husband I would not encourage her to become attached to another man, if you understand what I mean.'

'Of course I do Doctor, no I just think that Stephen is a bright and engaging young man. He is very fond of Meg and he has the knack of being able to make her smile.'

'Very good then. Well, so long as there is a spark of life in her and if you think she appears to be able to take care of herself then I am happy to clear her to return home.'

When Gladys broke the news to Meg she was thrilled.

'Oh Gladys, I have so appreciated staying here with you all, but I am anxious to get back to my own home. You do understand, don't you?'

'Of course I do my dear. The only thing is Henry and I don't want you to go back on your own so once Stephen gets back from the Autumn muster we are going to get him to accompany you home and get you settled in. James is probably there waiting for you.'

'I wouldn't be too sure about that Gladys; it's been weeks now and still no sign of him. To be perfectly frank I couldn't care less if he was there or not.'

'Meghan,' gasped Gladys, 'please don't think like that. You need to give the man a chance to explain himself.'

'Very well,' said Meg, 'if he's there I will let him explain himself and then I will ...'

'You will what?'

Meg smiled and relaxed, 'I don't know Gladys, I truly don't know what to think or how I will feel when I see him. I have been so angry, and I feel so let down, all my emotions seem to be spent. I barely feel anything at all these days. I just want to gather up Jasper and my beautiful dogs and go home. Thank you so much for arranging for Stephen to take me home, he has become a good friend these past weeks. He's such a thoughtful and caring man, I just wish James was more like him.'

When Stephen returned from the muster and learned he would be accompanying Meg back to Stony Downs he was elated. He had visited her almost every day, as much as his work would allow, and had succeeded in bringing a smile to her face. Meg was pleased that Stephen would be taking her back home. She was nervous about seeing James again and was grateful that she didn't have to face him alone. How would he react? Would he even want her there anymore? What would become of her if he didn't?

Stephen walked up behind Meg and as if reading her thoughts, said, 'Don't worry Meg, I won't leave you alone with him if you have any concerns. If he decides he wants to be alone then we will ride back here together. I won't leave you unless I am completely comfortable with the way things are between you two.'

They took it slowly. It was late April and autumn was well upon them. The rivers were starting to fill up but still low enough to cross in carefully selected places. They travelled along side by side with the dogs excitedly sprinting off ahead of them and doubling back again. Meg said very little, she would stare off in to the distance with eyes full of sadness reflecting the pain in her heart. It upset Stephen to see her this way, but he felt it best to leave her to make conversation when she was ready.

When they reached the house on Stony Downs it was empty. There was no sign of James anywhere.

'I don't think he's been gone for too long Meg,' offered Stephen. 'Bessy certainly needs milking though. I will get on to that right away. The hens are roaming free out of their cages. At least we had Buster and Sally with us. I'm glad he didn't take them with him, I know how much you love those dogs. It seems it is just James and his horse that are missing.'

Meg didn't seem to react to what Stephen was saying. She got down off her horse and walked into the house. She stopped just inside the doorway and put her hand to her mouth when she saw the baby's crib all smashed up and lying in bits on the floor. By the time Stephen followed her in she had climbed on to the bed and lay down facing the wall, clutching her precious cream wool blanket around her. Stephen saw the broken cradle and quickly gathered up the pieces and put them outside. He set the fire going, noting that the ashes were stone cold so it must have been out for some time. He wondered if James had simply gone down to the Arrowsmith hut to check on the stock down there. Once the fire was going and warming the house up he went out and tended the horses. When he came back, Meg hadn't moved. He heated up some water and made Meg a cup of sweet tea with honey and some of Bessy's fresh warm milk. He was surprised Bessy's milk hadn't dried up from not being milked for who knows how long.

Meg didn't stir when Stephen offered her some tea, so he sat down on the bed beside her and pulled her up into a sitting position drawing her close to him for support. She sipped mindlessly at the tea for a while then he let her lie back down again. He wasn't sure what to do for her. She seemed to have been drifting off into a world of her own the closer she got to her home. He was angry about the broken cradle, was that what caused her to withdraw again? He wondered. Was it a mistake to bring her back here so soon? He thought being home would bring back a flood of happy memories but there sitting against the wall was a box full of baby clothes and beside it had been the shattered remnants of a cradle which James had obviously been building. Stephen gathered up the remaining wood fragments and threw them on the fire then took the baby clothes out to the shed and stowed them out of sight.

146

The rain that had been threatening all day started to fall as early evening descended upon the valley. The weather had been fine and settled for the past few days although the temperatures were cooler. Stephen kept the fire going, made up a broth which he managed to get Meg to take a few sips of and slept on a makeshift bed by the fire.

By the third day it was still raining. Stephen was beginning to wonder if James had maybe met with an accident, or if he had decided not to come back or, with all the rain, had been trapped and unable to get back up the river. He wanted to go and check the Arrowsmith Hut, but he didn't want to leave Meg. He knew if he hadn't been spoon feeding her, she wouldn't have taken any nourishment. He was becoming more and more concerned for her. She was losing weight and was in need of a good wash. In despair he crawled on to the bed one morning and took her in his arms stroking her and murmuring in her ear.

'Meggie my beautiful lady, please come back to us, we need you. Buster, Sally, Bessy, Jasper and the chooks, but most of all me. I miss you Meg, where are you?'

Then he had an idea. Pulling himself gently away he went and opened the door to call the dogs in.

'Come in and see if you can rouse your mistress,' he smiled. He had been keeping them close to the house under the verandah, he knew how much they were missing their mistress.

'Maybe you can break through her pain and misery,' he whispered to them ruffling the fur around their necks.

The dogs sensed what was going on and immediately raced over and jumped up on their mistress's bed. They leapt about excitedly, licking her face and nuzzling her. Slowly Meg started to respond. She opened her eyes to see two large black and white furry animals trying to get her attention. She put her hands up to protect her face from their wet tongues. They nudged away at her hands thinking she was playing a game with them. The more she tried to protect her face the more they persisted. Stephen didn't interfere. They were getting a reaction which was more than he had been able to do. Finally, slowly, she sat up and embraced the furry bundles. She looked up at Stephen.

'Hello,' was all she said, but that was enough for Stephen. He knew she had reached a turning point and he was happy with that.

147

Over the next few days Meg slowly returned to her old self but there was still an air of sadness about her that Stephen knew would probably never go away.

'Do you want me to go and find James?' he asked her one morning when he felt she was strong enough for him to leave her.

'James? Do you know where he is?'

'No, but I suspect he might be down at the Arrowsmith hut. Do you want me to go and bring him back? He won't know that you are here?'

'Stephen,' she said sitting down on the bed, 'before I answer that I want you to tell me everything that's happened since the night I lost the baby. It's all a bit of a haze for me. What happened to James, why did he not stay?'

Nobody had had the heart to tell Meg what James's true reaction was. Instead they fobbed her off with stories of him being distraught about the loss of the babe and having to tend stock on the farm and that he would be there when she was well enough to travel home. She had believed them then but now she had her doubts. Something just didn't add up.

Stephen drew a deep breath and sat down beside her taking one of her hands in his.

'He was angry when he learned the baby had died Meg. He just got on his horse and rode away. Henry tried to stop him, but he just wouldn't listen to reason.'

'I can understand him being upset but why was he angry. Who was he angry with?'

Stephen didn't answer.

'Stephen please, you must tell me, I need to know. So much has changed, I need to make sense of it all.'

'Very well but you're not going to like it Meg and I am sorry to be the one who has to tell you. James was angry because the Doctor said that because you had been riding horses all these years your thighs and pelvic muscles were too tight to allow the baby to come through naturally and by the time the midwife got him out with forceps the wee chap had given up.'

Meg started to cry. 'Oh, so that's what it was. I didn't really understand what happened with the delivery, nobody said anything about it, and I didn't ask,' she sobbed. 'So it was all my fault, no wonder James is angry.'

'Meg it wasn't your fault, these things happen. You have always been a strong and capable woman and because of the life you have led your body has been strong too. The Doctor said things would be easier next time and that they would keep you in hospital to make sure.'

Meg got to her feet and stood in the doorway.

'You and I both know there won't be a next time Stephen. How long has it been since he left?'

'About eight weeks I think?'

'I don't think he will be coming home any time soon. I know him well enough now to know that this is something he will never forgive me for.'

Stephen came and stood behind her and put his arms around her waist. She allowed herself to relax back into his strong vibrant body.

'I will always be here for you Meg; you can count on me.'

It was the end of May when Marshall arrived. He had been sent by the Hopkins' to find out what was happening at Stony Downs and why Stephen hadn't returned. He stayed a couple of days and did a boundary run with Stephen before heading back with the news. When Marshall reported back to Henry that James was not at Stony Downs and that Stephen had decided to stay on and help Meg with the farm, he was not overly comfortable with the idea. He had said as much to Gladys one night as they lay in bed talking.

'I don't like it Gladys, I don't like it one bit that Meg and Stephen are down there alone together, it just doesn't seem right.'

'Henry, you have to admit that Meg should not be left on her own right now, especially if James doesn't turn up before the snows come. And besides Stephen has been very good with her, he is a patient man and she seems to enjoy his company.'

'That's what I am afraid of my dear, that she enjoys his company too much. What happens when James comes back?'

'What happens if he doesn't?' replied Gladys. 'Now stop your worrying and go to sleep,' she said as she rolled over. She did not want to worry Henry further by admitting that she too was concerned at what might be brewing between Meg and Stephen. She had seen something

149

between them when he was visiting her after the death of her baby. 'It should have been James,' she had thought to herself at the time.

It was the 29th July 1867, more than twelve weeks after Meg and Stephen had arrived at Stony Downs and still no sign of James. Meg was beginning to think he may never come home. Certainly, if he didn't come back very soon, he may be unable to get back until the Spring or even Summer.

Stephen broke into her reverie.

'Do you feel up to doing a boundary run with me today Meg? It won't be long before the snow comes, and we need to make sure the stock are down in the lower pastures. I'm not sure if James has moved them down or not. I haven't wanted to leave you. There is a chance we will see James down there, are you ready for that?'

'Yes, I think the ride and the fresh air would do me good and yes I feel ready to face James if we should see him. Let's go first thing in the morning, I will get some food organized. I need to make some butter and bake some bread.'

Stephen breathed a sigh of relief, 'She's back,' he thought to himself, 'thank God she's coming back to her old self again.'

They set off the next morning taking enough provisions to get them to the Arrowsmith hut and back. They planned on checking the Stony Downs stock first before heading on down to the Arrowsmith run. The dogs seemed restless and as Meg and Stephen mounted their horses, they noticed they too were a bit skittish. Stephen looked around at the cloudy skies, a mist was forming. That wasn't a comforting sign.

As they neared the hills to check on the stock, they were surprised to see a steady stream of sheep making their way down off the hillside to the flats below. They pulled the horses up and sat and watched them for a while.

'I have never seen sheep do that without being rounded up by the dogs,' Meg commented. 'I don't see any dogs or hear any whistles or commands, do you? Maybe James is about somewhere and we can't see him?'

'No. Something is not right Meg; I can feel it in my bones.' Meg turned around to look back up the valley. 'It's getting quite misty and gloomy; perhaps we are in for a bit of a storm. The sky has that sort of blue grey tinge to it, like it does just before it snows. I feel very uneasy Stephen, is it just me or do you feel it too?'

'I have been caught out in my fair share of storms over the years I must admit, but I have never felt...... well, yes, uneasy is the best way to describe it, best we get back to the house and batten down the hatches I think.'

'Let's make sure the sheep are all down safely first. I would hate to see them caught up the hill if the snow is going to be heavy.'

Stephen watched the steady stream of sheep through his eye glass as they descended the mountain side ahead of the creeping mist. He scanned around to see if he could spot James but there was definitely no sign of a horse and rider anywhere.

'I can see the tail-enders, with any luck that is the last of them. There seems to be a pretty big mob down here on the flats. They look unsettled too. Nothing we can do for them now, better get ourselves back to the house.'

Rain started falling just before they reached the shelter of the house.

'Meg I think it's best if we let the horses roam free. They can go into the stables if they want, I will put some oats out for them. If it snows heavily, they will keep walking around in a circle to create a bit of ground space for themselves.'

'That's clever, I wonder who taught them to do that,' laughed Meg. 'I'll go shut the chickens in the hen house with plenty of food and warm straw in their beds and make sure Bessy is warm and comfortable and has plenty of food too. I might shut her in, don't want her getting caught out in the snow.'

'What are you going to do with the dogs Meg? I'll get them some bones from the futtah shall I?'

'Yes please. I want the dogs inside with us. James doesn't like it but he's not here to object is he.' Stephen caught a tinge of bitterness in her voice.

Stephen understood Meg's need to protect her dogs and the comfort they gave her; he knew how much she loved them, and he didn't feel she could cope with losing anything or anyone else right now.

They stoked up the fire as the temperature started to drop and cooked up a big pot of stew to keep themselves nourished for a few days

151

if need be. Meg went out and gathered some vegetables to add to the stew.

They stood side by side looking out the window as the rain fell. The skies darkened, there was an eerie sense of doom pervading the atmosphere.

'Fancy a game of cards?' Meg challenged Stephen.

'Have to warn ya, I'm pretty darn good,' Stephen met the challenge.

They played until well into the night stopping now and then to have a stretch and something to eat.

'Might take a look outside and see what's happening,' said Stephen. 'Can't see much out the window.' He opened the door. 'Yep looks like we are in for a bit of a dumping alright, that rain has turned to sleet, won't be long before it snows.'

Meg came to stand beside him. 'Well I hope James has done something about fixing up that Arrowsmith hut because it sure won't be the warmest place to be.'

Stephen noticed some concern in her voice. 'We don't even know if that is where he is Meg, we just have to hope that he is looking after himself. He's a grown man and he's been out in all weathers, I'm sure he will be alright. To be honest I doubt he would have spent all this time at the hut, my guess is he's gone into town for a while. Let's hope he gets himself sorted out soon eh.'

'Yes, maybe you are right,' she sighed. 'Brrrr it's cold out here let's get back in by the fire.'

The temperature continued to drop, and the dogs were happy to be sprawled out in front of the fire.

'Stephen, why don't you share the bed with me, you can't sleep down there with the dogs. There's plenty of room for the two of us.'

Stephen was a bit hesitant. He knew where it would lead to if he had half a chance. It was all he could do to keep himself from reaching out to her and holding her close whenever she was close to him. It was agony for him to keep his love for her bottled up inside. He wasn't sure if this was such a good idea.

'Oh come on Stephen, we are both adults here, look I will put a barrier up between us if that helps. Better still I could get the dogs to sleep between us. I know they wouldn't let you get near me,' she laughed.

152

Stephen blushed.

'Come on let's make a barrier down the middle. You need to get some decent sleep.'

The stillness of the night and the warmth of the fire lulled them both into a deep sleep. When they woke up in the morning there was an uneasy eeriness hanging in the air.

Meg got up wrapped a shawl around her shoulders and went over to stoke up the fire. When she looked outside she wasn't surprised to see that snow was still falling. The gloom hadn't lifted.

It snowed thick and fast all that day and continued on unabated into the night. Meg and Stephen went out to check on the animals before nightfall.

'I wonder if they would be better under the verandah?' Meg suggested.

'If the snow gets too heavy they won't have any protection from the snow falling in on them if they are under the verandah, at least in the shed they can move to the back and hopefully stay dry. We must milk Bessy though and you'd best give the chickens some more feed and collect the eggs.'

The horses had been wandering about foraging in the snow, their tracks to and from the shed had formed a pathway through the ever-deepening drifts.

The snow kept falling all through the following day.

'Meg I'm not sure how long this snow is going to keep falling like this but I think we need to try and maintain a clear pathway to the animals so we can keep an eye on them and keep them fed. And besides, it will be better than just sitting around inside all day.'

Meg agreed and so several times a day they would go out and re-clear a pathway to the sheds. The snow continued to fall steadily, the sides of the pathway becoming several feet deep. There wasn't a sound outside, no birds, no animals, no sheep bleating, just an eerie silence. The horses helped them by walking around clearing a patch of ground for themselves which was eventually surrounded by a deep wall of snow. They got Bessy out of the shed and walked her around for a while with the horses before milking her and putting her back in the shed with some hay.

'It is almost to the top of the roof Stephen,' Meg exclaimed on the fourth day. 'Surely it must stop soon. I've seen snow falling off and on

153

over several weeks but not as heavy as this and for days on end. It's quite frightening.'

'Unfortunately, it does happen from time to time in the high country, but I've never seen anything quite like this either.' Stephen was getting worried.

On the fifth day the snow stopped falling but a cold frost formed an icy cover over the snow. Meg and Stephen cleared their pathway of the overnight snow and climbed up the hill behind the house. All they could see was the basic contours of the landscape completely covered in deep white snow. There were no distinctive features to be seen.

'How deep do you think it is?' Meg asked.

'Hard to tell but the fact that it has covered the roof of the shed and is more than half way up the apex of the house roof I would say about eight to ten feet.'

'The sheep won't have survived this will they?' Meg's voice choked on the words in sudden realization.

'No, I'm afraid there will be stock losses Meg, big losses, you need to be prepared for that. It is not going to be pleasant when the snow melts.'

The next day it started to rain, heavily. It began to wash the snow away and slowly over the next couple of days the snow levels lessened as the river levels rose. The roar of the water raging down the valley was deafening after the quietude of the snow. As soon as the rain abated Meg and James saddled their horses and went in search of the sheep. The river was full of dead trapped and floating white bodies. The water had come up and washed the dead sheep off the low-lying areas beside the river where they had gone to find shelter among the rocks.

Meg put her head in her hands and wept. 'Do you think any of them might have survived?' she sobbed.

Stephen reached across and took her hand.

'I'm sorry Meg, I doubt it very much.'

The dogs suddenly started barking and digging in the snow part way up the hill beside them. Meg and Stephen both leapt off their horses and ran to help the dogs. Just below the surface were two sheep huddled up together still alive but in a pretty bad way. They dug them out and pulled them to the surface where they flopped down, too weak to stand. Meg, Stephen and the dogs carried on digging.

'If these two have survived, there might be more,' called Stephen, there may be some under the rocky overhangs up there and maybe down there along the river bank.'

They dug for several hours not wanting to give up hope of finding more sheep alive. They were wet and sore and tired, but they did indeed manage to find a few survivors. There were some lucky ones who had taken shelter at the back of rocky overhangs by the river and had somehow managed to resist being swept away in the fast-flowing waters. They dragged each animal up on to an open patch away from the river's edge. Small patches of tussock started to appear for the sheep to forage on. Meg and Stephen were very tired, but they did not give up. They found twenty more sheep that had found shelter in amongst the rocks where they found a pocket of air to keep them alive. They weren't in very good condition, but they were alive and there was a chance they might survive. They managed to get to their feet and forage after a while and those that couldn't forage for themselves, Meg grabbed handfuls of tussock and grasses to take to them.

'How many do you think we've got?' Meg asked

'I've counted thirty-five.'

'Do you think they will lose their lambs?'

'Not sure, I guess we will just have to wait and see.'

'James will be devastated. I don't know if we have enough money to buy more sheep.'

'Speaking of James, do you want me to ride down to the Arrowsmith hut to see if he's there?' asked Stephen.

'Would you? Oh yes please that would be great. At least it would put my mind at ease, and I will know for certain if he is there. At the moment I don't know whether he is alive or dead or if he is ever coming back.'

Tears welled up in Meg's eyes.

'Don't worry Meg, he'll come back. He would be a fool not to.'

He took her hand and held it to his lips staring longingly into her moist blue eyes.

Meg allowed him to hold her hand for a moment then pulled away, embarrassed by the emotions that were welling up inside her. Living in such close quarters for all these weeks had brought them closer together and a strong bond was forming though neither of them had made any move to cross the boundaries of propriety, yet.

155

'I'll head off first thing tomorrow,' Stephen choked over the lump in his throat. He'd fallen in love with Meg the day she got up on Marshall's horse and whistled to the dogs when they drove the first flock of sheep on to Stony Downs. He never admitted it to himself but over the past several weeks it was getting harder and harder for him not to make love to her. She was a married woman and she still had a husband, somewhere, and this wasn't the time.

Stephen rode back into the yard four days later, alone.

'Was he not there?' Meg asked.

'No, I couldn't tell if he had been there or not, the hut has caved in with the weight of the snow. I dug around in the debris, but I didn't find anything that would indicate someone had been living there. I'm afraid there didn't appear to be any surviving sheep down there either. I poked around with a stick for a whole day with no luck.'

The snow lay thick on the surrounding mountains and would stay that way for the rest of the winter. Meg and Stephen set about repairing the damage caused by the snow. All the chickens survived except one so that one became dinner and then soup for a few days. Stephen slaughtered a sheep, one of the weaker survivors, that would keep them and the dogs in meat for a few weeks.

'How long before you think we will be able to ride out of here; it's been fine for a whole week now?' Meg posed the question to Stephen. It was late September.

'River's still running pretty high, but I know of a place we might be able to get the horses across if you wanted to get out.'

'I'm just not sure what to do next Stephen. I need to know if James is still alive and whether he wants to re-stock the farm or whether he is happy to walk away.'

'What do you want to do Meg?'

'It would break my heart to leave here, I love this place but there's no use staying on if we can't make a go of it. And I certainly couldn't do everything on my own, I would need some help.'

'If James doesn't come back, I will stay on here with you Meg. That's if you want me to of course.'

Meg reached up and put her hand on the side of Stephen's face. 'I would like that very much.'

Stephen impulsively leant down and kissed her on the lips, overcome by his emotions. Meg kissed him right back for a moment before pulling away.

'I'm sorry Meg I shouldn't have done that.' Stephen turned to walk away.

Meg reached out and put a hand on his arm to stop him. 'Stephen, please don't apologise, I feel it too you know.'

They spent a restless night side by side with the dogs sleeping between them. They agreed this would be the best way of stopping their emotions getting the better of them. It worked.

Next morning as Meg and Stephen were sitting having breakfast at the table they heard someone ride up. They leapt to their feet and ran outside and there dismounting his horse was James. Meg gave a cry of surprise and hesitantly ventured out to greet him. She wasn't sure how he would react, whether he was still angry with her or not. She was therefore pleasantly surprised when he leapt off his horse and pulled her into his arms kissing her soundly on the lips. Stephen stood to one side watching, his heart breaking.

'Where on earth have you been. Are you alright?'

'I'm sorry to have gone off and left you like that Meg. I behaved like an absolute bastard and I am truly very sorry. I was just so shocked to hear that we had lost our baby and I wanted to blame someone, so I blamed you.'

'So where have you been? Where did you go?'

'Can I get a cup of tea, I'm rather parched. Hello Stephen, how long have you been here?'

'I brought Meg back a couple of weeks after the baby...' he looked down and shuffled his feet, not sure what to say. 'When the Doctor cleared her fit enough to travel, and then we got snowed in.'

James did not seem pleased, but Meg distracted him by asking more questions.

'Sit down James, please. I want to know where you have been. We have lost most of our stock you know.'

James hung his head. 'Yes. I gathered as much. These ones out in the front paddock, that's all there is now?'

157

'Afraid so,' Stephen chipped in. 'No survivors down at Arrowsmith either.'

'You've been down there then?' James asked.

'Yes, I went down there looking for you James. The hut has been brought down with the weight of the snow.'

James sat with his elbows resting on the table, his head down.

'Damnation,' he swore.

After a few moments of silence he lifted his head.

'Do you want to start again Meg? Do we re-stock and carry on?'

'Well that's up to you James, do we have the money to re-stock?'

'As a matter of fact, we do,' his demeanour brightened. 'I've been doing some surveying work.'

'What?' Meg was horrified. 'All this time we have been worried sick about you and you were off gallivanting around the countryside?'

Meg burst into tears and started hitting James.

Stephen decided at that point that it was time he left. He quietly packed up his things, got on his horse and rode off back to Flaxbush.

By nightfall Meg and James were still sitting at the kitchen table. The fire was going out and they hadn't eaten all day. They sat and talked and cried between long silences. They talked about their lost child, the loss of the stock and the toll the past months had taken on everyone. Finally, James stood up, pulled Meg to her feet and they hugged each other for several minutes.

'Come on,' he said huskily, better get that fire stoked up,' 'I'm starving.'

Over the next few weeks Meg and James slowly mended the rift between them and got themselves back on an even keel, but Meg knew things would never be the same. As soon as the river was passable they rode out to Flaxbush to check on how everyone else got on in the storm. They were welcomed with open arms by the Hopkins family, even Marshall was overcome to see them. Stephen was nowhere to be seen. When Meg enquired after him when she and Gladys were alone, she was told he had gone to Christchurch for a while. Meg was disappointed. Gladys looked questioningly at her, but Meg avoided her gaze and the matter was dropped.

It had been the worst snow storm in recorded history and there had been massive stock losses right throughout the region. Henry's brother told them all this when he had ridden in from Christchurch to check on them. He brought newspapers filled with heartache and despair about the damage that had been caused. There was also tragic loss of human life as well as stock losses.

'This storm will go down in history, you mark my words,' said Henry.

Meg and James stayed on for a couple of days, restocked on whatever supplies they could carry with them on horseback and headed back home. James said he would be back to help with the muster and the shearing. There was very little for him to do on his own run until the sheep sales in March when he could restock again.

The Recovery 1867

James had earned enough money surveying to buy more lambs to restock the run-holding, but the numbers were well down on where he hoped to be by now. As they rode around the small flock one morning James pulled up and sat looking out over the mountains.

'Meg, I've been thinking. I need to go and earn some more money otherwise we are not going to be able to stay here. When the summer comes, I want to go back surveying. Would you be comfortable with that? I don't know how long I will be gone but I wondered if Howard would be able to come and stay while I am away.'

'I understand that we need the money James and yes I am sure I will be fine while you are away. And there's no need for me to have a baby-sitter, I am a big girl now and I can look after myself you know,' she laughed.

James smiled back at her, 'Yes I know you are more than capable of fending for yourself my love, but I just don't want you out here on your own. And I don't want Stephen here with you either. I've seen the way he looks at you. He's got a soft spot for you Meg and I don't like it.'

Meg blushed and turned away.

'James if we can be holed up together in a snow bound hut for several weeks without any improprieties then I don't think you have anything to worry about.' She gave him what she hoped was a confident and guilt free smile. 'Come on let's head back home, I'm famished.'

Meg and James spent the Christmas of 1867 with the Hopkins family. It was a quiet affair this year but no less a pleasant one.

On Christmas morning the children woke up at dawn and eventually the adults gave up trying to keep them quiet and got out of bed. They were sitting around the lounge in their dressing gowns clutching cups of tea chatting when Howard exclaimed, 'Oh look, there's a large parcel here. It's addressed to Mrs Meghan Morley.' He looked up at Meg. 'Did you know it was here?'

'No,' she said, her eyes bright with tears. She looked across at James. 'Did you know about this James?'

'I did,' me smiled smugly, 'Henry picked it up for us when he was last in Christchurch.'

Meg asked the children if they would like to help her open it. They didn't hesitate. Soon there was wrapping paper and string in all directions. Finally, the contents were revealed. A large grey bundle lay before them. Meg carefully rolled the grey fabric out knowing that there would be smaller gifts inside. She had written home about the Hopkins children on a number of occasions and was delighted to discover a beautifully wrapped parcel for each of them inside.

'Presents all the way from England,' exclaimed Jenny delightedly. 'It looks so pretty I don't want to unwrap mine.'

'I don't mind,' said Howard, 'I want to see what's inside mine.'

He ripped open the parcel to find a small leather pouch containing a folding knife which locked down inside a handle and when opened revealed some tools which would be useful for cutting, scraping and putting holes in hides. He was thrilled with it.

'I told them about your ability to tan hides, Howard, and it appears my lovely, thoughtful parents have found something which will help with that.'

She couldn't stop the tears that sprang up in her eyes. She missed her family so much at times like this.

Clementine and Jenny were equally thrilled with their trinket boxes which, when opened, played a wee tune. They happily went off to their room to find a special place for them and to play the tunes over and over again.

James was pleased to receive a new pipe and some tobacco which was not easily procured in New Zealand. Meg gently picked up the grey garment and smiled broadly when she stood and held it out at arm's length.

'Lawdy me, this is so beautiful but where on earth am I going to wear such a thing?'

It was a long grey coat with three large round black buttons to the waist. Once on, the coat would splay open from the waist and sit nicely over a skirt and hooped petticoats.

'We will just have to find suitable occasions for you to attend so that you can wear it,' smiled James. 'Try it on and let us have a look then.'

Meg and Gladys went off to the bedroom and came back some time later with Meg fully dressed and wearing one of Gladys's fine gowns complete with hooped petticoat and the new grey woollen coat over top. Gladys had even piled Meg's hair in a stylish array on top of her head. As they walked into the lounge there was stunned silence.

James spoke first. 'Oh Meg, that is becoming on you. I don't think I have ever seen you look more beautiful. Except on our wedding day of course,' he added quickly.

Meg's eyes shone. She had been pleased and pleasantly surprised with her reflection in the mirror too. All she had at Stony Downs was the small bone handled hand mirror her mother sent her last Christmas.

The following morning Henry, James and the children went out to raid the orchard while Meg and Gladys prepared for lunch. There was a knock at the front door.

Gladys wiped her hands on her apron and looked out the window. 'I didn't hear anyone ride up; I wonder who it is.'

She looked out through the mesh screen door and had to stifle a gasp.

'Meg my dear, there's someone here to see you.'

'Me? Oh, who, Bradley? Oh, my goodness, I wasn't expecting you. This is a wonderful surprise. How are you? Here let me look at you. Oh, you do look well.'

163

Bradley picked his sister up until her feet no longer touched the floor and swung her around in a bear hug. She squealed with delight.

'You are looking bonny Meg, how are things with you? I got your letters.' He hung his head. 'I'm so sorry to hear about the baby. Are you alright now?'

'Yes, I'm fine, as you can see my lovely brother, don't you worry. Come sit down and tell me all your news because goodness knows I haven't had many letters from you,' she scolded him with a smile.

Bradley's visit was like a breath of fresh air to Meg. She did not tell Bradley about James disappearing after she lost the baby, she didn't want there to be any animosity between him and James. She knew Bradley only tolerated James because he was married to her and that it wouldn't take too much for him to turn against James.

Bradley was only able to stay a couple of days before he had to get back to his West Coast merchant store. He left the store in the hands of a man he befriended a year before and who had worked with him in the store during the busy times. But the man liked his liquor and had a penchant for the opium which didn't instil too much confidence in Bradley.

'Have you tried opium Bradley?' asked James. 'I hear it is quite prolific especially among the gold miners and the Chinese folk.'

'Yes, it is if you know where to look. Some of the women in the whorehouses indulge quite heavily. I guess it is a way of making their lifestyle more palatable.'

'So, do you indulge in either pleasure Bradley?' asked James again, noting that Bradley had evaded answering the first part of his question.

'Yes James, I do as a matter of fact. I make no excuses for my behaviour. I am a hardworking man, I have no wife, I do not drink heavily but I do like the occasional opium pipe.'

'Oh Bradley, what would mother and father say if they could hear you now.' Meg was shocked. This was her little brother, going to brothels and smoking opium.

'Well Sis, I guess they would be as shocked as you are, but you need to understand the type of life we live over there.'

'He's right Meg,' said James coming to Bradley's defence. 'It is a hard and rugged life with few pleasures. I can understand Bradley's stance on the matter.'

Bradley was pleasantly surprised at James's support, but he also wondered if James himself had imbibed in either pleasures during his long sojourns away from Meg and Stony Downs.

Meg was heartbroken to see Bradley ride away two days later, but she was thrilled at having seen him at all.

'Please come back again soon Bradley, I miss you so much.'

'I will Meg, I promise,' he called back as he rode through the gate and out onto the rolling pastures heading back towards Christchurch.

'One day there will be a track through the mountains across to the West Coast Meg and it will be a lot easier for us all to travel back and forth,' commented James.

James agreed to stay on to see in the New Year with Meg before he left to go back surveying. Meg stayed on with the Hopkins for a few more days after James left. She loved spending time with Gladys. She had become like a mother figure and Meg was learning so much from her. Early on a warm sunny clear blue-sky day Meg packed her saddle bags with as much as she could carry. She would need all these supplies and more to do the things she had in mind. Someone would bring more supplies when they came to check on her in a couple of weeks.

'You are going to be a busy lady,' smiled Gladys as she managed to pop a few more items into the tops of the over-laden bags. 'You take care you don't hurt yourself or wear yourself out. Be sure to eat plenty of nourishing food and keep yourself well. If you get sick there is no-one around to help so you must take care of yourself, you hear?'

'Yes mother, I hear you,' laughed Meg as she pulled herself up into her saddle. She leaned down and stroked her friends face. 'Thank you,' she whispered with a tear in her eye, 'I honestly don't know what I would do without you.'

She turned her horse and rode off as tears started down her cheeks. She turned back and waved to the beautiful smiling faces that were seeing her off. She allowed the tears to flow for a while. It was a good release of a myriad of emotions that had been bottled up inside her for some time. She was going to miss James and the Hopkins and although she was ashamed to admit it to herself, she would miss seeing Stephen. She had watched out for him from time to time, but he hadn't returned to the farm before she left.

After an hour of wallowing she sat up in her saddle, wiped away the tears, took a deep breath of fresh mountain air, looked up at the beautiful blue sky and gazed around at the majestic mountain scenery surrounding her.

'What have we got to be sad about eh my lovelies? Life doesn't get much better than this now does it. Come on, let's go home,' she said to Buster and Sally who were happily trotting along beside her and Jasper.

Meg spent the first week airing out the linen, spring cleaning and resurrecting the gardens that had been hit hard by the winter snows. The roses had enjoyed the cold and were now a blaze of unruly colour climbing all over the walls of the house and along the vegetable garden fence. She would need to trim them right back after the flower heads died off. She preserved vegetables as Gladys had shown her and when the fruit was ripe on the trees, she would preserve them as well. Her next task would be to try her hand at drying meat and then she planned on tanning some rabbit hides. She loved rabbit fur and imagined the luxury of a blanket or a coat made of their pelts.

Meg settled down well into her new solitary life. She loved the freedom of being able to be herself and do whatever she wanted, whenever she wanted. During the hot summer days she began to wear less and less clothing, initially removing her clinging petticoats followed by her bodice top. She was small breasted and decided there was no point in wearing a support bodice where it wasn't needed and there was no-one around to see her anyway. She loved the freedom of just wearing a blouse with the sleeves rolled up. She also experimented with an old skirt that had seen better days and by unpicking the side seams and removing a large portion of material made the skirt lighter and straighter and much cooler to wear.

While she was doing the spring-cleaning Meg took everything out of the trunk under the bed to air it out. She discovered some of James old clothes and hung them out along the verandah rails to air. When she went to get them in at the end of the day, she held up a pair of trousers

166

against her body and decided that they might fit her. She giggled at the thought of wearing men's trousers but how much more suitable they would be for horse riding? She tried them on and with a few minor modifications she fashioned herself a pair of trousers. They felt very awkward and uncomfortable for a while but once she got used to them she found them rather liberating. She could throw her leg across the horses back with much more ease than having to work around her skirts.

Within a couple of weeks Meg had changed from her tidy appearance wearing bodice, pantaloons, petticoat, long sleeved blouse and a skirt; to a loose-fitting blouse with the sleeves rolled up and a pair of James trousers, with pantaloons underneath. She was grateful she didn't have a large mirror to scream back at her and show her how unladylike she must look. She felt free and unencumbered and that was all that mattered. Gone also was the neat little bun she always wore at the nape of her neck. Instead she untied her hair in the morning, brushed it out vigorously until it shone and let it hang loose about her shoulders. Her hair was fair with glints of gold running through it and it hung down below her shoulders. It got lighter now that it was out loose and being kissed by the bright sunlight. She had asked Gladys to cut it for her as it had been down to her waist and was too hot and heavy in summer. Gladys was reluctant when she saw how beautiful Meg's hair was, but Meg was insistent.

'It's always tied up Gladys, who will notice if it is long or short? I'm sure James won't mind, and it will be grown again by the time he comes back anyway.'

The big Flood of 1868

Meg might have settled quickly back into her life after the fun and bustle of Christmas, but her peaceful lifestyle would not last for more than a few weeks.

The days leading into February were hot and dry. Meg was sure the she had not known hotter days than these. There was an unusual sultry air hanging about the valley and on one particular evening when it was too hot to even think of sleeping, she had gone outside and sat on the wooden seat she had fashioned for herself beside the anvil and the blacksmith pit she had built. She was worried there might be a drought, the ground was parched and dry and brown. It wouldn't take much to set the countryside alight, she thought.

'What a good thing the run is not well stocked right now,' she said to the dogs as they sat panting at her feet.

They too were feeling the heat and were restless and uncomfortable. There wasn't enough water in the trickles that ran down the river for them to get any more than their feet wet. Meg only had 30 sheep left in her care now and she allowed them to roam wherever they could to get food and water. Lately they had spent more and more time down by the river where they could at least get a mouthful of water.

On the first day of February the sky darkened, and a feeling of unease came over Meg reminding her of the time the year before when she and Stephen got caught in that dreadful snow storm. She allowed her mind to drift back to the days when they were trapped in the house together. She was deep in thought and miles away when she was brought back to her senses by a cold drop of water on her nose. She wasn't sure what it was for a moment until more and more drops started falling and she realized it was raining. She leapt up from her seat and started dancing around in the ever-increasing fall of welcome water from the skies. But then, all of a sudden, the heavens opened up and the rain was coming down in sheets. She and the dogs ran for the cover of the verandah, shaking the excess water off themselves.

'Now that is heavy rain,' she said to no-one in particular. 'But very welcome rain at that.'

The air started to cool down and she decided she might now be able to get some sleep.

But sleep didn't come. The sound of the rain on the roof was deafening and sounded very different to any rainfalls she'd experienced in the past. It was heavy, extremely heavy and with the strong building winds behind it was finding its way in through holes and weaknesses in the roof. She lit one of the lanterns and was alarmed to see how much water was coming in. She quickly packed up the bedding and pushed it to one side of the bed where it was still dry and started to move things around the room out of harm's way. It rained and blew solidly all night without letting up.

As soon as it was light enough to see the next morning, she ventured outside to see how bad the flooding might be. She was not prepared for the sight before her. The river had risen alarmingly and she at once feared for her small flock. She dragged a reluctant Jasper from his stall and rode out towards the river's edge to see if she could see any of the sheep. She breathed a sigh of relief to see that they had made their way up a nearby hill and seemed to be out of reach of the river, for now. She turned back to the house and put Jasper back in his stall. The dogs had opted not to venture out on their mistress's latest foray in the rain but were eagerly awaiting her return.

'You were wise to stay here my darlings, it is dreadfully wet out there,' she giggled as she stripped off in the doorway.

169

The rain poured down in great volumes for the next five days. Meg was exhausted; she hadn't slept much at all as the storm raged unrelenting in its fury. At around midnight on the fifth night the noise suddenly stopped. Meg leapt out of her chair, the dogs sitting up wondering what was happening. They all ventured out to the verandah. Water lapped at her feet. The river had reached the house. She hoped and prayed that the rain had stopped at last and that the water would recede otherwise they might all be washed away. The flood waters did start to fall away but there were still sporadic downpours throughout the following day threatening to bring the flood levels back up again. By late afternoon the rain finally stopped and a weak pale-yellow sun was trying it's best to shine through the remaining straggling clouds.

Meg and the dogs slept well that night but were up early next morning to check on the stock. The flood water had still not receded back to the edge of the river and was flowing alarmingly high and very rapidly in places cautioning Meg not to venture too far in case they got caught up in the fast-flowing waters. She made her way as slowly and as carefully as she could until she could see the spot where she had last seen the sheep. They were still there. She breathed a sigh of relief and made her way back to the house. As the sun came out, she dragged all her wet belongings out and draped them over the verandah and fences to dry out. It had been a mighty savage storm, but she was not to know the full extent of the damage it caused until James would come home with newspaper clippings telling of the horrific loss of life and livestock across the country once again. Twelve ships were wrecked in the storm and the streets around many towns were under water.

'Another devastating storm that will go down in history,' she thought to herself.

True to his word James arrived with a new flock of sheep in late March. They were settled onto the hill pastures and once again Stony Downs was fully stocked and on target to succeed.

James stayed on the run right through until Spring but his resolve to stay put was wearing thin.

'Meg, I want to go back to my surveying again for the summer. I'm sorry but I can't seem to settle in one place anymore, I am so used to roaming the hills and....'

'Hush my love,' Meg put her hand out to stroke her husband's cheek. 'I know, I have been watching you these past few months and I can see you are restless and unhappy again. I knew this day would come.'

'You know me so well don't you. But I just can't leave you here on your own when there is stock to take care of.'

'Then we will just have to take on another cadet, won't we. It's a pity young Howard is away doing his studies; he was a lovely lad to have around and work with.'

James was thoughtful for a moment. 'Why don't you come with me.'

'What?'

'I still haven't fulfilled my promise to Henry to survey Flaxbush Station so we could start there then we could both survey Stony Downs and the Arrowsmith properties after that. We could get Marshall to run the farm again and you can come with me, even if it's just until Christmas. I would love to share my work with you Meg, you could be my right-hand man, so to speak.'

Meg sat quietly for a while, twiddling her fingers in her lap.

'I have sometimes thought about going surveying with you. You know, it might be fun, yes, maybe we could try it. I have been longing to ride up into these glorious mountains that surround us. Yes, maybe this would be good for both of us. When do we leave?'

'Let's ride over to visit Henry and Gladys day after tomorrow when I will have finished up all the things I need to do around here, and we can discuss the idea with them. I think we should go sooner rather than later and be back before Autumn sets in. The weather in these mountains can be so darned unpredictable at that time of the year.'

'Oh yes haven't we already learnt that lesson,' Meg sighed.

Marshall was only too happy to move into the house and run the farm for the Morley's while they were away. He would be his own boss again at last. So it was that in February 1869 James and Meg Morley began their new adventure together as surveyors.

Surveyors at large – January 1869

We will only go out for a week or so at a time on our first trips Meg. You may not like it,' James had warned when they were packing to go.'

'I'm sure I will like it James, you know how much I love being out and about in the great outdoors.'

He nodded, 'We'll see.'

Henry was delighted to hear that Meg would be accompanying James on the survey and had suggested to James that perhaps they start with the Stony Downs property first.

'It would be wonderful for Meg to see your property from the hilltops James, and if she doesn't want to continue on to do the Flaxbush Survey she has at least seen Stony Downs and perhaps the Arrowsmith property as well.'

'Thank you, Henry, that's not a bad idea. I've been a fair way up both sides of the ranges and I have spotted some markers already placed by a boundary surveyor some time ago so it should only take me a week or two to cover Stony Downs, three if we include Arrowsmith.'

Meg and James packed their saddle bags with a good supply of provisions. James's surveying implements took up a fair amount of space in a canvas bag which had seen better days. When it was full of equipment it was rather heavy, so it was tied to the lightest saddlebag in order  to balance the weight on the horses back. The metal linked chain used for measuring was the heaviest of all the items. Meg had done her best to darn the small holes which had begun to appear in the bag as a result of some of the sharper pieces piercing through, but it would need to be replaced soon. She made a mental note to look for one next time she was in Christchurch. She wanted to give it to James for his birthday in September.

Along with the chain measuring rods was a dozen or so marker pegs that James called 'dumpys' and a sturdy compass which looked like a fob watch. This had been a farewell gift for James from his parents when he left England and he was never without it. His theodolite measuring instrument was his pride and joy. Not all the surveyors had them, but he was lucky enough to have acquired one when he was working out of the Christchurch office.

As she watched James tying the theodolite box on to one of the saddle bags Meg remembered the day James had brought the sturdy wooden box home, his face beaming with pride. The most awkward piece of equipment was the wooden tri-pod which James used to fasten his theodolite to when finding his landmarks. It had pointed ends so it could be pushed into the ground for stability and a round metal plate at the top to attach to the base of the theodolite. Metal hinges just below the plate allowed for the tri-pod legs to be pushed apart and set to the desired height. The theodolite had confused Meg. James had tried to explain the intricacies of the mechanism to her, but she had shaken her head and said the compass she could understand but the theodolite was a bit beyond her. James was hoping he might get Meg to have another go at understanding the instrument on this trip.

Their bed rolls were strapped behind their saddles along with a couple of squares of canvas which would serve as both shelter and ground cover.

James pulled out a well-worn map and spread it out on the table.

'We'll cross the river here and go on up to the top of Mount McRae and start there. I saw a boundary marker up there near the bend in the river when I was mustering last year. It would be a good starting point.'

Carefully refolding the map, he turned to his wife, 'Are you ready to go Mrs Morley?'

'Ready to go Mr Morley,' Meg replied, saluting her husband in mock subservience.

They said farewell to Marshall and the dogs and headed off. Meg hated leaving the dogs behind, but they would have to carry so much more food for themselves and this just wasn't the right kind of trip to take working dogs. They barked and howled as she left but she kept looking stoically forward ignoring the tears running down her cheeks. James reached over and took her hand.

'Marshall loves the dogs Meg he will look after them well.'

'Oh yes I know that James, it's just that I will miss them so. I will be fine as soon as we are out of earshot.'

By mid-morning they had crossed the river and were beginning their ascent of the Cloudy Peak Range. James located the boundary marker he told Henry about and took longitude and latitude readings so he could use it for his next measurement from further up the hill.

'Let's stop and have a rest here for a while Meg, we are making good time and there's certainly no rush. One thing I love about this work is that there is no need to hurry so long as you get the job done within the expected time frame.'

As they sat on a grassy knoll and sipped on the warm tea that Meg had made and put in a bottle earlier that morning, she looked around her at the scenery.

'You know I have ridden a fair distance up the ranges on our property and it never ceases to amaze me that no two vantage points offer the same view. There is always a different view of the river or there is another mountain range which can be seen from a different angle. As the sun travels across the sky the colours of the mountain ranges change from deep blue in the mornings to bright gold in the evenings.'

175

'Yes, I know exactly what you mean Meg, it never ceases to thrill me too. You can understand why I love to be out here so much can't you?'

'I can indeed. I love being out and about riding around our farm too. I don't think I was ever meant to be a domestic housewife,' she laughed.

'You are a wonderful home maker my love,' James winked at her. 'Now let's get going. It would be good to get higher up before it gets too hot.'

Every now and then James stopped and took readings and made notes in his grubby well-worn note book with the corners curled up from being shoved in and out of his pockets. By the time the sun began to drop behind the mountain ranges in the distance they had stopped and set up camp. James built a fire, Meg put some mutton and vegetables in a pot over the fire and they both sat back leaning on a log watching the multitude of colours dancing across the sky as the sun set. Once the sun had disappeared the temperature dropped, and they snuggled up together for warmth.

'I wonder how many people have been up here,' Meg pondered as she lay snuggled up in James' arms.

'Well I know for a fact that Edward Jollie has been hereabouts because that range over there is named after him. I met him and his partner Edward Lee while I was in Christchurch. The majority of surveyors are in their early twenties so it was good to be able to converse with these older gentlemen from time to time and exchange experiences, they must have both been close to forty I suspect.'

'I know you have talked with me about your work and some of the people you have met when you are away working James, but I'll bet there is a lot more to this life than you have told me so far'

'Well I didn't think you would find it very interesting my love and by the time I have ridden back home my thoughts are resettled back with you and the farm. You did meet one or two of my colleagues when we were in town, don't you remember?'

'Of course I do, but they were just names and faces in passing.'

'Exactly my dear, my talking of them would have meant nothing to you.'

176

'Is there any one particular place you really liked or are all the mountain ranges fairly much the same?'

'Heavens no, every mountain range and surveying job I have done has had its moments, but I think the Kyeburn trip was possibly the most surprising.'

'Surprising?' queried Meg, 'in what way surprising?'

'It was one of the first jobs I was assigned to when we arrived here. Two of us were sent across the hills to the East to a place called Danseys Pass Coach Inn. We set up camp there and used it as our base while we surveyed the surrounding mountain ranges. The surprising part was that we discovered large swathes of quartz gravel being sluiced by gold miners up there, hundreds of them, over 4000 feet up in the mountains. I had always thought gold mining was done mostly down in valleys and along river beds.'

'Were they finding much gold?'

'By all accounts, yes, it appeared to be a rather successful find although how on earth they located such a site is beyond me.'

Over the next few days Meg proved herself useful by standing beside markers and helping James to build rocky cairns which would serve as marker monuments in the future.

'Whatever markers we leave have to be clearly marked and able to withstand all weather,' James had explained to Meg. 'Rock piles, well built, should stand the test of time. The ones I have come across are sturdy and easily identified which makes the next surveyor's work that much easier. I only use these pegs if there is no other way to leave a clear marking.'

Meg was beginning to understand the surveying process now that she was actually observing it in practice. She was even beginning to understand how the theodolite worked and although she had a spy glass of her own, she marvelled at how much closer she could see the ranges through the sight glass of the theodolite.

'Meg, Meg,' James was calling out to Meg, but she was lost in her own world taking in the early afternoon vistas of her majestic surroundings.

'Meg,' he called again. She suddenly snapped out of her reverie and spun around to look at James. 'For goodness sake Meg, I have work to do, here grab the chains would you.'

Meg went straight to the canvas bag containing the metal links that James used to measure distances. She'd learned that when the chain links were pulled out to their full length, they measured one chain.

'Sorry darling,' she said apologetically, 'I was lost in thought.'

'I could see that,' he smiled. 'I know it's difficult to concentrate sometimes but I just need to get this done and then we can relax and set up camp.'

Once the mutton stew was in the pot and hanging over the fire cooking Meg settled herself between James' outstretched legs and snuggled her back into his lean, strong chest. He wrapped his arms around her and together they silently watched the colours of the sky dancing and changing hue upon the backdrop of white fluffy clouds. When the last vestiges of light disappeared and the fire was their only source of light until the moon came up, Meg leaned forward and stirred the stew before settling herself back into James arms again.

'Tell me some stories,' she said.

'What sort of stories?'

'Oh, I don't know, you must have heard stories of people and happenings on your travels didn't you?'

James was thoughtful for a moment and then, 'Well, yes, I suppose there are some things I have heard that you might find interesting. Let me see now, did I ever tell you about Cheviot Hills?'

'No, I haven't heard of Cheviot Hills. Is it a sheep station?'

'Yes, probably one of the biggest around. I remember they were discussing it in the surveyors' office when I first started there. It was quite the talking point back then. The property is 85,000 acres if I remember correctly. Here, I'll show you on the map', he said as he reached behind him into his saddle bag.

He spread the map across Megs legs and leaning over her shoulder pointed to landmarks.

'It stretches from the Hurunui River here to the Waiau River round about here and then across to Lowry Peaks.'

'Whew,' whistled Meg, 'that is a very large property indeed. Do you know who owns it?'

Yes, I understand John Caverhill sold it to a chap named William Robinson who later bought the freehold title and stocked it on a pretty big scale. It was possibly the largest transaction ever made, apparently.'

He gave a chuckle before carrying on, 'I remember they called him Ready Money Robinson because he was always paying cash for everything. I remember that bit clearly because I thought at the time how incredible it would be to carry around wads of cash to pay for all your purchases no matter how large they are.'

'Incredible for the pickpockets and thieves too I should imagine,' laughed Meg.

Meg leaned forward to stir the stew again, 'Dinner's ready.'

They ate in silence, and after a hot drink they settled down for the night.

James was wakeful for a while remembering his time as a newly appointed surveyor to the Christchurch office. 'Was it truly almost 10 years ago,' he pondered. Maybe it was because he was lying atop a very large mountain range that he began to think back about some of the surveyors he knew, and those he knew who had lost their lives on mountain surveys. It didn't take much for someone to fall prey to the elements as he well knew. The main issue was that a creek which was easy to cross one day could well become a raging torrent the next with a good fall of rain overnight and the melting of snow. They would become cut off from supplies and if they didn't risk the danger of drowning by attempting to cross a swollen river they could die of starvation. Many of them were so young and inexperienced, in their twenties a lot of them. James shuddered.

'Are you alright James?' Meg reached out a hand to stroke his face.

He held her hand and kissed the palm. 'I was just thinking about one of the surveyors I met.'

'Do you want to talk about it? I don't mind, I'm not really sleepy yet.'

'It's not a happy story Meg, are you sure you want to hear it?'

'Yes of course, what is it?'

'It's about a chap called Henry Whitcombe. He and a Swiss guide were commissioned to find a route across that pass I was pointing out to

179

you yesterday. He's been on my mind ever since. I have a newspaper clipping tucked in the back of my notebook which I had almost forgotten about.'

He fumbled around with his clothing until he found the notebook in his pocket. He took out the piece of paper from the back of the notebook and carefully unfolded it.

'Do you want to read it?'

'How about you read it to me,' she said lying back on her bedroll and plumping up her coat which served as her pillow.

James took a deep breath and holding the clipping so he could read it in the glow of the camp fire began,

'They started off on the 22nd May 1863. Whitcombe and his companion Jakob Lauper, a Swiss alpinist planned to journey across the alpine pass and down the Hokitika River to the coast. Soon after they started the weather deteriorated and in heavy rain and snow, they made their way downstream. It was soon evident that Whitcombe had seriously underestimated the difficulties of the passage and their food supplies, estimated to last a fortnight, were exhausted or spoiled by the rain and the ubiquitous blowflies. The terrain was much worse than either could have imagined. They were delayed by the precipitous country which necessitated lengthy detours and having to cross and re-cross the swollen river. Day after day with no shelter from the elements, drenched to the skin and rarely able to light a fire, their food supplies spoiled and sadly diminished, the pair struggled along and, despite their greatest exertions, gained little more than three miles a day at times. At length near the coast they came across two Maori whares where they had expected to obtain food, but the place was deserted and all they found was a handful of small potatoes and a little Maori cabbage (Puwha).

Next day, thirteen days after setting out from the top of the pass, they reached the mouth of the Taramakau River. The actual distance they had travelled was about sixty miles. Across the Taramakau they could see the Maori kainga but there was no sign of life as it also was deserted. Despite the fact that Lauper could not swim, Whitcombe decided to attempt to cross the river rather than face the prospect of dying of starvation in the forest.

They found the water logged remains of two canoes which they lashed together with flax, making a rough raft, and set out to cross the deep, fast flowing river not far above the breakers at the river mouth. So

decayed was their primitive craft that by the time they reached the middle of the river it sank, leaving them at the mercy of the breakers. Whitcombe attempted to swim ashore but Lauper clung to the raft which was eventually driven ashore with Lauper more dead than alive, but Whitcombe was drowned.

Next day, when he had sufficiently recovered, Lauper retrieved Whitcombe's body which he buried in a shallow grave above high water mark. Lauper then set out to reach Howitt's survey camp at Lake Brunner. Fortunately, he met two small groups of Maoris on the way and although they also were desperately short of food, they were able to provide him with sufficient to enable him to reach Howitt's camp.

It was mid-winter and Harper's Pass was in a dangerous condition but Lauper, with the aid of two horses provided by Howitt was able in the course of two days to cross over the pass and reach Henry Taylor's station at Lake Sumner and a few days later return to Christchurch.'

'Oh,' said Meg sitting up, 'that's terrible. Did you know him?'

'I knew of him, he worked with Samuel Butler and I remember it was the talk of the town for quite some time. Do you recall the name Julius von Haast?'

'Yes, I think so, why? Was he in the surveying party too?'

'No but he did name Mount Whitcombe in Henry's honour which shows how well respected he was. A year later Arthur Dobson made the crossing.'

'Ah, Dobsons Crossing, yes I remember seeing that on the map.'

'I wouldn't mind a cuddle to take my mind off all this doom and gloom,' James smiled at Meg with a gleam in his eye.

'Is that all you wouldn't mind?' she giggled

James lost himself in the arms of his beautiful wife and for a while was able to forget the disturbing story and the thoughts that had been troubling him.

It was three weeks later that James and Meg arrived back at Flaxbush Station with completed survey maps of Stony Downs and Arrowsmith stations.

Meg and James regaled everyone with stories of their adventures over the next three days. By all accounts Meg had really enjoyed the time she spent working with James, but she had missed the farm and the animals more than she thought she would and was eager to get back home again.

'I will take Meg home and get her settled in, check on the animals and see how things are going then I will be back to survey Flaxbush Station,' said James as he shook Henry's hand.

'No urgency James, I will go over what you have given me and when you are ready just come on by and maybe I will come with you this time.'

'I would enjoy your company,' smiled James.

Marshall had loved his sojourn on the run and was disappointed when he spotted the two riders heading his way. The dogs were so excited to see Meg and James they almost turned themselves inside out. Meg leapt down off her horse and was immediately smothered by two balls of bouncing fluff, tongues licking at her face. She rolled around on the ground in fits of giggles. James sat astride his horse and laughed at the sight. Meg looked so young and beautiful and happy these days; he was most pleased to see her so full of life after the tragedies of the previous year.

'So how have things been going here Marshall?' James asked as they sat around the table enjoying a cup of tea.

'Very well Mr M, very well indeed. To be honest I am sorry to be going back to Flaxbush, I have really enjoyed my stay here.'

'I'm sorry for you too Marshall, I can well imagine it has been most gratifying to have been your own boss for almost a month. Rest assured if we both go away again you will be most welcome to repeat the exercise.'

After Marshall left James and Meg picked up their familiar routine and before long it was like they had never been away. The dogs followed Meg around constantly not wanting to let her out of their sight.

'They would sit and watch for you each night you know,' Marshall had told her. 'Bit sad really.'

Meg reached down and ruffled the fur on their necks. 'I missed you too my darlings,' she said huskily.

Once James was confident that everything that needed to be done had been done, he rode over to Flaxbush Station to begin surveying. This time his companion would be Henry.

182

As soon as James was out of sight Meg donned her old shirt and James trousers, untied her hair and shook it out, then went outside and took a deep breath, spread out her arms and yelled out to the hills – 'I'm baaack.'

184

Declaration of Love – Winter 1869

James left again just before winter. He had become more and more restless as the months wore on after his surveying stint on Flaxbush Station had come to an end. Meg didn't have to ask; she knew instinctively he would be leaving again.

Marshall and Henry came to help Meg with the stock work and Marshall came and spent a few days with her from time to time to do any odd jobs that needed doing around the house but for the most part Meg was left to her own devices. There was still no sign of Stephen and Meg didn't like to ask after him.

Stephen was back at Flaxbush and would love to have taken Marshall's place and come to see Meg, but he knew it would only lead to trouble. He knew it wasn't right, loving another man's wife, but he just couldn't seem to bury his love for her. He knew she felt it too. She spent an unhealthy amount of time alone while James was away. She was a young woman and it was only natural that she might miss the company of a man sometimes.

It was a particularly calm, blue-sky day when Stephen rode around the bend towards the Morley house on his first visit for quite some time. Marshall had taken a tumble off his horse the previous week and wasn't able to ride so Henry had suggested Stephen ride over to check on Meg instead. Henry caught Stephen's hesitation but chose to ignore it. James was a damn fool to leave his lovely young wife alone for such lengthy periods, it would serve him right if she took up with someone else. He knew that wasn't the right way to see it and if he ventured such a thought to Gladys she would have been furious with him.

It was a tricky journey and a bit dangerous in places, but Stephen was determined to see her. It had been too long. He hadn't been to Stony Downs for almost a year. Spring was just around the corner and would be turning the brown to green and no doubt James would be coming back sometime soon. He had been gone for several months now with no word of his impending return. In fact, as far as he knew, Meg hadn't heard from him since he left.

As Stephen got closer, he could just make out the house in the distance nestled into the base of the bush clad mountainside. A comforting trail of smoke lifted softly into the still air. He was almost at the house when a movement to the left caught his eye. It was Meg, across the other side of the river on her horse with her beloved dogs running along beside her. She hadn't seen him yet, so he dismounted, threw the reins over his horse's head to let him roam and forage for a while and sat down with his back resting against a sun warmed rock.

With one leg lying flat, the other raised with an arm draped over it and his hat pulled down over his eyes one could be forgiven for thinking he was asleep. He took this golden opportunity to watch Meg unguarded, allowing himself to feel the full force of his love for her without anyone around to raise an eyebrow at him.

'God she's beautiful,' he whispered huskily. Her hair was loose and flying free, she looked happy and at peace with her surroundings. She slowed down and made her way to the edge of the river; it was still flowing quite strongly but Stephen knew Meg would have found a good crossing point. Sure enough, the dogs leapt animatedly into the water yipping and barking as they frolicked through the icy cold water. Meg gently encouraged Jasper into the water and allowed him to take his lead as the water rose up over his shoulders. They all made their way to the bank safely, the dogs shaking themselves vigorously causing Meg to

186

laugh as they sprayed her with water. Stephen smiled at the sound; it was music to his ears.

She still hadn't spotted him yet, so he continued to stay put. Meg dismounted and walked across to the edge of the bush that ran up from the river towards the house. She stooped to pick some wild herb or flower. As she stood back up he noticed her clothing. What on earth was she wearing, he had only ever seen her or any woman in a dress yet here she was – in trousers? He was stunned but then he laughed. 'Oh Meg, you never cease to amaze me', he chuckled to himself.

At this point Meg looked up and after a brief pause raised her hand and waved. She put her hand up to shield her eyes to see who this stranger was and then waved exuberantly when she realized it was Stephen. She waited where she was while he got up, mounted his horse and rode quickly down to meet her. As soon as his feet hit the ground, she threw herself into his arms and hugged him tightly.

'Oh Stephen, I have missed you so much, it is so good to see you,' she gushed.

Stephen was a little taken aback by Meg's demonstrative greeting but his heart was leaping about all over the place. She released him from the embrace, turned to grab Jasper's reins and said, 'Come on back to the house, I have a delectable treat I have been dying for someone to try.'

Stephen walked beside Meg towards the house. He noticed rabbit pelts draped over the fence drying out.

'My you have been a busy girl,' he commented, picking up a skin to examine it. 'You've done an excellent job Meg, these are lovely. They are soft and pliable, well done.'

'Wait till you see what else I've been up to,' she blushed.

She led him around the back to the futah and prized open the door. It was full of pumpkins, potatoes, kumara and bundles of onions tied together hanging from the roof. There were parcels of dried meat cut into strips, honey and honeycomb was packed tightly into glass jars. There were blocks of cheese in a variety of conditions as it matured and then went past maturity, unused.

'Whew,' whistled Stephen, 'You are an absolute marvel Meg.'

She giggled at his comment. She knew that she had surpassed even her own expectations and was extremely proud of her achievements, but it was uplifting to hear someone else acknowledge them.

'Come see what's inside the house,' she smiled, grabbing hold of his hand.

An overwhelming vista of colours and aromas greeted him as he stepped inside the door. Dried flowers and herbs hung from the rafters. The shelves were stocked with jars of preserves and honey alongside unmarked jars of dried matter which Stephen presumed to be herbs. He was about to ask when Meg excitedly gestured to Stephen to sit down. She was animated, smiling and flushed; he thought he had never seen her look more beautiful than she did at this moment. On impulse he reached out and pulled her to him and kissed her soundly on the lips. She didn't pull away at first but then as her reeling senses began to calm down, she gently pulled back to look into his eyes.

'I, I'm sorry Meg,' he stammered, 'I shouldn't have done that, it's just that...'

'Hush,' she whispered placing her finger on his lips, 'don't spoil the moment. It happened and I liked it, let's leave it there for now.'

'For now?' Stephen's head was all over the place. 'What did she mean, for now?'

Meg pulled back the curtain which hung below the bench and reached in to lift out a small wooden barrel which was obviously full. Stephen jumped up to help.

'What on earth have you got in here?' he asked.

'Plum wine,' Meg answered proudly. 'Made it myself and it's pretty damn good too.'

Stephen roared with laughter. 'You are the most amazing and surprising young woman I have ever met in my life Meghan Morley.'

'Then you can't have met many women Mr Sangster,' she laughed.

She took two tin mugs from the shelf above the bench and allowed Stephen to fill them from the barrel. They both sat down at the table, raised their mugs in salute and took a sip of the deep burgundy liquid. Stephen shook his head and gasped.

'Good Lord Meg that's a pretty potent brew you've got there.'

'I know,' she laughed, 'the first time I drank it I was pleased there were no witnesses. Except for the dogs of course and they have been sworn to secrecy.'

She got up from the table and went to a cabinet on the wall.

'This is one of my favourite treats, I have it with my toast in the mornings.'

She produced a jar of yellow liquid and taking the lid off dipped her finger into it then put the sticky finger into Stephen's mouth. The sudden sharp tang on his tongue contradicted the sweetness of the wine and he was quite taken aback by the taste sensations.

'That is delicious,' he said grabbing her hand and dipping her finger into the substance again. 'What is it?'

'Lemon, honey,' she smiled, allowing him to keep sucking on her finger.

'Where did you get the lemons from?'

'I have a lemon tree. Not a very big one and it does take a lot of care and attention but in the summer time I am rewarded with a few pitiful but juicy little lemons. At least enough to make several jars of lemon honey. You like it?'

'I love it,' he said looking into her eyes, his words loaded with double meaning.

'Before we have any more wine, I think we should best get Bessy milked, collect the eggs, see to the horses and feed the dogs otherwise I fear they may get neglected,' giggled Meg. 'You are staying for a while, aren't you?'

'I'll stay for as long as I am welcome,' responded Stephen weak with lust and longing.

Once the outside chores had been completed Meg set a rabbit stew to cook over the fire. She added her fresh dried herbs which only served to add to the variety of heady aromas already hanging in the air. Stephen refilled their cups and they wandered outside to sit under the verandah and watch the kaleidoscope of colours dancing above the mountain tops as the sun planned it's decent over the horizon. Between the pleasant silences Meg and Stephen talked about their lives and shared secrets they had never shared with anyone else as the potent liquid took its effect.

'Meg, can I tell you something,' Stephen ventured cautiously.

'Of course, what is it?'

'Do you know I fell in love with you that day when you were riding Marshall's horse and you whistled to the dogs, do you remember?'

189

Meg laughed, 'Yes I do remember. Oh Stephen, I love you too, but I don't know when it happened, it just seems to have always been there.'

She was thoughtful for a while and they both let the silence settle between them.

'I love James too,' ventured Meg eventually, 'but in a different way. I guess it's a love borne of the commitment we made and the promise to look out for each other. It's more of a solid, grounded kind of love really.'

'So, what kind of love do you have for me then?' Stephen enquired, the alcohol giving him the boldness to speak his mind.

Meg smiled and looked across at him taking his hand.

'With you Stephen it is a light hearted, free flowing kindred ship that just sort of feels right, when nobody else is around. Does that make sense? I just feel so free and comfortable with you; I can say anything to you. I don't have to be something I'm not. You didn't even comment on the fact that I am wearing trousers. James would have a fit if he saw me sitting here in trousers drinking homemade wine.'

Their eyes met and they both laughed until tears ran down their faces.

'It is beyond me that James could leave you on your own for such long periods Meg. In fact, it makes me damned angry. What is wrong with the man?'

'Don't be too hard on him Stephen it's just the type of person he is. He's always been a loner and the surveying life suits him well. He loves being out in the wide-open spaces and is happy to be on his own. I knew that when I married him.'

Meg got up to stir the stew.

'Dinner will be ready in about an hour. I'm wondering if we will be sober enough to eat it by then,' she laughed as she stood in front of Stephen.

He pulled her down on to his lap.

'Maybe we could find something to distract us from the wine for a while then,' he teased.

He picked her up and carried her to the bed and laid her down gently, pushing her back into the pillows. He took off his shirt and trousers then gently, deliberately began releasing Meg from her attire. By the time he had finished they were both so hungry for each other that he

190

thrust into her without any further preamble. They lay spent in each other's arms and dozed off for a while, satiated and released from their years of pent up sexual tension. The heady aromas in the room and the wine had worked their magic.

Meg stirred first. It was dark outside. She raised her head to look at the fire and the pot hanging over it. She tried to extricate herself from Stephen's arms without waking him, but he stirred.

'Where are you going young lady?'

'Just checking on the stew,' she whispered back. 'I'll be back in a moment.'

'You better be,' he smiled, eyes still closed.

They sat at the table and ate their stew in silence, the consequences of their actions beginning to take hold in their minds.

'Stephen,' Meg began, 'I'm not sure we should do this again. I mean go to bed together. I would still love for you to come visit but I must admit I do feel a little guilty now.'

'I understand Meg, truly I do,' whispered Stephen reaching across the table for her hand. 'We both understand and accept our feelings for each other so let's just leave it there. We will always have this night to remember, at least I will.'

'Me too Stephen, me too. I think with James being away so much it was bound to happen at some stage and now that it has, we can leave it at that. It will be our secret.'

Stephen held Meg in his arms all night as she slept but he didn't make a move to do anything more than that. They were comfortable with their declared feelings for each other, they had expressed them intimately and although they would love to have allowed it to continue, they both knew it was not the right thing to do. What was done was done.'

Stephen kissed Meg gently on the lips next morning before he leapt up on his horse.

'I doubt I will be back again on my own Meg but trust me, I will be back soon.'

Meg stood and watched Stephen ride away until he was out of sight. He didn't turn back. He couldn't, he daren't, he didn't trust himself not to race back and take her in his arms again. He knew he probably wouldn't see her again until the Spring muster.

James returns – Summer 1869

The door was wide open but there was no sign of Meg. James walked around the back of the house to the shed. Bessy was sitting in the sun lazily chewing on her cud. She mooed softly at James as he scratched her on the nose. He smiled at the chickens busily scratching away in Meg's vegetable garden. There were rabbit pelts draped over the fences. There was a pile of ashes in the fire of the blacksmith's pit, cold now, and there was an anvil on a block nearby. 'Where on earth has she gone?' he pondered. There was no sign of Jasper or the dogs.

James wandered into the house and was taken aback by the dried and drying flowers and herbs hanging from the rafters. The shelves were stocked with preserves, strips of dried meat and honey in jars. There was dried matter in a variety of containers, unlabelled. 'Identifiable by smell,' assumed James as he replaced the lid of one of the containers which proved to be dried lavender. The place definitely had Meg's stamp on it, to such an extent that he felt like an intruder in his own home and if he was honest with himself, it did not sit well.

He heard a high pitched 'cooeee' from somewhere down by the river. He went to the door and there riding at full speed was Meg with her hair flying out behind her, laughing and waving and looking for all the world like a wild creature with her two dogs running along beside her their mouths open, tongues hanging out as if they were laughing too. She brought Jasper to a screeching halt beside James and laughing said, 'Might you be one James Morley perchance? I haven't set eyes on him for so long I fear I might not recognize him anymore.'

'You don't recognize *me*?' he laughed, shaking off his annoyance, 'My dear girl I hardly recognize you. My word but you look like a wild thing.'

Meg laughed and throwing herself off her horse leapt into James arms and kissed him longingly.

'Hmmm I might have to go away more often if this is the greeting I get on my return.' He picked her up and took her straight to the bed, Meg was more than willing to tempt him on, she had missed being with her man. It was late November; he had been gone for eight months.

When they finally got up it was getting dark, so they lit the fire and prepared dinner. While they waited for their meal to cook James questioned Meg about all the activities he had seen around the place. She pulled out a rolled-up map from under the bed and spread it out on the table. It was James map of their farm, but it was now covered in lines and scribbled words.

'On a good clear day when the weather is settled and all the stock work is done I stand outside with the compass, pick a direction and we head off in as straight a line as possible for a whole day taking note of the plants and animals and birds we see along the way, then I come back and write my findings on the map. See, here is a wild honey hive and another one here and here. All these places show where there are various herbs and edible plants.'

She babbled away almost oblivious to James presence while he watched her with a stupid smile on his face. She might be a crazy wild woman right now, but she was his crazy wild woman and he rather liked it.

When Meg had finally filled James in on all her activities, she turned to him.

'Now Mr Morley, where on earth have you been and why have you been away so long this time?'

James pulled a pipe out of his pocket, packed it full of tobacco from a pouch, lit it and leaned back in his chair. 'Well, where do I begin,' he smiled through a cloud of smoke.

194

'The tobacco smell works in well with the dried herbs up there in the rafters,' laughed Meg.

'It does indeed,' James laughed and began his story.

'I was sent to do some surveying in Rees Town, it's further south and to the East of here. While I was there I met a chap by the name of Buster Manson, bit of a character as his name might suggest. He had been sluicing for gold up the Skippers Canyon and doing quite well until his friend got injured and ended up in hospital. He was looking for another man to work with him so I decided I would give it a go. Meg, I'm telling you, it is damned hard work but look, look at what I have found already.'

He pulled a small leather pouch out of his pocket and shook out a dozen or so reasonably good-sized nuggets.

'And there's more where that came from. Meg I have to go back. This is too good an opportunity to pass up. You do understand, don't you?' he pleaded, pulling her to sit on his lap.

Meg was hesitant for a moment.

'So how long do you think it will take to get as much as you think you will need for whatever it is you think you want?'

James was a little perplexed. 'Uhm, well, I don't rightly know. I mean it's just the thrill of the find I guess.' He didn't know quite how to answer Meg's question.

'Well, you go figure it all out Mr Morley and no doubt you will come back when you are good and ready.' Meg was disturbed by what James had said.

She got up off his knee and tended to the simmering pot hanging over the fire. James watched her. She had changed, but then what could he expect being out here on her own for long periods of time. But he did wonder about her state of mind. She seemed happy enough if a little strange. He would keep a close eye on her while he was at home. If she was beginning to show any signs of losing her sanity he would need to do something about it. In the meantime he would try and pick up where he left off last time he was here at home.

'Tell me what's happening with the sheep Meg, how are they doing?'

'Well then,' she said wiping her hands on her breeches, 'where do I start?'

Meg filled James in on all that had happened on the run since he left and over the next couple of weeks they settled back into their familiar patterns once again

.

Gone again – Winter 1870

It was another long, hard cold winter and Meg was pleased to have James there with her. They squabbled and fought a lot more than they used to, but they accepted that they had both changed during their times apart and put it down to that. The closeness they once enjoyed seemed to have gone, replaced by a comfortable if somewhat fraught companionship. They both knew they had to get along being cooped up in the house for days and weeks on end trapped within the boundaries of the raging river and deep snows surrounding them, so they had to work hard to keep things amicable between them.

After James got back from his last trip he suggested to Meg that perhaps they could try again for a baby. Meg was hesitant but seeing the want in James eyes she couldn't refuse him.

'It's an ideal time really Meg,' he'd said. 'Cooped up here for days on end with nothing else to do and you won't be out riding so much so that must be an added advantage surely?'

Meg caught the undercurrent of his remark. He would never forgive her for losing their precious baby. 'Maybe it would help if we did have another baby,' Meg thought, 'maybe it would bring our marriage back on track.'

Unfortunately, as the weeks and months went by with no sign of a pregnancy James became more and more morose. Meg knew in her heart that as soon as it was safe to leave he would be gone. She didn't even know if he would return this time such was his mood.

As the darkness of deepest winter began to turn into brighter days James and Meg would ride off as far and for as long as they dared. They rode further than they intended one day hunting rabbits and lost track of time. Darkness descended upon them before they realized it. They were worried about not getting home, they had left their return run too late. The darker it got the more they had to rely on the dogs to lead them home.

As they stripped their coats, hats and boots off under the verandah James breathed a sigh of relief.

'I don't know how we would have fared getting home if it hadn't been for the dogs Meg. They are worth their weight in gold aren't they.'

Meg nodded and smiled but didn't say anything in return, she already knew the value of her beloved furry friends.

Spring came and as soon as he deemed it safe enough to get out of the valley James rode over to the Hopkins farm to help out with the spring muster. He and Meg had checked on their own in-lamb ewes and were happy with the lambing numbers again this year. James couldn't wait to report the good news to Henry.

Once the shearing was done on the Hopkins station James rode back to Stony Downs with Stephen, Marshall, Henry and two other shearers to shear his own flock. The weather had been settled for some time and Meg had managed to round up most of their sheep and bring them to the flat area beside the pens in front of the house.

'Good job Meg,' James remarked. 'Do you think you have them all?'

'No. I left a mob behind but they were heading in this direction so I knew they would be easy for us to go back and bring them in.'

Stephen jumped in to the conversation. He had avoided making eye contact with Meg but had been watching out for her since they rounded the corner further up the valley.

'Marshall and I can go get them while you instruct the others on how to put the shed together if you like James.'

'Good idea, thanks Stephen.'

'Meg you might need to come with us and show us where they are,' he turned his attention to Meg trying not to let any emotion show.

James turned to look at Meg and suggest that she didn't need to go but she got in first.

'It's okay James, it will be quicker if I go with them and show them where they are then they can take it from there. I will be back in time to get lunch on the table.'

James hesitated but then not being able to come up with any good excuse why she shouldn't go he had to agree. He'd gone off Stephen a bit, he couldn't put his finger on why exactly, but he suspected Stephen didn't have much time for him either. They were polite to each other but that was about as far as it went these days.

As soon as they were out of sight Stephen sent Marshall off with his dogs to round up the sheep that were slowly making their way down the side of the mountain. When Marshall was out of earshot Stephen turned at last to look Meg in the eye.

'How have you been beautiful lady? I see you have conformed back to being a respectable house wife and wearing your dresses again.'

Meg scowled at him but then smiled. 'Yes, I have settled back into my old routines with James for now, it keeps him happy. He said he was going back to the gold diggings after Christmas so I will be able to discard the dresses and put on my trousers again.'

'It's good to see you Meg, I have missed you terribly.'

'I have missed you too Stephen, how have you been?'

'I have put my shoulder to the grind and worked my way through these long lonely months without you,' he smiled ruefully.

'Don't.' Meg whispered.

'Don't what?'

'Don't say things like that, I can't bear it. I feel torn between the two of you. I have James, my husband on one hand whom I still love in a way and then I have you.'

'What about me Meg, how do you feel about me?'

She sighed and looked down at her fingers that were fidgeting with the leather reins she held in her hands.

'I relive that night we spent together over and over until my heart aches. Then I feel guilty and turn my thoughts back to James, but we have grown apart these past months and the closeness we once knew is no longer there. He is different now, more distant. It's almost as if he can't wait to leave. I hate to admit it, but I am not too concerned, I'm secretly looking forward to seeing James riding away again and leaving me in peace, to be free to come and go as I please and do what I want, when I want. Does that sound really bad?'

'I understand Meg, believe me I do. I will come back and see you after he leaves and we can talk more then, but for now I think you had best get yourself back to the house. I can see the rest of the sheep from here.'

He leant over and picked up her hand bringing it to his lips, his eyes probing into hers as if to see in to her soul. She took her hand back and quickly turned and rode back to the house before he could see the tears beginning to well up and run down her cheeks.

Meg was relieved when the shearing was done. She had felt awfully uncomfortable being in such close proximity to both James and Stephen at the same time. During the days she was able to concentrate on sorting the fleeces and keeping out of their way and at meal times she would leave the men at the table which had been set up outside under the verandah while she would sit on a makeshift stump around the corner beside the house. There were other stumps set around in a circle which they used in summer as an outdoor dining area. Sometimes the men would stay at the table to talk about the day's proceedings, other times they would come and join her. This was the most uncomfortable time for Meg. If James came out before Stephen made a move Stephen would stay at the table. One night though Stephen and Marshall came over together and sat opposite her. Meg could hardly swallow her food; she knew Stephen was watching her and it made her feel very self-conscious. The very worst time of all was when Meg was lying in bed beside James trying to sleep knowing that Stephen was on his bedroll right outside the door.

They didn't go to the Hopkins for Christmas that year, instead choosing to have some quiet time by themselves. On Christmas morning James produced a parcel from under the bed. He'd hidden it there when he came back just before winter. There had been no parcel from home this year yet but there was sure to be one waiting for them at the Hopkins. Meg giggled with delight when she saw the tiny box with its white ribbon. She tugged one strand of the narrow strip of satin allowing it to drop to the floor. She gently lifted the lid. There nestled in a bed of deep blue satin was a glistening diamond ring. She gently picked it up and held it to the light.

"Oh my goodness James, that is the most beautiful ring I have ever seen in my life. Surely it is not a real diamond?'

'Yes it is a real diamond my love and it is long overdue. I am sorry I never got to give you an engagement ring when we got engaged but better late than never eh.'

He took it from her and placed it on her finger.

'Oh,' she gasped, 'It's stunning and it fits perfectly.' She reached up and kissed him tenderly on the lips. 'You know I never expected a ring; we were saving for our trip to come here.'

'I know but with this gold I have found we will be able to afford a lot of things Meg. If I thought you would wear them I would buy you pretty dresses but I think perhaps I should buy you trousers and dungarees instead,' he laughed.

James went to pour them a cup of Meg's plum wine. She looked down at the sparkling diamond on her finger and felt sad.

"Here we are growing apart,' she thought, 'and now he gives me this beautiful ring.' She thought back to the day he proposed to her.

James handed her a cup and raised his in a toast.

'Here's to fame and fortune, well fortune at least,' he laughed.

Meg was stunned. She stared at James with her mouth open. He lowered his cup.

'What Meg? What is it?'

'Oh, I thought, I mean, you have just given me this beautiful engagement ring and I thought you were about to propose a toast to us.' Her eyes were brimming with tears. 'I was just thinking about the time you proposed to me, how happy we were then.' She took a deep breath, 'I guess we are very different people now aren't we, wanting different things.'

She put her cup down on the table and rushed out the door, tears rolling down her cheeks. The dogs immediately got up and followed her.

James wasn't sure what had just happened. It was just a ring, he had wanted her to wear it and show it off, especially in front of Stephen. He wanted people to know that he wasn't a poor struggling farmer anymore, that he was well off enough to buy his wife a real diamond ring. He hadn't even considered Meg's reaction to it; he was unsure how to react. He decided to leave Meg to come back on her own accord, which she did when it was time to put dinner on.

Dinner was a very quiet affair and they went to bed without speaking. The silence between them became a large gulf as the days passed. Meg was bitterly disappointed at the distance that had grown between them. She had thought James was making inroads to bring them closer together again and James was disappointed that Meg didn't share in his penchant to better themselves.

After a week of awkward silence James finally broke the ice.

'Meg, we have to talk. The Hopkins will be here tomorrow, and we need to at least appear to be happy, even if we are not.'

Meg stopped kneading the dough she was preparing for the bread she was baking in preparation for their arrival.

'I know,' she sighed. 'I'm sorry James; I just got the wrong idea about the ring that's all. I thought you were trying to revive what we once had.'

James hung his head. 'Oh Meg,' he sighed looking back up at her. 'I didn't realize it would mean that much to you. I knew you would like the ring and I guess I just wanted you to show it off to everyone, I didn't think you would place that much importance on it. I'm disappointed you don't share my enthusiasm to better ourselves, I thought that's what you wanted.'

'No James, I don't need wealth. As far as I'm concerned we have all we need right here, right now. I know you get restless being stuck here with me for too long and I understand that, but I have no desire on this earth to be anywhere else or be anything other than who I am. I'm sorry if that disappoints you but that is just the way I feel. I'm happy here, living this life.'

'I'm not unhappy here with you Meg, it's just this lifestyle suffocates me. I admire the way you can live here on your own. God, you seem to thrive on it, especially when I am not here. But I need to be moving around, travelling, exploring. I guess that has always been my nature, that's why I became a surveyor, the nomadic life suits me well.'

There was silence for a few minutes while each of them digested the others words.

'I don't know where we go from here Meg but please believe that I do love you, we may have a different viewpoint on life and we may want different things but I still love you and I want you to be by my side when I find my fortune.'

'I tell you what James, let's discuss this when you return with your wealth shall we, you may not even find your pot of gold. And just in case you were wondering, yes I do still love you.'

James got up from the table and came around behind Meg and gave her a cuddle and kissed her on the neck. He dipped his hands in the flour and flicked them at her, she flicked her floury fingers back at him and when he ran outside she chased after him. They ran around the house ducking and diving and hiding from each other the dogs joining in the game. Finally, James snuck up on Meg and tackled her gently to the ground. He rolled her over; kissed her on the mouth, pulled her to her feet them smacked her bottom and sent her back to her bread making. The stand-off had finally ended.

On New Year's Day the entire Hopkins family, along with Marshall and Stephen arrived with food and gifts and the much anticipated parcel from England. After the happy new year's hugs, kisses and handshakes were over the children went running off down the paddock towards the river with the dogs while James and Henry set up the refreshments table and Meg helped Gladys to unpack the food parcels. Stephen and Marshall unsaddled the horses, gave them a rub down and took them down to the river for a drink, joining the children in a game of skipping stones.

'My, my, young Meg, look at what you have done here. I am impressed, I truly am.' Gladys pulled out a jar containing a yellow substance and took the lid off. 'Let me guess, this is lemon honey is it not?'

'It is,' beamed Meg. Come let me show you all my treasures, I have had the best time, I really have.'

'But where did you get all these things Meg, I mean, lemons, lavender, honey?'

Meg took Gladys's arm and showed her the garden and small orchard around the back that Meg had been nurturing over the years.

'My plum tree blessed me with abundance last season, so I made plum wine, wait until you try it. It is a bit strong though,' she smiled apologetically. 'Oh, and this climbing rose along the side of the house has been marvellous, I made rosehip syrup this year. As for the lavender and honey that you asked about, I have found wild honey hives and patches of plants and herbs when I go out on my wee outings with the dogs. I will show you my map when we have a moment to ourselves.'

'Your vegetable garden seems to have done well this year Meg, I'm afraid the house cow found her way into mine and did quite a bit of damage before we could get her out. I did manage to bring you some fruit from the orchard though so you can make some preserves. And I thought you might be running low on jars, so I have brought some of those too.'

'Bless you Gladys, yes as you can see I have filled every container I own with preserves of one kind or another. Thank you.'

Gladys picked up the fur quilt lying across the foot of the bed.

'These pelts are excellent Meg, are these the ones you cured yourself?'

'Yes, it was hard work and it took me ages to make them soft and pliable like that, but I am pleased with the result. I used a sacking needle to join them together and ended up with very sore and bloodied fingers, but it was the only way I figured it could be done.'

'Well you have done a wonderful job; I am very impressed. I noticed the anvil out back; do you still do a bit of smithy work?'

'Yes, I do now and again but I have run out of iron now so apart from keeping an eye on the horses' shoes there's not much use for it I'm afraid.'

'Oh, that reminds me, Henry popped in some spare horse shoes for you. Thought your horses might need some new ones,' she smiled.

Meg smiled conspiratorially at Gladys and pulling aside the curtain under the bench showed her the small wooden keg.

'Is that the plum wine?' she laughed.

'Sure is. Want to try some?'

'Why not.'

Gladys produced six glasses from a sturdy wooden box.

'These are my gift to you dear Meg, how well planned was that?' giggled Gladys as she set the glasses up on the bench, the table having been taken outside.

'Oh, it will be so much nicer drinking wine out of a glass instead of a tin cup,' she enthused. 'Thank you Gladys. Gosh where would I have been without you all these years eh.'

Meg and Gladys took the glasses filled with the rich ruby red wine out to the men and handed them around. Stephen glanced furtively at Meg making sure James wasn't watching and raised his glass to her. She smiled back and gave him a quick nod. They were both remembering the night they drank this very wine together.

'By God but that's a might powerful brew Meg. Can you make a whiskey too?' laughed Henry sputtering a little as the strong liquid hit the back of his throat.

'I don't know, but if you get me the recipe and ingredients, I am sure I could set up a still and start a moonshine business.'

Everyone roared with laughter. 'I have no doubt that you would be very good at it too.'

Gladys was the first to notice Meg's ring. Meg had worn it but hadn't tried to show it off and hadn't even mentioned it to Gladys.

'My oh my Meghan Morley, that ring on your finger, it surely can't be a real diamond, can it?'

James puffed his chest out proudly, 'I can assure you Gladys that it certainly is a real diamond.'

He went inside and came out with his pouch of gold nuggets. 'I struck it lucky in Rees Town last summer. And there's still more there to be found I'm sure. I'm going back next week.'

There was a stunned silence while this news sunk in.

'Going back?' said Henry. 'You're leaving Meg and going back again? How long for this time James?'

James didn't seem to take any offence at Henry's questioning.

'Not sure Henry, depends how my luck holds out. I have been itching to get back there all winter. Sorry Meg, that's no reflection on you, it's just something that seems to have taken a hold on me. I think they call it gold fever,' he laughed.

Stephen was quietly thrilled to hear that James would be going away again, and soon. He was already planning his next visit to see Meg.

'So, how much do you think that little lot is worth then James?' Henry asked. 'Can't say I've had much to do with the gold myself.'

'I'm not sure to be honest Henry. I haven't had it valued yet, but I exchanged one nugget for Meg's ring and that diamond was not an inexpensive one believe me.'

Everyone was quiet for a moment not knowing what to say. Next thing the children came charging up towards the house from the river laughing and quite out of breath.

'Is lunch ready yet?' asked Clementine, 'We're starving.'

'It will be soon, now off with you. We will call you when it's ready. Don't go too far away hear?'

'We won't,' they chorused back disappearing around behind the house to play chasey around the sheds and garden.

'And don't you go running through Mrs Morley's garden either.'

'We won't,' Jenny called back over her shoulder.

Lunch was a grand affair. The table groaned with the weight of all the delectable delights that Meg and Gladys had spent days preparing.

Everyone sat back at the end of the meal their appetites more than satisfied.

They spent the next two days wandering around in the hills and along the river beds and just relaxing and chatting in the sun feasting on leftovers. Then all too soon the visit was over. Meg was sad to see Gladys go; she missed female company. Most of the time it was just the menfolk visiting and she only ever saw Gladys on special occasions or on the rare occasion she went into town.

Silence settled on the house when everyone rode off back to Flaxbush Station. As soon as she had waved them out of sight Meg pulled the unopened parcel out from under the bed. She wanted to open it by herself without anyone else around. She became quite tearful whenever she read the letters from home and was even more melancholy when parcels arrived. James was out checking on the stock, so she was quite alone. It was just as well as the first thing she picked up was a light blue pair of dungarees. Meg held them up against herself and laughed.

'Oh mother, how wonderful you are.' There was a wee note tucked in the pocket of the bib on the front.

'My darling daughter,' it read, 'I was shocked but highly amused when you wrote and told us you had been wearing James trousers and shirts. But I can well understand that if there was no-one else around to see you they would be a lot more serviceable considering the work you are doing. I do hope you are not overdoing it my dear. I have also made you some linen shirts to go under your dungarees, I hope you like them. My loving thoughts are always with you my beautiful girl. Love Mother.'

Meg quickly tried on one of the shirts and the dungarees before James came back and was delighted with the way they fitted and how comfortable they were. She decided she must send a letter away with James when he went back to Rees Town, thanking her mother for her loving and thoughtful gift.

James packed up and rode out the following week. Meg watched him go with mixed emotions. She would miss him, but she was also anxious to get into her dungarees and pick up her life where it had left off.

The calm before the storm – 1871

Meg slipped straight back in to her old ways with ease. It got to the stage where she didn't care whether James bloody Morley ever showed his face again. She was angry and disappointed with him for leaving her so early after the New Year. She was under no illusions that he was anxious to get away from the farm, but he could have at least stayed for a while longer. Though she had to admit she was just as eager to see him go. What had their marriage become, she wondered.

The hot lazy days of the January summer gave way to the equally hot summer days of February. Meg would often watch out for Stephen when she was out riding. She missed him and hoped he would come and see her soon, she ached for him. She no longer felt guilty about her feelings towards him. James obviously didn't love her enough to want to stay. He was more in love with his gold than he was with her she decided angrily.

Then finally in the third week in February there he was, her beloved Stephen. This time there was no preamble; he rode straight up to the house, picked her up and took her to bed. Their first encounter was wild and rushed as they tried to satisfy the hunger that burned bright within them both. At last they lay back on the pillows smiling and contented, the sheets drenched in sweat. They continued to make love for the rest of the day and into the night. Somewhere during the night when the air had cooled down, they got up and made something to eat before heading back to bed.

It was late morning before they dragged themselves out of bed, weak kneed and giggling. The dogs wouldn't let them be, they jumped all over the lovers demanding food.

'So, what brings you here to see me now?' Meg asked as they sat and ate.

'I asked Henry for some time off, told him I had a few things I needed to do.'

The smile on his face left Meg under no illusion as to what that meant. 'And Henry was only too happy to let me go; I haven't had a holiday for the past three years. He thinks I've gone to Christchurch.'

Meg giggled as Stephen told her of the extra-ordinary lengths he had gone to, to make sure he wasn't seen heading up the valley. He'd packed some belongings in his saddle bags and headed off up the track as if he was going to town. As soon as he was out of sight and off the property, he rode the neighbouring fence line up and over the hill into the valley below, the valley which would lead him to Meg.

'I scouted the property while I was mustering last Spring and found a way down in to this valley which was out of sight of anyone who might be working at Flaxbush. It took me a lot longer to get here but at least I am here. I doubt that Henry will be sending anyone here to check on you for a while. More than likely it will be early Autumn and then again before it snows.'

Stephen stayed at Stony Downs for three weeks. It was the happiest three weeks of his entire life. He was madly in love with Meg now and dreaded having to leave her and return to Flaxbush.

'If James doesn't come home before winter sets in I could ask Henry if he thinks it wise that perhaps I come and stay with you. I don't think he suspects how we feel about each other.'

'Let's wait and see when the time comes,' said Meg hesitantly. 'I think you will find Henry suspects more than you think.'

The last thing she wanted was for James to turn up and find Stephen there again. She wasn't sure how she would handle such a situation.

210

After Stephen left, Meg picked up the reins of her solo life again and carried on. Summer turned into Autumn and then late Autumn. Chilly rains beckoned the winter snows but there was still no sign of James. Meg wondered if perhaps he might not come home this winter. Stephen had told her about how the gold fever took hold of people and consumed their lives.

'If he has gold fever Meg, he won't want to leave under any circumstance if there is any possibility of finding gold no matter how slim the chances,' Stephen had warned her.

Meg wasn't sure whether James could be lured into such an addiction but then she remembered how his face had lit up when he spoke about his findings and how proud he was of his leather pouch of nuggets.

The first snowflakes started falling in late June. Stephen had been back three times but only for two days at a time. On the last occasion he had come over at Henry's insistence to see if Meg was prepared for the winter and to bring her back to Flaxbush if he had any doubts.

Stephen had reported back to Henry that Mrs Morley was in good spirits and well ready for another dark winter sojourn. He did suggest however that, as James hadn't made an appearance and hadn't sent word of his whereabouts or impending return that perhaps he might go and stay at Stony Downs to look after the stock and the property, and Meg of course,' he'd added as if it were an after-thought.

'I know Marshall has usually been the one to go but since his mother has taken ill I think he wants to be able to go and see her whenever he can. I think he would fret if he was stuck in the valley.'

'Yes, yes you are right of course. Let's leave it for another week or so Stephen and see what happens,' Henry had said. 'I'd hate to think of James returning and finding you there and you not being able to get back. The three of you stuck there living together doesn't sound like an ideal situation to me. I have noticed that you and James have never really cottoned on to one another. Is it just a personality clash? What is it you don't like about the man?'

Stephen was a bit taken aback by the question but recovered quickly and said, 'No I don't like the man much Henry. I can't understand why he would leave his wife and property to go off gallivanting around the countryside all the time. Either he wants to be married and be a husband and farmer; or he does not. It just doesn't make sense to me. I worry about Meg, she's a lovely woman and deserves better than the way James treats her. At least that's the way I feel.'

'I understand Stephen and if truth be told I heartily agree with you. Let's see if the man turns up over the next few days and as soon as it looks like heavy snow we'll make a decision then shall we?'

Stephen watched the weather closely and prayed it would turn to snow before James turned up.

The days dragged by with no sign of James then finally Henry called Stephen inside to discuss what they were going to do.

'I've had a chat with Marshall and as you say he's not at all keen to be too far away from being able to get to his Mum if her condition should worsen. It could be that we are in for heavy snow in the next couple of days, so I guess it's up to you. If you want to go then I won't stop you, but I will need you back here as soon as the way is clear for you to get back safely.'

Stephen fought hard to contain his excitement. A whole winter holed up with Meg, nothing could be better. He was beside himself. He went straight to his bunkroom and started packing. Little did he know that his world was about to change, dramatically.

'Stephen, Stephen, come quick, it's Ma, she's sick.'

Stephen threw open the door of his bunkroom. It was still very early in the morning; he was just finishing up the last of his packing ready to head off down the valley to his beautiful Meg.

'What is it Howard?' He could see the boy was upset. He was shaken and pale and there was fear in his eyes.

'Dad doesn't know what's wrong with Mum. He couldn't wake her up, she won't wake up,' he sobbed.

Stephen was stunned. He was talking with her only yesterday and she seemed fine. He put an arm around Howard and led him back to the house.

'Stephen, thank God you are still here. I don't know what's happened. She was fine when we went to bed last night, I could feel her tossing about in the night, but I didn't think it was any more than restlessness. I've sent Marshall in to town to get the Doctor. Stephen, I think she's dead. I have no idea how I am going to cope without her,' he said looking back at the bed and the woman in it whom he loved so dearly.

Stephen put the kettle on and fussed about making a pot of tea. He didn't quite know what else to do, his mind was in turmoil. On the one hand he was shocked and very upset about Gladys and how Henry was going to cope; but on the other he was bitterly disappointed that his opportunity to spend precious time with Meg was slowly slipping away.

Stephen sat with Henry beside the bed while they sipped their tea in silence. When Henry reached for Gladys's hand and started talking to her Stephen left and went in search of the children. They were huddled on Jenny's bed. The girls were crying and Howard was trying to calm them.

'Stephen, is Mother dead?' Clementine's wee voice stirred his heart.

'Yes Clemmie, I'm afraid she is.'

He sat down with them on the edge of the bed as they dissolved into tears of utter despair.

The Doctor confirmed that Gladys died of a heart attack. Marshall didn't come back with the Doctor, he stopped along the way back to let friends and neighbours know of the tragedy.

'Doc says she knew there was something not right with her heart. They talked about it at her last check-up, but she never said anything to me about it. Damn, why couldn't she have told me, warned me, instead of this,' Henry was angry.

He sprung up out of his chair, grabbed his coat off the peg by the door and went outside to put his boots on.

'Where are you going Henry?'

'I need to be by myself for a bit. You keep an eye on the children for me will you Stephen, see if you can get them in to bed, not that the poor little buggers are likely to sleep much anyway.'

Stephen and Howard got the girls into bed and left them crying quietly into their pillows then they made sure the Doctor also had a bed for the night.

'Howard, how about you get yourself off to bed now too, I will wait here for your dad. I can sleep on the couch tonight.'

'Thanks Stephen,' Howard said as he headed off to his room. He stopped at the door and turned back. 'Stephen,' he said quietly.

'Yes Howard, what is it?'

'I'm glad you're here.'

'Me too Howard, me too.'

And he was. Despite his disappointment at not being able to get to Meg he was very glad to have still been here when Henry and his family needed him the most.

The following days were a blur of people sitting around in tears trying to console each other and making vain attempts to eat and drink. The Doctor rode back to town to talk to an undertaker and make arrangements for the funeral.

A carriage arrived early one afternoon.

'Probably another one of the neighbours,' Stephen said as they all craned their necks to look out the window.

But it wasn't the neighbours it was Gladys's sister Eunice and her husband Mark. The children ran out and threw their arms around their beloved Aunty and Uncle sobbing and all trying to talk at once. Eunice was overcome.

'Come on children let's get you inside, it's cold out here,' she managed through her tears.

Henry was visibly relieved but surprised to see them.

'How did you get here so quickly?' he asked releasing his sister in law from a warm bear hug.

'Young Marshall sent word to us when he was in town fetching the Doctor. I guess he thought we might be needed here.'

'Smart lad,' smiled Henry. 'Gladys died of a heart attach; did you know?'

'Yes, we passed the Doctor along the way and he told us. Oh Henry, I am so truly sorry. Gladdy was such a lovely woman and the best sister I could ever have had; she was such a love to me when we were growing up. Always the bossy one because she was the eldest, but I did love her so.'

Mark wrapped his arms around his wife and held her close as she sobbed into his shoulder.

'There's a lot to talk about and sort out,' mumbled Henry. 'But let's not get into that now. All I want to do is give Gladys the send-off she deserves, will you help me with the arrangements please?'

The children kept themselves occupied decorating the wool shed where the service would be held. Marshall and Stephen dug the grave in the white picket fenced off area behind the house. The small family cemetery began 50 years earlier with the first occupant. Gladys would be

214

the fourth, Meg and James' baby, although not a true family member, was the third. Howard found some bits of wood and made a cross using some of his mother's white wash to paint it with. The girls found some wild flowers and one or two late roses from their mother's garden to put on the table that would serve as an altar. One of the roses was tied to the centre of the cross.

Despite the recent snowfall people came from miles around to pay their respects.

'Meg should be here Stephen,' said Henry as he watched people arriving. 'She would want to be here. She will be heart broken when she learns of Gladys passing.'

'I know Henry. I did consider trying to get down to bring her back but even if I could get through it would all be over by the time we got back. The main river crossing is well up and almost impassable already. I went down and had a look a couple of days ago and we've had more rain since then. I'm afraid Meg is trapped now until the Spring thaw.'

Unwelcome visitors – Winter 1871

A shot rang out echoing around the hills splitting the peaceful silence like a knife. A stillness hung in the valley as it always did right before a storm. Maybe it was thunder, Meg thought. She grabbed her coat and went outside.

'Maybe its James, come home at last,' she said to the dogs.

They weren't so sure, the bristles on the backs of their necks stood straight up and they were sticking close to Meg, protecting her from whatever danger they perceived was out there. Meg's heart was pounding as she cautiously stepped out from under the verandah into the gloomy overcast light. Seeing nothing untoward she turned to go back inside when she heard voices whooping and hollering from up the hill behind the house. She watched, stunned, as three riders came crashing out through the trees each carrying a gun. The dogs started barking wildly at the intruders. The riders stopped short when they saw Meg standing beside the house, the dogs snarling protectively beside her.

'Well, well, well, what have we here then,' said one of the men smiling broadly. 'Didn't s'pect to find any habitants hereabouts did we boys?' he laughed. 'This looks like a mighty fine place to hide I reckon.'

Meg stood defiant, hand on hips feigning a courage she didn't feel.

'Where have you come from? Who are you? I know you aren't from around here.'

'No Ma'am we're from the army. We got us some leave and thought we might get us some wild venison.'

'Be a mighty nice change from bloody mutton,' laughed another of the men. 'Sorry to frighten you. We've come us a long way, any chance of a nice brew and something' to eat?'

Meg was hesitant. She was on her own now. Since the last heavy rainfall she knew the valley was no longer accessible from either end.

'How did you get in here, the rivers are flooded, there's no way in or out.'

'We got across the river just in time. We've been making our way across this ridge back there looking for a way down into the valley.'

Meg decided she didn't have much of a choice but to do as the men asked. She was trapped here on her own now. If they wanted to harm her there was nothing she could do about it. The men dismounted and tied their horses to some matagouri bushes behind the house.

'Where have you come from?' Meg asked again.

'We came up from Hakatere across this mountain range behind us. Bit of a wild ride, taken us a few days. Thought we might find a way across to the West Coast.'

'I do have a surveyors map that shows a crossing,' hope rose in Meg's heart.

The men crowded into the house filling the room with their stench. The dogs were not at all happy with the invasion, but they took their lead from their mistress. The men acted like they hadn't eaten in days and they certainly hadn't taken the time to wash. They didn't appear to be carrying any supplies with them and she didn't like the way they started rummaging through her shelves.

'Why don't you go and wait under the verandah and I will get you some bread and cheese and a cup of tea. I can't do anything while you are all crowded around in here.'

They didn't move for a moment, one of them eyeing her with a lascivious leer.

'Morty, get your damned arse out there and keep an eye out and leave this poor woman alone.'

The two dogs were standing beside Meg, soft threatening growls rumbling in their throats. The dirty stinking letch grunted his disapproval but did as he was told. The others grabbed up Megs chairs and took them out under the verandah. Meg's mind was racing as she prepared the men some food. The dogs stayed close beside her. She had no doubt that they would attack to protect her, but she didn't want any harm coming to them either. She took bread and cheese out hoping it would keep them happy for a while.

'Why did one of them have to keep an eye out,' she wondered.

The men shovelled the food into their mouths and asked for more.

'All I can do is put on some stew,' said Meg sullenly. She wasn't happy watching her precious food supplies disappear down the throats of these awful men.

'I guess we can wait for that, can't we boys,' grunted the larger of the three men, the obvious ring leader. 'Might give us a chance to get some shut eye, haven't slept much lately.'

Meg busied herself with the makings of a stew. The thought went through her mind that perhaps she could put some poison in it but quickly dispensed with the thought before it took hold.

'You are not a murderer Meghan Morley,' she chastised herself.

The men ate the whole pot of stew and another loaf of bread along with some more cheese.

'The food won't last long if you continue to eat like that,' she scolded them.

'Don't worry ma'am we don't plan on stayin long, we still need to get across to the West Coast. Now where's that map you was talkin about?'

Meg rummaged under the bed and dragged out the wooden box containing James old maps. She looked through them selecting one and brought it to the table to spread it out in front of the men. She didn't like the way they leant over her; it was unnerving. The dogs must have sensed it too because they nudged the men aside to get closer to her.

'Now here is the crossing. If you follow the track to here, you will have to get across the river here. It is wider and doesn't flow as fast as this one out here does so you might find a good place to cross if it doesn't rain or snow again before you get there.'

219

'Worth giving it a try I guess, thanks for this,' said the ring leader as he rolled up the map intending to keep it. 'Right, now boys, best we get some more shut eye, we got an early start in the morning.'

Two of the men curled up in front of the fire much to the dogs' disgust. That was their space. The ring leader was eyeing up Megs bed which made her feel sick to her stomach.

'I don't share my bed with anyone but my husband,' she said defiantly with hands on hips.

The man laughed. 'Until now sweetie, until now.'

He reached out for her and she stepped backwards until her back hit the side wall of the house. The dogs were snarling and growling and creeping slowly towards the man with full menace. He turned and looked at them then back at Meg and shrugged deciding it wasn't worth getting attacked for.

'You're lucky I don't shoot those damn dogs of yours. But you bein out here all alone I figure you need them more than they need you.'

Meg let out a sigh of relief, 'Yes you are right about that, I don't think I could survive out here without my dogs.'

The man backed down. 'Just why are you out here alone anyways?'

'My husband has caught the gold fever, he goes away a lot but he's due back any time, in fact I thought that was him when you showed up.'

'Hmmph,' the man uttered pondering this bit of information over. If her husband was due back soon then it was probably best he didn't generate any more trouble than they were already in. A jealous and angry husband was more likely to use a gun than words and he didn't fancy the idea of being shot.

'Right then, I'll just sleep over here by the wall. G'night ma'am and thank you for feeding us it was mighty neighbourly of you.'

Relieved, she climbed into bed fully clothed the dogs snuggled up close beside her. Despite her nervousness she did manage to get some sleep.

Early next morning Meg cooked up some eggs for the men, served up with more bread and cheese. They thanked her for her hospitality and saddled up ready for their journey.

Just as they were about to mount their steeds a voice rang out from the hill behind the house, making Meg and the dogs jump in fright.

'What now?' she thought wildly staring up the hill, 'more of them?'

The dogs started barking, they were already on high alert, the hair on the back of their necks bristling.

'Put your guns down on the ground and raise your hands in the air boys,' called the authoritative voice. 'This is the end of the road for you, there's four rifles aimed on you right now so you might as well come peaceably.'

Sighing, the men reluctantly put their weapons on the ground at their feet as four armed Policemen came out from behind the bushes. Their horses were tethered further back up the hill when they spotted the escapees horses and crept down to the house to surprise them. The Sergeant came over to Meg.

'Are you alright Ma'am? Did they hurt you?'

'No, I am fine thank you Sir, just a bit shaken.'

'I'm sorry they frightened you.'

'It's not every day I get visitors way up here and these types of visitors are not the sort I want to see again any time soon,' she attempted a smile.

'Don't worry Ma'am, I doubt you will be seeing their likes again, it's quite a hike they've been on, we came up the river hoping to cut them off. They have been eluding us for several days now. Glad we finally caught up with them before they did any harm.'

'Would you like some tea and something to eat Sergeant?'

'Thank you, Ma'am, but no we need to get these guys locked up before nightfall if we can. There is a wagon waiting for us back up over the hill on the neighbouring property that will keep them secure until we get them back to the gaol in Christchurch.'

'I thought the only way in and out of here was via the valley?' Meg said.

'Well yes, it is, unless you want to spend several days bush whacking and getting cut to ribbons fighting your way through brush and scrub and climbing over mountains,' he smiled ruefully.

'Is that what you have to do to get these men back to Christchurch then?' asked Meg taking in his dirty ragged and torn uniform.

'Yes, I'm afraid so. I just hope we can get down the other side of this range before we get any more snow; it's getting pretty deep up there already. We have more men waiting on the other side and we will need to

221

camp out on the way back, but the farmers are more than happy to let us use their sheds when we are passing through their properties.'

'They didn't tell me they were escaped convicts,' said Meg. 'How did they escape?'

The Sergeants cheeks reddened.

'They were being transported from the courthouse to the prison when they broke free of their bindings, overpowered us and took off with our horses. I'm sure there will be some explaining to do when we get back,' he grinned sheepishly.

Finally, the Sergeant turned and instructed his men to get everyone saddled up ready for the return journey over the hill.

'Best we get back up and over the top to the others before sundown,' he instructed his men. Meg was relieved to see the seven men all heading back up the hill, three of them heavily trussed and tied. As soon as they were out of sight she sank down on to one of the chairs shaking like a leaf, a huge lump in her throat. Buster and Sally came up to give her wet soppy kisses. She bent over and buried her face in their fur and sobbed.

'I am so glad you were here with me my darlings. What would I have done without you?'

Meg didn't sleep well for several nights after the men left and would spend her days wandering around the house muttering to herself incoherently. Eventually the tiredness crept up on her and sleep took over. The dogs progressed from sleeping in front of the fire to sleeping at the foot of the bed and were now sleeping on top of the bed with her.

'To hell with what James thinks my darlings,' she told them, 'you are my protectors now; he's not here to do it.'

She giggled as the dogs snuggled up one on either side of her as she slid down into the middle of the bed.

One – James's Folly

As James rode in through the front gate of Flaxbush Station the impact of the previous months hit him hard. His friends were no longer there. Henry, Gladys and the children were all gone now. The place had an air of sorrow and loneliness about it that was almost palpable. He slid off his horse beside the gate leading to the house, the house that he now owned. It seemed to be a hollow victory right now as he stood looking at the home that held no life.

'So, you finally decided to show up again.'

The voice startled James; he hadn't heard Stephen walking up behind him.

'Yes Stephen, I'm back. Thank you for looking after the place for me, I really appreciate it.'

'I didn't look after it for you,' spat Stephen. 'I'm looking after it until the new owners arrive.'

'You're looking at the new owner.'

Stephen was stunned. 'You?' he spat. 'How is it that you are the new owner?' He was none too pleased about the idea of James owning Flaxbush.

'I arrived in town a couple of weeks ago and heard about Gladys. It must have come as a great shock to the family. And Meg too of course, she was very fond of Gladys.'

'Meg doesn't know.'

'What do you mean Meg doesn't know. Gladys died months ago, why didn't anyone go and tell her, she would have wanted to be at her funeral.' James' fists were clenched and his jaw tightened.

Stephen was incensed.

'You limey, selfish, fucking bastard. How the hell can you stand there and begin to know anything about what has gone on here while you were away doing whatever it was you were doing with whoever you were doing it with.'

He stood nose to nose with James ready to take a swing at him. James took a step back, drew a deep breath and let out a sigh.

'You're right Stephen, I'm sorry. I have no idea what has been happening here. Look, I'm pretty beat from riding all day, why don't we go inside and sit down over a beer and have a chat. I think we both owe each other that much. I know we will never be friends but at least let's try to get along for now. In the long term I would like to keep you on here to manage the property if you have a mind to.'

Stephen dropped his hunched shoulders and also took deep breath. He hated James for the way he treated Meg, but he also loved Flaxbush Station and if he wanted to stay on he would have to toe the line. He accepted James's offer of a beer.

The house hadn't been lived in since the family moved out. Some of the basic furniture still remained but all the soft furnishings and memorabilia that make a house a home were missing. James shuddered.

'Not the same anymore is it.'

'Nothing's the same any more James, it never will be.'

James pulled two bottles of beer from his saddle bag and placed one in front of Stephen.

'Right then, let me tell you what I know then I would very much like to hear everything about what has been going on here since I left, especially about Meg. How is my wife these days?'

Stephen bristled but kept his cool.

'I wouldn't rightly know how she is James. Meg has been holed up alone since the first heavy rains back in May. Nobody has been able to get in to check on her since. I have tried, believe me I have tried.'

James was concerned. 'So Gladys passed away late May and by then Meg was already trapped in the valley?'

'Yes, we knew she would be devastated and want to be there but there was no way in, the rivers came up after the first heavy rains then it snowed and that was that, the valley was cut off completely. Every now and then I try to find a way in but the rivers are still running too high although I noticed yesterday that the levels are starting to drop now that the spring thaw is almost over. We haven't had a decent snow fall since the end of August.'

'Five months,' James hung his head. 'That poor girl has been trapped in there on her own for five months.'

'James you bloody astound me. How can you sit there and worry about your wife now? You have been gone for almost a year and only now you worry about her? What is wrong with you? She's a beautiful woman, you have neglected your duty as a husband and provider. You have left her to fend for herself while you just ride off and leave her. Where the hell have you been anyway?'

James drew a deep slow breath, let it out and slumped down in his chair.

'Stephen, everything you say is true. I've allowed myself to get caught up in my own selfish dreams and desires. By that I don't mean I have been with other women, far from it, no I have been chasing the gold. Once you get a taste of it, the gold fever takes you over. At least it did me. I have been down in the Skippers area sluicing, and doing pretty well I might add,' he smiled ruefully. 'Found enough to buy Flaxbush Station outright and still have plenty left over.'

Stephen was shocked. 'That's an awful lot of gold, I thought Skippers was running dry on gold.'

'My partner seemed to have a nose for it, and we were lucky enough to come across an area that appeared to have been worked over but when we sluiced it we found an untouched seam underneath that had been missed. Of course, we didn't mention it to anyone, we just let everyone go on believing the place had been well worked over. And to all intents and purposes it had, we were just lucky enough to find what we did.'

Neither men spoke for a while, they both sat in silence deep in thought. Then Stephen spoke up.

'So, you are the new owner then?'

225

'Yes, I surely am. It's a bitter sweet victory being that the Hopkins family had to undergo such a tragedy and fall apart before I could purchase this land. I'm going to need all the help I can get Stephen and I am hoping you will stay on, as I said before, and manage the property for me. I will increase your salary and catch you up on any monies that are owed to you since Henry left.'

Stephen nodded his head slowly looking James right in the eye. He held out his hand.

'Thank you James, yes I would be happy to take up the position.'

They shook on the deal. 'So, what about Meg?' Stephen asked.

'What about her?' asked James raising an eyebrow.

'Well, she's not going to like leaving the valley is she. I mean, she's been happy there, I can't see her wanting to move back here to this place, it just isn't her.'

James was affronted. 'Don't begin to tell me what my wife might or might not like Stephen. I'm sure being stuck in the valley for the past five months has put her off staying there now. Besides I plan to build on to this place and turn it in to a fine homestead for her.'

Stephen held his tongue. He knew full well that Meg would probably not want to move away from the valley, despite being trapped there all winter. He figured he knew her better than her husband did. He was curious to see if he was right, and if he was, how was James going to deal with it.

Two weeks after James arrived at the farm the management duties were all sorted out and assigned to Stephen. He would pretty much run the property the way he thought best with the help of two newly hired hands. Marshall left soon after the Hopkins moved out leaving Stephen to look after the property the best he could. The neighbours had been a godsend though, calling in every week to offer whatever help was needed.

The builders and building materials arrived and James hoped the renovations to the Hopkins home would be completed by Christmas. He planned on riding to Stony Downs in a couple of days to see Meg and surprise her with the news that he had purchased Flaxbush Station. He was confident she would love the house and become the perfect hostess for the many parties and visitors he planned on having out to visit his new estate. He was a wealthy landowner now and he was determined to behave as other landed gentry did. He decided that he would leave her in the valley until the house was finished if she wanted to.

Stephen watched the progress of the renovations with interest. He was pretty sure James had no idea what a challenge he had coming up with regards to getting Meg to move. And while he was anxious for Meg, he was keen to see how James was going to handle it. The main reason he accepted James' offer was so that he could stay and keep a close eye on Meg. He wasn't about to let her out of his sight again. He just prayed that she was safe. He had been itching to have another go at getting in to see her, but his farm management duties and the new hired hands were keeping him well occupied with the Spring muster just around the corner.

Meg's dogs were the first to spot James as he rode up towards the house. He was relieved to see smoke wafting up lazily from the chimney forming a white streak against the clear blue of the sky overhead. The air was dead still. It was a perfect Spring day. Meg appeared at the door wiping her hands on her trousers peering out to see what or who the dogs were barking at. She shaded her eyes against the rising sun then realizing who the rider was let out a shriek and ran up to meet him. James's horse shied away and he had to rein it in. He slid off the horse and held his arms open to greet his wife. She leapt into his arms and clung around his neck, feet lifting off the ground.

'James, oh my goodness, is it really you? I had almost given you up for dead. Where have you been all this time?'

She loosened her grip from around his neck and he took her arms pushing her away from him so he could look at her.

'Meg, you are a sight for sore eyes. I wasn't sure if or how you survived the winter. I heard you have been trapped here since May. Are you okay? You certainly look well and healthy.'

'I am James, I am. It was a very long and difficult few months, but we survived, didn't we my darlings.' She ruffled the dog's fur.

The dogs were standing protectively beside Meg but relaxed when they had sniffed out the intruders were family.

'Come, let's get you inside, the kettle is on the boil.' Meg linked her arm through James' and they walked back to the house.

As soon as they both sat down James took Meg's hand.

'I have news Meg, lots of news and not all of it good I'm afraid.'

Meg sat for a moment preparing herself. She took a deep breath and letting it out slowly said, 'Alright James, what is the not so good news. Tell me.'

'Meg, I'm so terribly sorry to have to tell you this but Gladys has passed away.'

Meg was stunned. James allowed time for the news to sink in.

'Gladys is dead? No, this can't be. Not dear Gladys. Oh no James this can't be true, please tell me it isn't true.'

'I'm sorry Meg but it is true.'

Meg jumped up from her chair.

'Henry, the children, we must go. They will need us. Gladys, oh my dear sweet Gladys.'

Tears were streaming down Megs cheeks. James got up and sat her firmly down in the chair again.

'Meg sit down. There's nothing we can do. Gladys died back in May.'

'In May? In May? All those months ago and nobody came to tell me?'

Meg was furious. She stood up again and started pacing around the room fists clenched, her face contorted with grief and disbelief.

'At the time she died Meg the weather packed in and nobody has been able to get in until now. They did try, truly they did. Stephen said he has been trying to get in to see you ever since.'

'Well if Stephen wasn't able to find a way in then I guess nobody could have,' cried Meg and walked off outside.

James could hear her sobbing, but he decided to let her to grieve for a while on her own before he told her the rest of his news.

After about an hour Meg took off on Jasper, the dogs following. James did not try to stop her.

It was dark by the time she returned home. James had a pot of mutton stew on the fire and some of Megs red plum wine at the ready. Megs eyes were red and puffy from crying so James decided to leave the rest of the news until morning, hoping she would at least get a little bit of sleep.

Meg didn't look much better the next morning and she was still distant from James. Despite his being away for almost a year she didn't seem to want or need any comfort from him. This disturbed him a little, but he decided perhaps it was just the grief that was holding her back. After all she had been pleased to see him the previous times he had returned after being away for months at a time. He would wait until she had gotten over her grief before he tried to approach her again.

Later in the day Meg sat down at the table with James.

'So, what other news do you have for me James. I trust no one else has died.'

'No Meg, I promise, no one else has died. In fact, I think you will be pleased with the rest of my news, at least I hope you will be.'

'Well then you had better tell me what it is.'

There was no life in Meg's eyes, only sadness and despair. James was hoping to change that.

'I was in Christchurch on my way back to see you last month when I heard the news about Gladys. Upon making further enquiries I learned that Henry and the children had gone to live with Gladys's sister Eunice and her husband Mark, and that Henry had put Flaxbush Station on the market. So I enquired at the Land Office to see if this was true and when I found out that it was I purchased it.'

Meg looked disbelievingly at James.

'You purchased Flaxbush?? With what? How could you have purchased that whole station? Did you get a loan without talking with me first?'

James reached out and took Meg's hand, but she pulled away from him.

'It's alright Meg I purchased it outright, in cash. I found more gold Meg, a lot more gold. We are rich, beyond our wildest dreams.'

He let the news sink in for a few moments.

'I am renovating the Hopkins homestead for you Meg. It will be grand, two stories and big wide verandahs and....'

'Stop. Please just stop James. How could you. How could you do all this without talking it over with me first. Are we not a married couple anymore? Do we not do things together now? You go your way and I go mine, is that it?'

Megs words were bitter. James was shocked.

'Meg I know you are grieving for Gladys right now, maybe we should talk about this another time.'

'Talk about what? It appears to me you have already made all the decisions.'

229

'I wanted to surprise you, I wanted to get the house finished so that when you moved to Flaxbush at Christmas it would all be done and ready for you. I would like to consult with you on the furnishings though. Would you like that?'

'No, I would not. I do not want to move into that house. Not now, not ever. It was Gladys' house; it will never be mine. I hate you James, I hate what you have become, and I hate what you have done. And if truth be told I hate that you keep leaving me for so long. What kind of a man does that to his wife?'

She went and sat on the side of the bed. The sound coming from way down deep in her soul began as a deep guttural moan rising up in her throat and spewing forth in a scream of such torment and anguish it frightened James. He watched in horror as his lovely Meg transformed into someone he no longer recognized. Her face was contorted with grief and pain and she hunched over hugging her knees to her chest rocking back and forth, howling like nothing he had ever heard before. He had no idea what to do. Dumbfounded he sat and watched her. The dogs jumped up on the bed and snuggled in around her in attempt to offer comfort. James also tried to get close to her, but the dogs snarled at him, so he backed off. Not knowing what else to do he grabbed up his hat and pipe and went off for a walk down by the river out of earshot.

When he returned over an hour later, she was curled up on the bed in a foetal position eyes open and staring at the wall.

'Meg?' he reached out to touch her. The dogs growled but he ignored them. He knelt down beside the bed. 'Meg?' he tried again. She didn't respond, she didn't seem to know he was there.

'Meg, I am so very sorry to have brought you such bad news and caused you so much pain. I don't know what to do for you right now. Can I get you some water?'

He went to the earthenware jug at the end of the bench and filled a cup with water. He took it back to the bed and offered it to her. She didn't move. He shifted the dogs to one side ignoring their distrust and pulled her into a sitting position and tried to get her to drink. She was like a floppy rag doll; she didn't respond to anything. He placed the cup of water on the floor, threw his legs up on the bed and pulled Meg into his arms and cradled her. Eventually she fell asleep. He decided all she needed was a good night's sleep; she would be back to her old self again in the morning.

But she wasn't. Far from it. The Meg he knew was not the Meg who lay curled up in the bed, unmoving, unresponsive.

James had no idea what to do for Meg. He had never had to deal with a situation like this before. Meg had always been the strong capable one in their relationship and, much as he disliked it, he drew comfort from knowing that he could leave her when he went off on his jaunts knowing that she could look after herself. But this Meg was a different being altogether.

He had to get back to Flaxbush and keep an eye on the building and renovations. He didn't want them making any mistakes or taking matters into their own hands when it came to decision making. He stayed for another night hoping that Meg would come around.

Early the following morning he woke up to see Meg standing beside the bed looking at him.

'I won't move to Flaxbush James. I won't live in poor dear Gladys' home. It was her home it will never be mine. I'm staying here, you can do what you want.'

With that she turned on her heel and went and sat outside under the verandah. James lay in bed for a while trying to get his head around Meg's behaviour. He was getting angry now and short of patience. This was not what he planned; this was not how things were supposed to be. He needed Meg to be by his side at the new Flaxbush Station homestead, to be the gracious hostess when they had visitors. He would get servants to do the housekeeping and cooking, all she had to do was play the dutiful hostess and run the household and hopefully in time bear him healthy children. He got up and got dressed and went outside to relate his thoughts to her. She listened in silence then turned to look at him with such disgust that he recoiled at the look on her face.

'I will never be that person James. How could you ask that of me! What do you see before you? Do I look like a dutiful gracious housewife? I am a free spirit James, I am broken by grief, I have been so used to living wild and free all these years, do you honestly expect me to become what you are asking? If you do then you don't know me at all. I will not move to Flaxbush. I don't care what you do,' she spat, 'but I will be staying here and that is the end of the matter.'

She stood up and walked off down towards the river with the dogs trotting along beside her.

231

James was furious. He leapt out of his chair knocking it over and ran after her. He grabbed her arm and spun her around. She pulled away from him.

'Let go James, you are hurting me.'

The hatred and bitterness in her eyes shocked him but he didn't let go.

'You will come with me,' he hissed, 'and you will be my wife in every way and that includes running my household as I see fit. I have left you to run free for too long, it is time I took you in hand and brought you back to live life as a normal human being, not this wild free spirit you claim yourself to be.'

Having said his piece James let go of her arm, confident that he had gotten through to her and expecting her compliance. But to his utter surprise she drew back and slapped him hard across the face and snarled, 'Never. Never will I ever conform to your wishes. You are not my master and hell you haven't even been my husband for a very long time so no, you no longer have any control over me, I am staying here and that is that.'

She turned and ran. She ran as fast as her legs could carry her. She ran away from her husband and all that he had told her. She ran from the grief and pain of losing her dearest friend. There was no way on earth she was going to go and live the life James had described, it sounded utterly dreadful.

James stood and watched Meg until she disappeared around the bend in the river. He was trembling. He hated confrontation at any time but this altercation with Meg was so totally unexpected and uncharacteristic that he was at a loss as to what to do. He decided it might be best if he just left her for a while and went back to Flaxbush. Give her some time to calm down. He brought some fresh supplies with him when he arrived, and he could see she had done well to provide for herself during the winter. She looked well and healthy; it was just her mental state that he was concerned about.

'She'll come around,' he thought to himself as he saddled up and rode off back towards Flaxbush.

Meg watched him ride away as she sat down by the river.

'Don't care if I never see that man again,' she whispered to the dogs then giggled and began playfully splashing them with water, much to their delight.

'So, how was Meg?' asked Stephen. 'Did she survive the winter without any trouble?'

James was reluctant to answer; he wasn't sure what to say. Stephen noticed his hesitation and tried to hide a smile.

'She didn't take the news too well did she? About moving back here I mean. No doubt the news about Gladys came as a terrible shock too.'

James nodded, 'Yes it did Stephen, she was extremely upset.'

And with that he walked away. Stephen wasn't sure what to make of James response, but he could tell something was troubling the man. He would talk with him later and see if he could get him to open up about what happened on his trip to Stony Downs.

The renovations to the new homestead were progressing at a steady pace. James was well pleased with how it was shaping up. It was becoming as grand as he hoped it would be. Next would be the furnishings. He planned on having only the best. He doubted Meg would have the class or the knowledge to select such things, so he planned on bringing someone in to do the interior designing and requisitioning. But first he had to make another trip to Stony Downs to see how Meg was coming along. He knew she would come to her senses eventually, she had to, he needed a hostess and home maker.

Meg was not pleased to see James riding back down the valley three weeks later. She hadn't changed her mind and she wasn't about to give in to him. If she was about to lose her husband in the process, then so be it. He hadn't been around for her for a long time now and she had proved she didn't really need him anyway. She would live her life here at Stony Downs alone and she would be happy.

James was hesitant as he approached Meg. She didn't run into his arms this time, nor did she greet him with a smile. She was stony faced, and her eyes held no light or promise. His heart sank. He knew before she even spoke that she hadn't come to her senses, but he didn't give up hope.

'Have you thought about what I asked of you Meg? Are you ready to come and be my wife and my homemaker? I need you to help me run the household. We will be having people to visit on a regular basis, we will be socializing and holding dinner parties, wouldn't you like that?

233

You won't need to do any of the hard work, I will get staff in to do everything for you, you just have to manage the household like the other landed gentry do.'

Meg looked and James and a smile formed on her lips. She started to laugh. The laughter became louder and almost hysterical before she took a deep breath, tears streaming down her cheeks.

'James do you have any idea how pompous and ridiculous you sound. Landed gentry?' she spat. 'Landed gentry! For goodness sake we are no more landed gentry than the dogs here. Just because you found some gold doesn't make you landed gentry, it just makes you pretentious and arrogant. Being gentry is in the breeding James not your mind. Look at me. I mean really look at me. What do you see? You cannot make a silk purse from a sow's ear; do you not understand that? I am not in the least pretentious and I will never be able to become what you expect of me. I suggest you leave me here and go find yourself another wife because I am happy to give you a divorce. You are not the man I married, and I certainly do not like the man you have become. Go back to your new life and leave me here in peace.'

James stood and looked at Meg, stunned. He didn't know this woman she had become. She was strong and resilient, but she was also defiant and angry. He had to admit he was a little afraid of her. She was no longer predictable and controllable. He had left her to her own devices for too long, he needed to bring her back into line again.

'Meg, there will be no divorce. I will not go through the humiliation and embarrassment of a divorce. You and I will present a united front to the world. I don't care whether we have separate lives and bedrooms, but we will live together in the Flaxbush homestead. So long as you play the dutiful wife and hostess, I care little for what else you might wish to do from day to day. I am willing to allow you that much freedom, but you will be coming back with me. The homestead will be completed within the month. If you do not wish to have a say in the furnishings, then I will employ someone to do it. If you do not wish to manage the household then I will employ someone to do that also. You have four weeks before I bring the dray back to get you and your belongings so sort out what you are going to bring with you and what you are going to leave behind.'

With that he remounted his horse and rode off back to Flaxbush before she could raise any more objections.

234

Little Girl Lost

Stephen was amused to see James return from Stony Downs once again without Meg. He knew she must be alright because he had left her there, but he was also extremely curious to know what was going on between them. He could see James was not a happy man. He was short tempered and impatient these days. Finally, one afternoon James and Stephen were sitting outside the shearing shed sipping on their cups of tea.

'James, if you don't mind me asking, what is happening with Meg. When is she coming back? I kinda miss her smiling face. I haven't seen her for nearly a year. Is she well and happy?'

James turned to look at Stephen but did not see anything other than curiosity in his eyes.

'To be perfectly honest with you Stephen I am at a loss as to what to do with that woman. She is adamant that she does not want to move here. I laid the law down to her on my last visit and I gave her four weeks to get herself sorted out before I go back and get her. I'm not sure what I will find when I go back but my gut instinct tells me she won't come willingly. I might have to call on your help. I will physically drag her out of there if I have to.'

Stephen was shocked, 'Surely you don't mean to hog tie her and drag her kicking and screaming back to where she doesn't want to be?'

'If I have to Stephen, yes that is exactly what I will do. She is my wife and she will do as I bid.'

'Look do you think it would help if I went down and had a chat with her. Got her to see sense?'

James stared at Stephen, 'What on earth makes you think you would make any difference Stephen. I know you have always had a soft spot for my Meg, but I can't see as how you could make her change her mind if I can't, you hardly know her.'

'Sometimes, someone outside the situation can take a different independent approach. Someone who is not involved emotionally; if you know what I mean.'

James was silent for a moment then he sighed and jumped down off the fence he had been sitting atop of.

'Well, I suppose it won't do any harm, you can give it a try if you wish. I'm darned sure I don't know what else I can do to persuade her.'

Stephen was beside himself with excitement at seeing Meg again. It had been far too long since their last meeting and he had missed her terribly. He rode up towards the house half expecting her to run out and greet him but there was no sign of life apart from the smoke drifting up from the chimney. No dogs barked or came out to greet him. He dismounted and left his horse to roam and forage. The door was open, but the hut was empty. He walked around the yard checking the sheds. Meg's horse wasn't there so he figured she must be out riding. He sat down on one of the blocks that served as an outdoor seat and lit a cigarette. He was lost in thoughts of Meg as he watched the smoke from his cigarette curl up and form patterns in the stillness of the air. It was peaceful and quiet, but he could hear the sound of the trickle in the river as it navigated a path through the rocky river bed. So lost in thought was he that he didn't hear Meg and the dogs coming towards him until the dogs gave out a yelp of recognition and came bounding over to greet him, the shock of their sudden intrusion knocking him off his seat. Meg sat astride her horse and roared with laughter.

'Gotcha,' she laughed as she got down off Jasper.

Embarrassed, Stephen hauled himself to his feet gave the dogs a quick hug, brushed the dirt off his shirt and trousers and walked over to take Meg in his arms. She backed away and put her hand up to thwart him. Puzzled, Stephen stopped in his tracks.

'Meg, is everything okay? I thought you would be pleased to see me?'

'I am Stephen, did you bring me some supplies? Gladys usually sends supplies; did she send some with you? I could do with another book or two.'

Meg walked over to Stephen's horse and started to undo his saddle bags. He walked after her, took her arm and gently swung her around.

'Get your damned hands off me,' she hissed.

'Meg? It's me, Stephen. You know I wouldn't hurt you.'

Meg looked a bit dazed and stared at Stephen for a moment before recognition dawned on her beautiful face.

'Oh Stephen, yes, yes of course. Yes, I know you wouldn't hurt me. Wouldn't hurt a fly, wouldn't hurt a fly. Come on my lovelies you must be hungry let's go see what's in the pot shall we. Stephen, are you staying to eat with us, I have plenty?'

She turned and walked inside, the dogs trailing obediently behind her.

As Stephen watched her disappear inside his heart broke.

'Oh my Lord Meg, what has he done to you. Where is my beautiful girl, where is my love?'

Meg popped her head out the door again.

'Well come on then Mr Sangster, it's almost dinner time, better go wash up while I dish up.'

Stephen looked up at the sky. It was barely past noon and here was Meg talking about dinner. He went along with her rambling nonsensical conversations and erratic behaviour but inside he was in torment. How was he going to get Meg to agree to leave this place and go and live in Flaxbush.

Stephen slept in the shed behind the house that night and hoped that by morning Meg might be over her delusional behaviour and be more like her old self again. He knocked on her door and when there was no answer, he quietly opened it. Her bed was made but she and the dogs were not there. He went back outside and scanned the horizon; it was still dark in the valley, but the rising sun was beginning to lighten the sky directly above the mountain tops. Once again Stephen lit a cigarette and sat down to wait for Meg to appear. This time he was listening out for her and had to smile when he could hear her whooping and hollering her way up the creek bed with the dogs barking in unison. She pulled Jasper to a breathless stop at the verandah rail and slid off his back. She hadn't even bothered to put a saddle on him.

'How long have you been riding bare back Meg?'

'What? Oh Stephen, there you are, I thought you must have gone home. Bare back, I have always ridden bare back, I think.'

'Meg, we have to have a serious talk. I need you to sit down and listen to me carefully, can we do that now?'

'Not now Stephen the dogs and I are famished, aren't we my darlings?'

They wagged their tails in agreement, anything for extra food. It didn't seem to bother them that their routines were in a shambles.

Stephen watched Meg fumble around with the fire and the hot water as she made a pot of tea. She didn't seem to be able to focus on what she was doing. He offered to help but she snapped at him and told him she was more than capable of making tea thank you very much. Eventually she sat down at the table with him. He reached over and took her hand. She tried to pull it away, but he held fast.

'Meg. Look at me. Look at me Meg. It's me, Stephen.'

'Yes, I know who you are Stephen.'

'But do you remember what we have been to each other Meg?'

'What do you mean Stephen? I know you work for Henry and Gladys and that you used to come over and help out sometimes but that was a long time ago. James is gone now and I am all alone, nobody comes to visit any more. But I don't mind, really I don't, I have a good life here now and I love my beautiful mountains.'

'Meg, listen to me. Look at me and listen to what I have to say.'

Meg looked at Stephen again, but he couldn't see the girl he knew and loved in her vacant eyes. He had to try and get through to her somehow even if he did risk upsetting her.

'Meg, James has bought Flaxbush Station. He bought it for you. He is building the house into a wonderful big homestead for you. Do you understand what I am saying?'

'What is he doing to Gladys's home, he can't do that. Henry wouldn't sell Flaxbush, he can't, they have to stay there. I need for them

238

to stay there, I need them, I need Gladys...I need my dear friend Gladys...'

'Meg, I am so sorry, but Gladys has passed away. Did James not tell you?'

Meg shook her head. 'No, Gladys wouldn't die, she wouldn't leave me here on my own. She just wouldn't.'

'Meg, Gladys got really sick and died. Henry was so upset he couldn't stay living in the house anymore without her,' so the children have gone to live with their Aunt and Uncle in Dunedin and Henry is living there now too. James came back from Skippers with a whole pile of gold in his pockets and bought Flaxbush Station when he heard Henry was selling up. The property belongs to James and you now. It belongs to both of you and James wants you to go and live there with him.'

'I don't want to live with James, he's not a nice man anymore and I don't believe Gladys is dead either. When did she die? Why did nobody come and get me?'

'She died in May Meg. Her heart gave out on her in the end.'

'May? What month is it now?'

'December, it's almost Christmas.'

'Christmas? Oh, there might be a parcel from home. Henry's brother might bring it over when he comes to visit.'

'Come back with me Meg so I can look out for you. You know how much I care about you don't you? You know I would never let you down or do anything to hurt you?'

'No, I'm staying here Stephen. You can go now I have things to do. Go on, off you go, we are busy here aren't we my darlings.'

239

The returning

When Stephen rode into the yard alone, James laughed.

'Ha, you couldn't get through to the stubborn woman either could you?'

Stephen slid off his horse, the look on his face wiping James's smile away.

'What's the matter, she is alright isn't she?'

'No James your wife is far from alright, she is half out of her mind. She seems to have lost her grip on reality. I am really worried about her.'

'What do you mean she's lost her grip on reality?'

James ushered Stephen up on to the verandah.

'Here, come and sit down, tell me what happened?'

Stephen recounted the conversations he'd had with Meg. 'She's not right in the head James, it's heart breaking to see her like that.'

James stood up. 'I will go into town first thing in the morning and go see the doctor and find out what I need to do to help her. Will you look after things here while I'm away?'

'Of course James, you don't need to ask. And don't take too long. I am worried about her hurting herself, she seems to be away with the

241

fairies at times and not concentrating on what she's doing, especially when she's cooking.'

James was alarmed.

'Right you are then, I will get there and back as soon as I can and then you and I can get down there and bring her home.'

'Home,' thought Stephen, 'I doubt she will ever call this place home.'

James was back within the week, but he wasn't alone. He had a woman with him, a rather elegant, handsome looking woman. Stephen stood to one side as James helped the woman down from the carriage.

'Ah Stephen, this is Martha, she is the widow of a former work colleague of mine. We did some surveying together a few years ago. Martha was looking for work, so I have hired her to run the household and help me look after Meg.' He took Stephen to one side.

'I have spoken with the doctor; he will come and see Meg next week as soon as we bring her home. He suggested I try and figure a way of getting her to come back to Flaxbush with me. He said it is vital she is not left alone. He believes she might be having a breakdown given all that she has had to deal with recently, especially with the death of her dearest friend. I will tell her that I am taking her to stay in Christchurch as a Christmas treat. That should do the trick and if I tell her there is a parcel waiting at the Post Office for her it should be enough to get her to come with me.'

'Meg did agree to a trip to Christchurch with James believing that this was a Christmas trip to pick up her parcel from home and to buy some treats. It wasn't until they reached the Flaxbush homestead that Meg became confused again.

'What has Henry done to the house? Doesn't it look grand James.'

'Yes, it does my love. They have gone away for the holidays and left it for us to stay in for as long as we like. Isn't that a wonderful Christmas surprise?'

'I suppose. It would have been better if they were all here with us though, I have missed them, especially Gladys.'

James looked across the top of Meg's head and caught Stephen's eye giving him a nod.

242

'Meg, what a lovely surprise. How are you? We have missed you around here.'

'Hello Stephen, you stayed behind then. Is Marshall here too?'

'No Marshall has moved back to be with his Dad since his Mum passed on.'

'Oh, sorry to hear that. James. Who is that? Who is that woman in Gladys's house?'

'That's Martha, she is the new housekeeper. The house got too big for Gladys to run on her own.' James hoped the lie would satisfy Meg for now.

'I see. Well, you'd best get our things James so we can settle in. It's getting late.'

James looked at Stephen and shrugged. It had only just gone past midday.

James got Meg settled into the house and she seemed to be quite happy to be there. She liked the new furnishings and drapery that she was told Gladys had picked out. During the day she would wander about in the yard or sit under the trees in the orchard singing softly to herself as she made daisy chains with the wild flowers.

Meanwhile James and Martha carried on as if the homestead belonged to them. Martha ran the household and the staff while James spent his time between keeping a watchful eye on the farm and going in to town to frequent his club and meet up with his new found friends. Sometimes he would take Martha with him and they would spend a couple of nights in the hotel together as if they were a couple.

James and Meg shared a bed, but Meg always turned her back on James and wouldn't allow him to touch her. As soon as she was asleep, he would slip out of bed and spend the rest of the night with Martha, creeping quietly back into his own bed before Meg woke up in the morning.

One day when James and Martha were away in town leaving Stephen and the staff to keep an eye on Meg, she went across to the yards to see Jasper and the dogs.

Stephen came out to see her.

'Meg, how are you today? I haven't seen you for a few days.'

'Hello Stephen. I was wondering. When are the Hopkins due back? They have been gone an awfully long time haven't they? And I don't like their new housekeeper, she has her eye on James, I can tell. I think it's time we went back home.'

'My dearest Meg,' said Stephen taking her hands in his. 'Come and sit down, I think it is time we had a chat.'

'What about Stephen? What is going on? Things don't seem right to you either do they?'

'Meg, this is your home now. You have to accept that this is where you belong. You will never want for anything and you will always be well looked after. You are happy here aren't you Meg?'

'No Stephen this is not my home, this is Gladys's home. What are you talking about?'

'Meg, look at me. This is your home now, yours and James. I am here too; I will look out for you. You are safe here. We all love you.'

Slowly realization dawned on Megs face. Her eyes welled up with tears.

'This can't be true Stephen. James has tricked me into being here hasn't he.'

'Meg, I am sorry, but it was the only way he knew how to get you to come here. He only wants what's best for you.'

Stephen knew full well that wasn't the case. He had watched James with that woman, Martha, had seen the way he was with her. He knew they slept together, that's why he decided to try and get through to Meg. He hated the way James treated her.

Meg got up and walked back to the house. Things were beginning to fall into place. She was beginning to remember things. Gladys was dead. This was not her home; James had renovated it. And as for that housekeeper. Yes, she knew he left her bed at night and went to sleep with that woman. She had feigned sleep one night and followed him.

Meg went to her room and dressed in suitable riding clothes. She searched around until she found some old saddle bags and filled them with supplies, including some food for the dogs. As soon as she thought the coast was clear she let her dogs off their chains, went over to the stables and saddled up Jasper. Quickly and quietly she rode out the gates and headed for Stony Downs. Nobody saw her go. The dogs, sensing the need to be stealthy, did not utter a sound when she let them off. She held a finger to her lips to silence them and they obeyed.

244

James and Martha returned the following day. Stephen walked across the yard to help unload the dray.

'How was Meg while we were away Stephen?'

'She was well. She came over to the sheds for a chat yesterday and seemed fine.'

'Good. Let's get these supplies packed away then shall we. We have guests arriving in a couple of days.'

Once the dray was unloaded Stephen began to lead the horses back to the shed.

'Stephen, do you know where Meg is? She doesn't appear to be in the house.'

'Jasper and the dogs are not there either. I think she must have gone for a ride.'

'Oh well that's a good sign. I guess she will turn up when she's ready. Come, Martha, let's get preparations underway for our guests.'

Stephen was concerned. In the weeks since James and Meg had been at Flaxbush, Meg had never once taken Jasper for a ride. She would visit the dogs every day and let them off their chains, but she hadn't been out riding.

'Perhaps our talk yesterday got through to her,' he thought, 'maybe this is a good sign.'

Later that evening James came across to see Stephen in his quarters.

'I'm beginning to get a bit worried about Meg. It's dark now and she hasn't returned. You don't think she may have fallen off her horse do you?'

'I'm not sure James. Have you checked to see if she has taken any clothing or food with her? Are all the saddle bags still there?'

'I never thought to check. Come with me would you please?'

Both men checked the sheds and the house for signs of missing food, clothing and saddle bags.

'There's two saddle bags missing James.'

'There seems to be some clothing missing too but I can't be sure, and Martha tells me there are some supplies missing from the cupboards.' He paused for a moment. 'You don't think she would have gone back down to Stony Downs do you?'

'It wouldn't surprise me James, it wouldn't surprise me at all.'

'Damn and blast that woman. We have got guests arriving tomorrow and she has to go and pull a stunt like this.'

'James, the girl is unwell, you know that. I'm sure if she has gone back to Stony Downs she will be alright there for a few days until you can get down there to bring her back.'

'Will you go Stephen? Will you go and bring her back? I just can't spare the time at the moment. Jack can take care of things while you are away can't he?'

'Yes, he is quite capable, but I really think it ought to be you going to get her not me.'

'Please Stephen, these people who are coming to stay are of high standing in the community and I need to gain their approval.'

Stephen was furious. 'I will go James, but I am not happy about this.'

'Thank you, Stephen. Oh, and please don't bring her back until next Monday, our guests will be gone by then.'

It was all Stephen could do not to punch the man.

Meg greeted Stephen with a warm smile when he turned up.

'Hello Mr Sangster,' she giggled. 'What are you doing here?'

'I have come to take you home Meg.'

'This is my home Stephen and why didn't James come himself? Too busy with Martha is he?'

'Meg I'm sorry it has come to this. James is an insensitive fool; he doesn't deserve you.'

'No, I don't think he does either,' she giggled again. What about you Stephen, do you think you deserve me?'

She fluttered her eyelashes at him flirtatiously.

'Meghan Morley,' he laughed, 'I have never known you to be such a flirt.'

'Neither have I,' she laughed, 'but there's always a first time isn't there.'

Stephen wasn't sure if Meg was in her right mind or not, it was hard to tell. He needed to spend some more time with her before he could make an assessment. He had until next Monday. That meant that taking into account the two-day ride back to Flaxbush, he had three days to spend here with Meg.

'Do you mind if I stay a while Meg? James asked me to come and make sure you were alright.'

'Of course, Stephen you are welcome any time, you know that.'

Over the course of the next few days Meg appeared to be more like her old self again much to Stephen's relief. She even allowed him into her bed. No longer did he feel any guilt about his actions considering the way James had been treating her. And Meg obviously felt the same. She didn't seem to have any regard for James at all going by the way she spoke about him.

When it came time to go Stephen wasn't sure whether he would be able to convince Meg to go with him or not. Sadly, she refused to leave.

'Stephen you are welcome to stay here with me, but I know you probably feel you are needed at Flaxbush, you are the farm manager after all. But I belong here. I will not return to Flaxbush, it is not my home and James is not my husband any longer. You can tell him that from me.'

'James was not happy to see Stephen arrive back alone.'

'Was she there?'

'Yes James, Meg is back at Stony Downs and she is quite well. Perhaps not fully back to her old self but she seems to be managing alright on her own for now. Maybe it is best to leave her there for a while.'

'I cannot leave her there Stephen. It does my reputation no good for anyone to think my wife would prefer to live alone in the valley than here in this lovely house with me.'

'And your fancy woman,' spat Stephen. 'Meg knows about you and Martha you know. She knows you slip out of bed at night and go to Martha's room. She's not as stupid as you might think.'

With that Stephen turned and led his horse to the stables to unsaddle him and brush him down leaving James stunned and a little unnerved.

James saddled four horses up to the dray the following day and rode down to Stony Downs determined to bring Meg back whatever it took. When he finally arrived at the property he was not surprised to find Meg wasn't in the house or in the gardens or the sheds around the house but he knew she would be there, somewhere, watching him. He stormed into the house and started packing up her belongings and stacking them on the dray. He was being none too careful with her precious jars of preserves and belongings. He knew full well this would bring her out of her hiding place, and he was right. Meg had seen him coming, had been expecting him, so she had taken Jasper, Buster and Sally and hidden in the trees alongside the house. None of them made a sound but James knew they were there. Eventually Meg appeared, raging at the way James was treating her precious belongings.

'How dare you come here and do this to me. You have no right.'

'I am your husband Meg and I have every right. You are coming with me whether you like it or not. I am not putting up with this silly nonsense a moment longer. For goodness sake woman, pull yourself together.'

Meg looked at the belongings piling up on the back of the dray and at the house almost bereft of its contents and realized she had lost the battle. There was nothing for it but to go along with him. For the time being at least. She reluctantly helped him to load the dray even if just to prevent him from doing any more damage.

It was a long, silent ride back to Flaxbush Station, neither of them had anything to say to one another. When they pulled into the yard at Flaxbush Stephen came across from the shed to help them unload. He had been waiting anxiously, afraid of what James might do if Meg refused to accompany him back to the homestead. But she had and he was relieved.

As soon as they pulled up outside the homestead Meg stormed inside and slammed the door. James looked across at Stephen and shrugged.

'At least she's here,' was all he said.

The days following Meg's arrival back at Flaxbush were not easy. Meg could be heard screaming at Martha calling her a whore and a husband stealer. Then James' voice would rise above the din trying to prevent the women from tearing each other's hair out. James was beginning to wonder if he shouldn't have left Meg where she was after all.

As the winter started to draw near, Meg became more and more restless. She desperately missed her life on Stony Downs. Here at Flaxbush she was no more than a burden and an inconvenience. Back there she was everything she had ever wanted to be. She was happy.

248

Stephen watched Meg from afar. He was reluctant to get involved but still wanted to keep a watchful eye on her. On more than one occasion he had seen her out at night in her night attire dancing around in the orchard, singing and talking to herself. He would see her run up to the windows every now and again and peer inside muttering under her breath.

One night he went across to talk to her.

'Meg what are you doing out here without a coat. It's getting cold.'

'I know Stephen, it will soon be winter won't it. The snow will come soon,' she smiled at him. 'They are in there, him and her, they are in there,' she was pointing to the windows. 'I see them Stephen, I know he loves her, I know he goes to her bed at night. But the snows are coming soon.'

She smiled up at him again and he got an uneasy feeling in the pit of his stomach.

'What about the snows Meg, why is that so important.'

She swung around and glared at him.

'Nothing, nothing at all. Now off you go, back to your room. You shouldn't be out here after dark you know. James will growl at you.'

She pushed a finger against her lips. 'Shhhh,' she said. 'Don't make any noise or he will catch you and then you will get a walloping.'

Stephen walked away. Meg's behaviour only served to twist his already broken heart.

'My poor darling Meggie,' he muttered. 'What has that man done to you.'

James knocked on Stephen's door two weeks later.

'Martha and I have business to attend to in town this week Stephen, I would be obliged if you would keep an eye on Meg for me please. She shouldn't be a bother, just treat her like a naughty child and mete out punishment for bad or improper behaviour if you see fit.'

'What? What sort of punishment have you been dealing to her James?'

'She knows that if she misbehaves she gets....'

'Yeah I know, a good walloping. Isn't that right! You beat her if she doesn't behave the way you want her to.'

249

'Sad to say it is the only way to keep her in line now Stephen, she acts like a child so she needs to be treated like one. Now will you see to her or not?'

'Yes of course I will, you know I will. How long are you going to be away?'

'Most of the week I suspect.'

'Right. I will see you when you get back then.'

Meg had been watching and waiting for James and Martha to leave. She overheard them talking and knew they would be away in town for at least a week. Now was her chance to escape. She could get her things together, as much as she could carry, and go back home where she belonged, back to Stony Downs. The snow was coming and if she timed it right he would not be able to follow her.

Meg had become adept at reading the weather over the years and even in her madness this skill was still intact. She placated Stephen and did as she was bid until she knew a snow storm was imminent.

The day finally arrived, her escape day. Stephen was away checking on the stock along with the farm hands and she made sure the two girls who worked in the household were busy with their chores. She walked nonchalantly across the yard to where the dogs were and let them off their chains. She grabbed the well laden saddle bags she had hidden in Jasper's stall and once she had him saddled up she walked him around behind the sheds, mounted him and rode off towards the valley, and home.

By the time Stephen and the men arrived back that evening the house lights were on and everything seemed to be in order so he didn't bother to go over and disturb them.

The next morning it began to snow so they left early to go and check on stock. They arrived back late in the afternoon. The snow was falling heavily and was forming a thick blanket on the ground. There was no sign of James and Martha and Stephen wondered if they might have left their run a bit late getting back and got caught in the snow. He walked over to the house to make sure everything was running smoothly there.

One of the servant girls was in the kitchen preparing dinner.

'Everything alright here Agnes?' he asked.

She nodded but didn't say anything.

'And Mrs Morley, is she alright?'

250

Agnes shrugged her shoulders. 'Don't know, ain't seen her for a while.'

Stephen was alarmed. 'How long is a while Agnes?'

'Dunno, ain't seen her all day today least ways.'

'Where's Ruth?'

'She's upstairs lighting the fires. She ain't seen her neither.'

Stephen bounded up the stairs hoping to get more sense out of the other servant girl.

'Ruth, when was the last time you saw Mrs Morley?' he asked breathlessly.

'I didn't see her when I went to bed last night and I haven't seen her this morning.'

They were in Meg's bedroom, James had moved in with Martha, leaving Meg in a room by herself.

'Ruth, I want you to look through Mrs Morley's things and tell me if you notice anything missing.'

Ruth was a little nervous about following Stephen's request.

'Now Ruth,' he demanded. 'Mrs Morley's life may depend on it.'

Ruth leapt up from the fireplace and began rummaging through Meg's drawers and wardrobe.

'Yes, there appears to be some clothing missing, and her grey coat has gone and some of the things off her dresser, her brush and comb set and a photograph of her family.'

Stephen's heart sank. 'By God she's gone back.'

'Back where?' Ruth was alarmed.

'The foolish girl has gone back to Stony Downs.'

He knew there was nothing he could do until morning and even then if the snow didn't stop falling during the night there was little chance he would be able to follow her anyway.

He was up with the larks first thing next morning after having had very little sleep. It was still snowing and getting deeper by the hour. He knew he had little chance of getting through to Meg, but he had to try. He saddled up his horse and rode in as far as he could but had to turn back. The snow was just too deep for him to even plough through, let alone his horse, and there was no way he could make it all the way to Stony Downs on foot. It would take days, even if he was able to survive in the cold weather. He reluctantly gave up and turned back.

James and Martha weren't able to get back for a further week until the snow began to melt away. When James heard what Stephen had to say about Meg's disappearance, he was angry.

'We can head off first thing,' offered Stephen, 'with any luck we should be able to get through now that the snow has started to melt. Let's hope the rivers are not too high. At least we know she can look after herself and she has the house for shelter.'

'No she doesn't,' said James softly.

'No she doesn't what?' demanded Stephen.

'She doesn't have the house, it's not there,' he hung his head. 'I put a match to it so she wouldn't go back. She didn't even know that I did it. I lit the fire and placed logs around it so that they would catch alight and eventually burn the damn place down once we were out of sight. She wouldn't have even known.'

'What! So Meg has gone off back to Stony Downs only to find it burnt to the ground and it's been snowing and she's trapped? My God man this just tops the lot. You do realize you have more than likely caused her death don't you. Don't you!'

Stephen grabbed James' collar and pushed him back up against the wall snarling menacingly right into to his face.

'You bloody bastard,' he hissed. 'You stinking rotten bloody bastard, I could damn well kill you right here, right now.'

'Stephen,' a voice shrilled out behind him. 'Stephen leave him alone. For goodness sake get a hold of yourself, what has gotten into you?' Martha was visibly shaken.

'Will you tell her, or will I?' spat Stephen as he stormed out the door.

Stephen sat up all night waiting for the first shafts of daylight to appear. He had his horse saddled up and ready to go. He was going after Meg with or without that bastard husband of hers, he could wait no longer.

The going was tough, but Stephen managed to get him and his horse through the melting snow. He found what he thought was a suitable river crossing. It almost took his life when his horse lost its footing and was swept down river for a short distance, but he clung on for dear life and the horse finally found its feet and was able to clamber up and out of the river. Both horse and rider were a little shaken, but Stephen walked alongside the horse for a while talking softly to reassure him and eventually they were both settled enough to carry on.

When Stephen spotted the site where the house used to be all he could see was a blackened spot on the ground. He started calling to Meg as he approached the ruins. The sheds were still standing as was the stone surround of the fireplace, but that was all.

'Meg, where are you? Meg,' he called anxiously.

Just then he heard a whimper as Buster appeared from Bessy's stall behind the shed followed by Sally, head down, her tail wedged firmly between her hind legs.

'It's alright little ones,' he crouched down calling them to him. 'Where's your mistress?'

They turned and walked back around behind the shed. Jasper was standing stock still beside the shed, his head drooping. Stephen looked inside the shed and there curled up in a ball was Meg wrapped up in a coat and blanket.

'Meg, oh thank God.'

He knelt down beside her and touched her face then pulled back in horror. She was stone cold, and her lips were blue. He let out a roar of disbelief and pain as he pulled her to him and held her cold body tight to his chest.

'Meggie, oh my beautiful Meggie,' he wailed.

The dogs came up and nuzzled him. He drew them in and cuddled them too. They would certainly be mourning their beloved mistress. Stephen stood up and stroked Jasper's nose whispering softly to him. He knew that all three of these animals were just as upset as he was. When he knelt down to pick Meg up, he noticed she had something clutched in her hands. It was a tin covered in dirt. She must have buried it in the garden. He took it from her and put it in one of his saddle bags. There was no way he was going to let James have anything that meant that much to Meg. He wrapped Meg tightly in the blanket and securing it with ropes tied her carefully on to Jasper's back all the time tears were streaming down his face. Jasper was a little unnerved to be carrying his mistresses' dead body, but Stephen eventually calmed him down and the two horses and two dogs all headed off back to Flaxbush Station.

They met James along the way; he had left later in the day behind Stephen but hadn't been able to find a safe river crossing. When he saw Jasper with a body tied to his back he knew immediately that it was Meg

253

and that she was dead. He leapt down off his horse and ran over to the blanket wrapped body and started to cry and call out her name.

'Don't you bloody dare pretend you are anything but relieved that Meg is dead,' Stephen sat protectively close to Jasper and Meg's body. 'You disgust me James; I will never forgive you for this. You are responsible for her death and I despise you for it.'

James looked up at Stephen.

'You have made your feelings very plain Stephen; you do not need to keep reminding me of the fact. Now if you don't mind I would like to take over from here. You are relieved of your position as Station Manager; your services are no longer required. I would be obliged if you would get out of my sight, I never want to see you again.'

Stephen's Story

'Sarge you gotta believe me, that son of a bitch killed his wife.'

'Now then son, settle down, you can't go around accusing people of murder like that. Get yourself into a powerful lot of hot water, that will. Just calm down and let's sit and have a chat about what it is that's got you so steamed up.'

The Sergeant of the Christchurch Police Station made two cups of tea and took them back into his office where Stephen remained seated, elbows on knees, head down, visibly upset.

'Now then Mr Sangster let's start at the beginning shall we. Tell me a bit about yourself, what brought you here to New Zealand?'

A bit stunned by the question Stephen hesitated for a moment then seeing the questioning look in the Sergeant's eyes decided maybe he should calm down and talking about himself might help.

'I came here from Australia in 1850 as a teenager Sarge,' he began tentatively. 'And yes, before you ask, I am an offspring of convicts. Suffice to say home life wasn't what you would call ideal. So I jumped on a ship when I turned 14 and landed up here. Managed to score myself a decent job and the rest is history. I love working on the land and

255

eventually worked my way up the ladder to head shepherd, thanks largely to the good heartedness of Alexander Formsby and Henry Hopkins. I met Mr Formsby at the sale yards. He was looking for a good reliable shepherd and said he liked the cut of my jib,' Stephen smiled at the memory. 'He was prepared to train me to be a shepherd and teach me all he could about stock management.'

Stephen stopped to take a sip of his tea, a rueful smile curling his lips. 'If it wasn't for those men I don't know where I would have ended up.'

He paused for a moment, then lowered his voice so that the Sergeant had to strain to hear his next words.

'And I would never have met Meg.'

'You were obviously very fond of Mrs Morley; I can see that. Is that why you are so angry towards James Morley? Is it out of some sort of jealousy Stephen?'

Stephen looked up and glared angrily at the Sergeant.

'Jealousy? No, it wasn't about the jealousy although I do admit I am guilty of that for sure. No Sergeant it was the way he treated her. He drove her to her death.'

'So just how did he manage to do that then?'

'He forced her into a life that made her desperately unhappy and he took up with another woman right in front of her. She knew about it; she knew they would sneak off to be together. She said it didn't matter but I know it tore her apart inside. She kept trying to go back to the house where she had been happy, but he kept dragging her back to Flaxbush Station.'

'The house?' queried the Sergeant. 'What house?'

'The house they built on the Stony Downs property. I have never seen her so happy as she was when she lived there Sarge. Why couldn't he just leave her there where she knew who she was. She was more than capable of looking after herself, hell she had to be, the bastard was away more often than he was home.'

'Where did he go, on these long periods away?'

'Initially he went off surveying so they could buy more stock for the farm but then he got gold fever. He would be away for months at a time looking for that damn gold. Oh yes he wanted to be somebody alright, he wanted the high life, the recognition. Well he damn well didn't deserve it. He had a beautiful talented wife and he just threw her and their farming life aside as if it never mattered. But it mattered to Meg.'

Stephen's throat tightened as he spat out the words. Talking about it brought up the anger, and with it came deep sadness. The Sergeant was sympathetic, but facts were facts.

'That may well be the case Mr Sangster but that doesn't make him a murderer does it.'

'Oh, but it does. You see Meg escaped Flaxbush and went back to the house a couple of times. She wasn't quite right in the head you know. But that was his fault too, he drove her mad. Then the last time Morley went to get Meg and drag her back to Flaxbush Station, he threw a match to the house and burnt it to the ground. Meg never knew. She never knew until the next time he went to town with his fancy woman and she high tailed it back to the house. The weather had been brewing up for rain and snow for a few days and I guess she knew that if she timed it right, by the time Morley returned from town and discovered her missing the weather would have set in and the rivers would be impassable for quite some time. And she would have been right; it snowed the night she left. By the time we found her she was dead.'

Again, he choked on his words. Then with tears rolling down his cheeks he said, 'I will never forget the sight. She'd made a straw bed for herself in the old cow stall and there she was, stone cold dead and clutching a tin to her chest. I was the first to find her, so I took the tin and hid it out of sight. Whatever it was it obviously meant a lot to her and I didn't want Morley to have it.'

The Sergeant was quiet for a moment as he sipped his tea.

'I can see why you are bitter Stephen and I would probably feel the same way in your shoes. But unfortunately, we can't convict somebody for being a bastard or for ill-treating his wife, even if it did ultimately culminate in her death. But I will tell you this Stephen, Morley and his lady friend have booked passage back to England. I only found out yesterday when I was checking through the passenger manifests looking for someone else. I think it best that we let sleeping dogs lie and let them leave. I will go down to the docks and have a wee chat with Mr Morley before he leaves and suggest he never returns to New Zealand. That's about the best I can do Stephen, I do hope it goes some way to alleviating some of your grief and anger.'

Stephen took a deep breath and let it out slowly.

'Thank you, Sergeant. Yes, it will be a relief to know that I won't be seeing him around anymore. I was afraid I might not be able to contain myself if we were ever to confront each other again. Thank you, it has been a relief to get all this off my chest. I haven't had anyone to talk to about it until now.'

'I'm glad to be of help son. Do you have any plans from here?'

'The first thing I am going to do is head over to the West Coast and see if I can find Meg's brother, Bradley Winstanley. Last I heard he had a merchant store in Hokitika. He needs to know about Meg, no doubt bloody Morley hasn't bothered to tell him. Bradley needs to know the truth so he can let their parents know. I can't see Morley going to the Winstanley's with the truth, can you? Especially since he's taken up publicly with that woman friend of his.'

The Sergeant caught the bitterness in Stephen's voice.

'I sincerely hope you will avoid making contact with Mr Morley, Stephen. He will be gone soon enough, and you can forget all about him.'

'Unfortunately, I will never forget him Sarge. But now that I know he is leaving there is something that I have wanted to do.'

'And what might that be?'

'Tell you what Sarge, if it happens you will be the first to know.'

The Sergeant smiled, stood, and held out his hand.

'All the best Mr Sangster, I do hope your plans come to fruition. I'm here if you ever need a friendly ear. Please give my deepest condolences to young Bradley when you find him.'

'I will and thank you for listening, I appreciate your patience.' Stephen responded shaking the Sergeant's outstretched hand

'All part of the job,' smiled the Sergeant as he held the door open. 'By the way, what was in Meg's tin?'

'Aha, that's my secret to keep Sergeant, that's my secret to keep,' and we waltzed off out the door

. As soon as Stephen left the Police Station, he saddled up his horse and went to collect his dogs from the sale yards where he had been working as a stockman. If he was to head over to the West Coast he would need to find somewhere for them to stay until he got back.

His dogs, Sally and Buster were Meg's two beloved collies. He had taken them with him when he left Flaxbush, he wasn't about to leave them with James. Meg wouldn't have wanted that. In the few weeks since Meg's death Stephen had formed a close bond with the dogs and now they were inseparable. He asked around town for a suitable sitter and found the perfect solution, a family with older children who absolutely loved the dogs on sight. The dogs in turn lapped up the attention from the children. Relieved, Stephen set about getting himself sorted to ride down to Dunedin and up the West Coast to Hokitika in search of Bradley Winstanley.

It took Stephen the best part of two weeks to reach Hokitika. He was very relieved to set eyes on a large bustling merchant store with the name 'Winstanley's' over the door. He tied his horse to the hitching post outside and walked into the dim interior.

'What can I do for ya,' called a friendly voice from the back of the store.

Stephen looked around to see a young man walking towards him. As soon as he saw who it was, he grabbed the man's hands in both of his and pumped them enthusiastically.

'My God if it isn't Stephen Sangster. What on earth brings you all the way from Flaxbush? Here, come on to the back of the shop, I've no doubt you could do with a drink.'

Stephen followed Bradley and sat down at a table covered in bills and paperwork. Bradley cleared a space and set down a couple of tin mugs tipping a tot of whiskey into each one.

Stephen took a large sip of whiskey and coughed as the burning liquid hit the back of his throat. He hadn't expected to find Bradley so easily; he still wasn't sure how to tell him what he had come all this way to say.

'It's good to see you Stephen, I know what a trek it is to get all the way around to Flaxbush, it will be great if they ever get a track across those damned ranges won't it.'

Stephen nodded. 'Bradley, I am very sorry, but I come bearing bad news.'

Bradley sat down heavily in his chair and stared at Stephen; dread written on his young face.

'Its Meg isn't it?'

Stephen nodded.

'Is she sick?'

'No Bradley, I'm afraid she is dead. She was buried a few weeks ago. There was no way we could get word to you for you to get there in time, I am so sorry.'

'So why are you here instead of James? Did he send you?'

'It's a long story Bradley and you are not going to like what I have to say. James won't be coming to see you, he has booked passage back to England, with his fancy piece.'

'With his what?' Bradley was stunned. 'You had better start from the beginning man,' he said as he got up to retrieve the whiskey bottle and top up their tins. 'If it's not going to be a pretty tale, we may need more of this.'

By the time Stephen filled Bradley in on everything that happened at Flaxbush and Stony Downs since he was last there, Bradley was incensed.

'That cowardly bastard,' he spat. 'Never did like the man right from the start. I knew he wasn't good enough for my sister.'

'Bradley, there is one thing I want you to remember through all of this. Meg was the happiest I had ever seen her when she was living on her own at Stony Downs. Before James found that gold and let it go to his damn fool head they seemed happy together. I've had the past few weeks to get the anger and bitterness out of my system and I have also had the privilege of seeing how happy Meg was, but I do understand the pain you must be feeling right now.'

'It's just as well the man has booked passage back home or I would not be held responsible for my actions if he crossed my path again.'

Bradley made a bed up on the kitchen settee for Stephen and offered him his hospitality for as long as he needed. The next morning the two men sat at the kitchen table nursing headaches from the amount of whiskey they'd had the night before. Bradley looked like he hadn't slept a wink all night.

'What are your plans Stephen? Are you heading straight back to the Canterbury?'

'I have never been over this side of the island before so I might stick around for a week or two and have a look around. That's if you can put up with me for that long.'

'Of course I can. I think I can safely say we have a mutual bond in the fact that we both loved my sister. I'm not wrong am I Stephen? You loved her, didn't you?'

'Yes I did Bradley, I loved Meg very much.'

'Then we are kindred souls in that regard,' he raised his coffee mug in salute. 'Now get out of here and go take a look around, I've got a business to run.' He laughed.

Stephen stayed with Bradley for two weeks enjoying the chance to have a good look around the area before he started on his long trek back to Christchurch. He was missing Sally and Buster and was worried they might be fretting having lost Meg and then himself. They were his only link with Meg now and he wasn't about to lose that link.

As Stephen saddled up his horse he turned to Bradley.

'What's in the future for you Bradley, now that Meg has gone. Does that make a difference to your plans?'

'Since you mention it Stephen, yes it does. I have given my future here much consideration over the past couple of weeks. I've decided to sell up and go back home to England. I have to admit I never really settled here. I've had the odd lady friend or two but it's time I settled down and started a family and I just don't feel it's going to happen here. What about you, have you got any plans?'

'As a matter of fact, I have. I've had a plan in mind ever since I heard that Morley was selling up. When you come to Christchurch before you sail home, I would be obliged if you would spare a week or two and maybe come to Flaxbush Station. I will leave word at the Post Office to let you know if things go as I hope they will or where you can find me if they do not.'

Bradley laughed and grabbed Stephen in a bear hug.

'You have me intrigued brother, but I have no doubt it has something to do with Meg so yes I will definitely allow some time before I sail.'

Stephen touched his forefinger to the brim of his hat, smiled and threw himself up into his saddle and rode off down the street with the smile still on his face.

Stephen didn't waste any time getting back to Christchurch. His first port of call was the land office.

'Yes, Mr Morley has departed these shores Sir and yes there is a new owner at Flaxbush Station,' said the man behind the counter.

That was all Stephen needed to hear. He didn't rush the trek from Christchurch out to Flaxbush, instead he took his time, stayed a couple of nights here and there and just savoured the journey. For the first time in a very long time he finally felt at peace within himself. Morley and his fancy woman were on their way back to England and good riddance. He smiled to himself. He might be able to put his idea into action after all.

The dogs were excited to be back on familiar territory again as they approached the fence line separating Flaxbush Station from its neighbour. Stephen laughed as they barked and yipped their way up the track towards the homestead. They had missed him as much as he missed them and were full of exuberance at being able to run free again. They were racing up the familiar dirt track towards the homestead when they suddenly stopped dead in their tracks. Off to the left across the paddock they heard a familiar neighing. Next thing Jasper appeared, galloping across the paddock at break neck speed coming to a screeching halt at the fence still whinnying and neighing. He stopped and leaned his head over the fence to nuzzle noses with the collies. The scene brought a tear to Stephen's eye.

'Hello old boy,' he muttered huskily reaching across to rub Jasper's nose.

Jasper hung his head enjoying the rub, eyes half closed. A voice hailing them from up the track brought all four of them out of their reminiscent reverie.

'Well, I must say I haven't seen anything quite like that before. You all must know each other then?'

John Bradley, the Station owner had heard the neighing from the homestead and came out to see what all the fuss was about. Stephen leapt off his horse offering his hand to the stranger.

'Stephen Sangster, I used to work here for Henry Hopkins a while ago. This horse belonged to a very dear friend of mine. These are her dogs so you can understand their excitement at seeing each other again.'

'I can indeed. John Stanley's the name. Sangster you say? Yes, I've heard about you. Worked here for many years I believe. You have a very good reputation Mr Sangster. Come on into the house, I've just put the kettle on.'

262

Stephen took hold of his horse's lead and they all walked up to the house with Jasper tagging along on his side of the fence. Stephen tethered his horse to the fence at the corner by the gate so the horses could be together. He knew the dogs would be happy to stay there as well, with Jasper.

Stephen and John talked at length about the history of the property and the people who had worked there.

'I've heard a few bits and pieces from some of the staff who stayed on after Morley left but I am grateful for the detail you have given me Stephen; it all helps to create a fuller picture of the property. I live here alone, my wife died in childbirth three years ago. We planned to get our own farm block eventually. After her death I rattled around in Christchurch for a while not knowing what to do with my life then a friend told me about this place. It had an appeal, remote and isolated. I purchased it on instinct and so far I haven't been disappointed. It's a great piece of property.'

'It certainly is, I loved working here. I left here for personal reasons, but I sure do miss it.'

'This could be fortuitous timing Stephen. I am looking for a head shepherd. My chap has taken off back home to England. Are you interested?'

Stephen smiled broadly, 'You bet I am, when can I start?'

John and Stephen quickly formed a very close friendship and easy-going working relationship. John was glad to have someone living in the house with him, he hated rattling around in the large homestead on his own. Although it evoked bitter-sweet memories for Stephen being back on the property and living in the house that Morley built and lived in, he loved the sense of feeling close to Meg.

One afternoon as they sat on the verandah after the spring muster was over Stephen raised the subject of the Stony Downs run.

'Have you amalgamated the two runs John?'

'Not exactly, I run the two properties together, but they are still under separate titles. Why do you ask?'

'I've been wondering if you would consider selling or leasing me a small block that surrounds the area where the old house was when Morley owned it.'

263

'Ah, I know the spot you mean, I have seen the remains of the old stone fireplace. But what on earth would you want that bit of land for? Would you not be better off buying the whole title? I would consider selling it to you if you like?'

'I wouldn't mind John but purchasing is out of the question for me financially, I would be happy to discuss a lease though.'

After much negotiation, a trip to the land office and discussions with a solicitor the deal was done. Stephen would lease the Stony Downs property and work for John Stanley. During the summer months he would live on the property at Stony Downs and look after the stock and return in the winter before the snows came so he was not trapped there for weeks at a time and unable to be on hand to help out at Flaxbush when needed.

'We will bring the Stony Downs stock back here for the winter Stephen and leave Stony Downs to recover and be ready for more stock in the Spring. We can always run some beef stock on there too I suppose, they pretty much look after themselves.'

Stephen could barely contain his excitement at the prospect of finally being able to begin the project that had been churning away in his mind all year.

John, on seeing the bond between Stephen, the dogs and Jasper, had decided to gift him the steed as a thank you for his friendship and hard work.

'He obviously belongs to you and the collies Stephen,' he said. 'Far be it for me to break up a family.' He smiled broadly at the tears in Stephen's eyes.

'Thank you John,' Stephen said huskily, 'you have no idea how much this means to us.'

'I think I do Stephen, I think I do.'

He turned on his heel and walked away before Stephen saw the tears in his own eyes. He was lonely too and would have loved to share such a bond with someone, or something. He would miss Stephen over the summer months; they worked and lived comfortably together. He would just have to wait until winter and look forward to cosy chats in front of the fire again, glasses of port in hand.

John and the staff helped Stephen load his wagon with timber and supplies and watched as he rode off and disappeared around the side of the hill with his family in tow. Jasper trotted comfortably alongside the wagon with the dogs. Stephen didn't need to hitch him to the wagon, he knew he wouldn't stray far from him and the collies, they were his family now.

Stephen borrowed six of John's Clydesdales to haul the heavily laden wagon across the stony creek beds. His own horse would stay at Flaxbush until he returned in the Autumn. The strong beautiful Clydesdales would be worth their weight in gold in the months ahead and he was very grateful to have the use of them.

During the second day of their trip to Stony Downs the team settled into a comfortable rhythm. Stephen stopped now and again to let the horses forage and take a break. It was a heavy load and he was in no hurry. When they were travelling quietly along the river banks away from the rough stony ground which required constant vigilance, Stephen would imagine Meg riding Jasper alongside him. Sometimes he could almost see her in her ill-fitting pants and loose shirt with her hair flying out behind her in the breeze, laughing and singing and calling out to him. The way Jasper behaved sometimes made him wonder if he could feel it too. He would suddenly race off ahead of them only to screech to a halt and turn to face them and wait for them to catch up, head tossing, mane blowing in the breeze. The dogs would be running after him barking and yipping in delight. Yes, he decided, she was definitely with him and he didn't have to share her with anyone except this wonderful animal family of theirs.

Stephen and the animals lived in the sheds behind the house site initially, which although still standing had become very run down. Stephen's first job was to tidy them up and make them habitable until the house was finished. He worked hard from daylight till dusk every day. It was a labour of love and he enjoyed every minute of it. The house almost built itself. Everything went together exactly as planned, there were no hitches or setbacks.

When Stephen finally lay down his hammer late that summer and walked back a distance to get a good look at the house, he couldn't believe it. It looked exactly the same as Meg's house had once been. Even the verandah had the same slight lean on it that Meg's house had which had annoyed James immensely but had never bothered Meg. When he walked into the empty interior, which was still to be furnished, he was

265

thrilled to feel like he was once again walking into Meg's house. He could sense her there, the energy, the excitement, the pure joy.

Stephen couldn't wait to furnish the house. It would look exactly the way it did before it was burned down. In the weeks and months leading up to the rebuilding of the house Stephen would purchase goods whenever he went into town. He would return with packages wrapped in brown paper, much to John's curiosity. Stephen never said a word about the packages and John never asked; although he would have loved to know what was in them. Stephen would wander through various shops in Christchurch and would feel himself being drawn to particular furnishings and household items, deciding they would be perfect for the house even though it hadn't been built yet. These packages had been sitting waiting amongst the building supplies and at last were ready to go into their new home.

Stephen couldn't believe his luck when he came across a tablecloth that was exactly the same as the one Meg used. The only things he knew he wouldn't be able to replace were the treasures her family sent her from home. There were a few small precious items in the tin she was clutching to her chest when she died, and Stephen made a beautiful hand carved cabinet to display them in. They were his closest link to the woman he loved and would continue to love for the rest of his life.

In the bottom of the tin was a carefully folded map and when Stephen finally got around to opening it up and spreading it out on the table, he felt a sudden surge of overwhelming love and satisfaction. The house was complete, his job was done, and Meg was happy with the result.

Stephen poured himself a cup of strong tea from the pot slowly bubbling away over the fire burning brightly in the old stone fireplace. He sat down and studied the map he'd just found. He wasn't sure what to make of the markings at first and then it slowly dawned on him what they represented. He laughed out loud, 'Oh Meg, you clever girl, this will prove very useful indeed.'

Stephen Sangster's dream had come true at last. He had rebuilt the home he once shared with Meg for a short time and knew in his heart that she shared with him again now.

Bradley, as promised, turned up on Stephen's doorstep about six months later and was suitably impressed with what Stephen had accomplished.

'The folks will be well pleased when I tell them about this Stephen, thank you.'

Bradley's eyes welled up with tears.

'Have you written to your folks and told them the news?'

'Yes. I also told them I was coming home, and I hope you don't mind but I told them about you too. I know they would find it a comfort to know how much people here loved her. I just picked up a letter back from them at the Post Office in town before I came out. They are heartbroken as you can imagine but have gained some solace knowing that I am on my way home. They asked me to thank you most sincerely for looking after Meg. They will be thrilled to know the extent you have gone to, to honour her memory. You loved her more than you let on didn't you.'

Stephen nodded. 'Yes Bradley, I did.'

About seven months after Bradley left for England a parcel arrived for Stephen and was brought to him at Stony Downs by one of John's farm hands.

'Looks mighty important,' grinned young Marcus. 'Thought we'd best get it to you quick smart.'

'Come on Marcus, you were just curious to know what was in it weren't you,' laughed Stephen ruffling the boys bright red hair.

Marcus watched sheepishly as Stephen started to unwrap the parcel. He'd never had a parcel before and this one came all the way from England. Inside was a brown envelope with a journal in it. Stephen picked up the folded piece of paper that fell out of the wrappings.

'Dear Stephen,' it read. *'When Bradley told us what you have done to rebuild Meghan's beloved house and how much you cared for her and looked after her, we decided we wanted to send you something special to put in her house. Something from us in remembrance of our beautiful Meghan.'*

Stephen gently opened the journal under the watchful eye of young Marcus. The pages sprang to life with photos, clippings and

267

handwritten copies of Meg's letters home to her family. Eyes filled with tears, he picked up the letter and continued to read.

'Please treasure it and find somewhere special in Meg's rebuilt house to put it. We know it will be in safe hands.
God Bless you, young man, we are disappointed we may never get to meet you, but Bradley has told us so much about you we feel you are a part of the family now. If you have a mind to write to us, we would love to hear from you and what is happening way down there on Stony Downs.

Our Love and Blessings to you
Your Winstanley Family.'

Stephen was overwhelmed. He could feel Meg sitting right there beside him. He imagined her arm around him, her head resting on his shoulder.

Marcus could see Stephen was overcome so he took his leave and went out to chop some wood for the fire.

Stephen turned his attention back to the parcel. There sitting amongst the brown paper wrappings was a beautiful grey homespun hand knitted jersey. He was stunned. Nobody had ever made him anything in his life. This was a wonderful thoughtful gift and it brought on more tears.

'Oh Meg, what a wonderful family you have.'

He could swear a voice in his ear said, 'And they are your family now too my love.'

AND SO IT WAS

To this day anyone riding through the area could be forgiven for saying they caught a glimpse of two riders and two happy collie dogs racing across the river or hear the echoes of laughter wafting down from the mountainsides.

'I could hear laughter, but it was a happy sound, not an eerie one', recalled one of the local musterers.

All that remains of Stephen's lovingly rebuilt hut is a crumbling pile of stones that once formed part of the fireplace. Every now and then a small bunch of herbs and wild flowers appears on top of the stones. Nobody knows who places them there.

Acknowledgements

I love reading and writing about the early settlers who came to New Zealand in the 1800's. I admire their strengths, their courage and their dogged determination to fight the odds and forge a new life for themselves. Among the characters in our history the following are some who inspired and enthralled me with their tales and gave me greater insight when it came to writing this book.

The inspiration for this book initially came from a visit to EREWHON High Country Station in Canterbury, New Zealand in 2017. Their fabulous fully illustrated book *Seasons of EREWHON* takes you right into the heart of the high country and tells you the fascinating history of the inhabitants of that area.

CRUSTS - written by L.J. Kennaway, is a true account of the experiences of two brothers in the Canterbury High Country of NZ. It tells of their struggle, hardship and courage. The fact that the author Laurence Kennaway survived to tell his story is incredible in itself. Mr Kennaway lived in New Zealand for 30 years before returning to his homeland, England, where he died at the ripe old age of 70. If you like reading about inspirational people with courage and strength, then this book will not disappoint.

You can find a free copy on line at: www.enzb.auckland.ac.nz. I loved this book so much I sourced a precious hard copy; they are still available in New Zealand from places such as Smith's Books in Christchurch.

STATION LIFE – by Lady Barker (1870) is a very entertaining novel of her life as a high country farmer's wife. Highly recommended. Lady Barker followed up this novel with another one three years later entitled Colonial Memories (1873). Both books are available in libraries or at ENZB.

SAMUEL BUTLER wrote several items and books mostly with a view to helping emigrants coming to New Zealand. Emigrants Handbook is one such publication. He also kept a very comprehensive journal of his trip out to New Zealand on the Roman Emperor and wrote a book entitled *A first year in Canterbury Settlement.* No doubt there are many more that I have yet to discover.

A FABLED LAND written and illustrated by Bruce Ansley and Peter Bush is a fabulous account of the history of Mesopotamia Station.

ENZB – Early New Zealand Books (www.enzb.auckland.ac.nz) is a wonderful reference source for NZ non-fiction publications dating back as far as 1807 right up to 2005.

I am happy to direct readers to other sources and help them to find out more information on this enthralling time in our history.

CPSIA information can be obtained
at www.ICGtesting.com
Printed in the USA
BVHW041343011120
592287BV00015B/287

9 780473 481667